DEATH
DO US
PART

MIRANDA GRANT

BY MIRANDA GRANT

WAR OF THE MYTH SERIES
Elemental Claim
Think of Me Demon
Tricked Into It
Rage for Her

FAIRYTALES OF THE MYTH COLLECTION
Burn Baby Burn
The Little Morgen
Bjerner and the Beast

TO LOVE AND TO PERISH SERIES
Death Do Us Part

DEATH DO US PART

authormirandagrant@gmail.com
mirandagrant.co.uk
tiktok @authormirandagrant

ISBN: 978-1-914 464-01-0

Cover by Magnetras Designs.
Edited and published by Writing Evolution.

DISCLAIMER

DO NOT FEED WASPS ALCOHOL

It makes them more aggressive and you're way more likely to be stung. They do not hold their liquor well. These are fictional wasps in a fictional world, drinking a fictional drink. They get sleepy. REAL LIFE WASPS DO NOT.

Again:

REAL LIFE WASPS GET ANGRY WHEN DRUNK!!!

To My Wonderful Monster:

So this was going to be properly dedicated to you given
how much of it is 'based' on our moments, but instead,
I'm dedicating it to Heather Harris and Michelle Carter.
You're supportive because you have to be (and you know,
sex); they are because they truly liked the book – a book
that would've been binned without their support.

So although I love you, babe, I'm dedicating this to them.

To Heather Harris and Michelle Carter:

Thank you for believing in me when I didn't.

ONE

Rules are meant to be followed.

UNLESS YOU CAN FIND A LOOPHOLE.

— RICHARD

I lounged back in my seat, a shot of ambrosia in my scarred hand. Swirling the honey-coloured liquid around the glass, I locked eyes with the high scholar.

"I've crushed the Vylian forces to the north," I said slowly. "I've fended off the Great Beast every year. And now you're telling me that I must bow to a single piece of paper?"

The man swallowed, his eyes flicking to the black and purple carvings beneath his feet. "Well, no. I mean, yes. I mean –"

"Breathe, scholar...while you still have the luxury of being able to."

The next swallow was damn near audible.

"It's not just..." The man pulled at his collar, the dark

purple fabric doing little to hide his paling complexion. "Not just a piece of paper that's...that's stopping you," he stammered. "It's a High Law of Oyveni's."

My eyes narrowed. I hated hearing that fucking name. If the bitch wasn't already dead, I'd kill her myself. And if I had the power to go back through time, I'd finish her whole damn line, including her pet toad. Oyveni's laws had been a pain in my ass since before I'd taken the throne. It was because of her that I'd been forced to kill my younger sister rather than just banish her.

I'd been forced to kill my older sister too, but she, at least, had deserved it.

My fingers tightening on my glass, I pushed the memories aside. "Which says what?" I demanded.

"That...that the Timeless Laws..." The high scholar took a deep breath, his hands fidgeting in his traditional robes. He twisted the fabric round and round his pudgy fingers before finally looking up – but his deep blue eyes never did find mine. "They cannot be changed without the signature of a king –"

"Which it has," I growled.

The man flinched. His eyes darted back down to the floor. "And a...and a queen."

Everything inside me stilled. I raised my glass to my lips, fury tightening my brows. For nearly two decades I'd ruled on my own, had protected them from every danger, and now they required me to have a queen? A *woman* I would be forced to share my power with? My vision? I took a sip from my glass and placed it lightly on the table. Smiling viciously, I drawled, "A queen, you say?"

The man's whole head ducked to the floor. "Y-yes." He gulped.

"And does the Court have anyone in particular in mind?"

8

"Evangeline."

Fucking Petre.

That snake had been trying to secure her daughter on the throne for over two decades. Evangeline was a beauty, sure, but she'd be so much prettier if she had been born mute. Our marriage would barely last long enough for the ink to dry. And then we'd be having a funeral.

"Can it be a queen of a neighbouring kingdom?" I demanded, thinking of the brownies to the south. Although our two kingdoms weren't on actual speaking terms, we were currently at peace with each other.

"No. No, it has to be the signatures of the fairy king and queen."

I bit back a curse. I didn't have the time nor the desire to find a wife. "Bring me this law of hers. I wish to read it myself."

"I assure you, My Grace, there is no loophole to exploit."

"Like your father had assured me with Oyveni's High Law of Accession?"

The high scholar flinched.

"If I'd listened to your father, I never would have been king." I leaned forward, my eyes hard. "Tell me, scholar, are you like your father?"

The man shuddered. "No," he whispered.

"Good. Then get me the original tome."

"Yes, my lord." Bowing until his head was parallel to the ground, he scurried out backwards.

As soon as he was gone, I swivelled to face my brother. "*A fucking wife!*" I growled.

"At least it's not a husband they're trying to push for this time," Nicholas said from his position in the corner. He leaned against the wall, his arms and ankles crossed, his face heavily cloaked by the shadows. He used to be the centre of attention, the magnet in every room. And now he clung to the darkness like a newborn to a teat. It was pathetic.

"Step into the light, Nicholas," I snapped, my annoyance making my tone harsher than I had intended. I knew all about PTSD and self-loathing. What soldier of mine didn't? But I didn't have the time for my brother's pain today. If we didn't come up with a solution, then the last six years of my hard work were going down the fucking drain.

After a brief second of hesitation, Nicholas did as requested. The left half of his once handsome face was twisted and melted like a wax doll that had been left out in the sun. The right had an ugly thick scar running from his brow to across his nose. The wounds not of battle but of domestic dispute. Of believed shame.

Forcing my tone to soften, I asked, "Where in Hel's realm am I going to find a woman who isn't going to be overcome with greed and power?"

"Any woman of the Court will try to kill you. They are all content with the Timeless Laws."

"I am aware of the desires of the Court." Just this morning, Josie had tried to push herself into my arms, a knife hidden up her sleeve. If she hadn't been Caroline's heir, I would've killed her on the spot. Instead, I had to let her go and wait for her to strike again.

"Then a servant?" Nicholas suggested.

Scowling, I shook my head. "They might be demure at the start, but give them a couple years and they'll grow into the role. They wouldn't be able to help themselves." Not when they'd always be addressed before me. Not when they would have the final say on every matter. And especially not when the fucking Court would push it into their head that I was no longer needed. I was the first ruling king and they were determined that I would be the last.

Furrowing my brows, I knocked back the contents of my glass, then placed the tumbler on the table.

"Find out who I can blackmail," I said. "She'll have to have something big –" My eyes narrowed in warning. "Don't you dare make one of your quips."

Wordlessly, Nicholas cupped his hands in front of his chest and squeezed. Although he *technically* hadn't uttered a word, I threw my glass at him anyway.

It shattered against the wall behind him. I was on my feet before the first shard hit the floor. "Nick, I'm sorry. I didn't think –"

He shook his head, brushing it off despite the paling of his complexion. "It is fine. Dorothy liked to throw plates, anyway, not glasses."

Forcing myself to nod, I sat back in my chair. I knew from experience he hated dwelling on the subject. I still didn't know how she'd managed to scar him so badly, so permanently. I'd just received a call in the middle of the night, his voice breaking as he'd asked for help.

"I know you don't like Evangeline –"

"She is not to be placed in the line-up," I warned.

"But she is likely to have the most secrets."

As she was head of FI9, that was a fucking given. She'd probably broken so many laws, her file would be as thick as her thighs. Thighs I'd once seen crush a man's skull.

"No," I repeated.

"I hear she's as wild in bed as she is on the battlefield."

"*No.*"

Chuckling, Nick finally relaxed. His complexion went back to his natural tan. His dark purple eyes, though still high on alert, were now softening. "I'll see what I can dig up on a few candidates," he said as he headed for the exit.

I nodded. Tapping my fingers against the table, I contemplated having a wife in silence. But just as my brother was about to shut the door behind him, I called out, "I'd prefer it if she was mute."

Nicholas stopped and turned around. A grin curved his twisted face. "If you stuck your cock in her mouth," he began.

"Don't!"

Chuckling, he closed the door, leaving me on my own.

The last of my amusement quickly faded, flooded under a new wave of annoyance.

Scowling, I opened the top right drawer of my desk and pulled out my set of throwing knives.

A wife.

I picked up a pitch black blade. Twirled it in my fingers.

How the hel was I going to handle one of those?

With a flick of my wrist, I tossed the blade into the target on the other side of the room. A perfect bullseye.

Slowly, a corner of my lips curled up into a smile.

TWO

A good brownie never ruins a party.

Unless it's Karl's.

— Arienna

"Arienna, stop!" Fabia hissed as she ran behind me, her black trousers allowing her to easily close the distance between us.

As I skirted through the sea of tables in my large fluffy dress, I tried not to trip over the hem. But the blasted thing was *everywhere*. And these oh-so-cute heels weren't doing much good either. Whoever had designed them seemed to have made them different heights. I cocked my head to the side. Perhaps it was a new fashion trend...

"Whatever you have, it is not a good idea!"

I ignored her. No, this was a *brilliant* idea. And everyone would love me for it. Well, everyone except Karl.

But Karl was a dick.

"Ugh, he had such a nice dick," I moaned.

Grabbing my shoulder, Fabia turned me around. I teetered on my feet, almost dropping the box I was holding as I did so. Digging my fingers into the carefully wrapped paper, I held on tight. Hyatt would *not* like it if he got dropped.

"One, that's not true. You sent me pics" –she wrinkled her nose– "which I have *not* forgiven you for by the way, and two, he came in like three seconds."

I hiccuped. "Four and a half." I giggled. "I actually counted."

Rolling her eyes, my best friend started dragging me back towards the main party.

"Wait! I need to add my box to the pile!" The table of presents was just there. I was so close to making it.

"*No.*" She yanked on my shoulder. The sound of funky music started to play behind us. I only had a minute left to add my gift to the pile and slip away unseen.

But my attempted step forward was immediately halted by her pull.

"Why are you being so mean?" I whined.

Sighing loudly, Fabia turned to face me. "Because you came here full on drunk–"

"Did not."

"And you *always* do stupid things when you're drunk."

"That's not true!"

She raised a pretty lilac brow. "Six weeks ago, you went home with Karl."

"He was sweet."

"He was a nobhead. Still is. And he's marrying your *mother*. After having cheated on you with your sister."

"But –"

"He broke up with you three days ago. Via an ad in the newspaper."

"That was because he was busy."

"Yeah, *banging your mother.*"

"But –"

"No. Stop making excuses for him." She snapped her fingers in front of my face. I followed the movement, swaying on my feet. I wondered if she'd ever tried taming a centipede. Perhaps I could convince her to give it a go... It would make a great anniversary present for Mum and Karl.

If Hyatt didn't already do the job.

I grinned.

"In fact," she added, "stop making excuses for your whole messed up family."

Hey! My family's not messed up.

"Yeah, well, at least I have a family." As soon as the words flew out of my mouth, my eyes widened. "Oh my gods. I didn't mean that. I'm so sorry."

She waved my apology away, causing me to frown. A good brownie *always* accepted an apology. But I guess, in this instance, I could ignore that. I had, after all, just used the family card on an orphan.

Maybe she was onto something about alcohol making me do stupid things...

But no, that couldn't be right.

Because the last time I was drunk, I got a gorgeous tattoo on my butt. Best decision ever.

"And two days ago," Fabia continued, "you tried to take out an ad telling everyone how lonely you were. And how even three seconds of action was better than the nothing you'd now be getting. You then went on to say how you didn't want the last guy you had sex with to also be the same guy whose balls had touched your mother's butt."

I nodded along even though I didn't understand her point. What woman wanted their mother's butt on theirs, transferred by their fiance's balls? I gagged. What woman wanted their mother's va–

"Don't say it."

My eyes widened. Could she read minds now? "How –"

"Because you wrote it in your ad. And you're lucky I was the one that saw it. Had Pram been working that day, she would've signed print faster than Karl would've come after three days of not having sex."

I giggled. He did come awfully quick.

"And just this morning," she said without a lick of humour, "you agreed to be the maid of honour for your mother. Who is marrying your ex-fiance. In the venue you picked out."

I blinked. "So? I wasn't using it. That's just what a good brownie does, and I'm a good brownie." I followed the rules and everything. Well, most of them.

She cocked a brow, her silver eyes dipping to the box I held in my hands. "Oh yeah? What's that then?"

"A box?" I smiled, so proud of myself.

"No duh. What's in it?"

"A present?"

"Which is?"

I glanced away. "Something nice?" Crap, if she asked anything else, I was going to be screwed. Coming up with technically correct answers was hard.

Just as I smiled most innocently, an angry buzz radiated from inside. Drat.

Her eyes widened as she took a few hurried steps back. "Is that a fucking bee?"

"Fabia!"

"Screw my language, Arienna. Answer the damn question!"

Geez. Someone was in a mood today. "No, it's not a

bee."

She stared at me in clear disbelief. The buzzing got louder. The box began to shake. Doing my best to hold onto it, I frowned. "The ambrosia should've kept him knocked out for at least another couple of hours."

"Drop the box!"

"What? No, that would be rude."

And a good brownie was never rude. Also, Hyatt would definitely stab us then.

"Arienna, that box is not strong enough to stop its stinger from stabbing you! Drop the box!" She waved her arms frantically. Cradling the box tighter against me, I protected it from my psycho friend.

"Stop shouting!" I shouted. "Hyatt doesn't like loud noises."

Or any noises really. He was kind of a dick. Which is what made him the perfect gift for Karl.

"One sting and you'll die," Fabia added, her voice strained. "Their venom is awful. Now put down the box."

"But –"

"Oh, there you two are."

We both froze as Gerald, the chief of helpers, stepped through the green archway separating the reception area from the dance floor. His pale pink suit was the exact colour of my hair. I'd been avoiding him all evening, certain he'd mention it, and *really really really* hoping he didn't.

Struck by a moment of clarity, I raised the box over my face.

"Um... That is some lovely wrapping you've done," Gerald said.

I nodded, tilting the box up and down as I did so. The buzzing got louder. The shaking intensified.

As my arms struggled to hold Hyatt still, Fabia blurted,

"It's a vibrator."

Oh, thank the gods. "Where?"

I lowered the box so I could look around. If I couldn't get laid tonight, that would do.

"*In your box*," Fabia said. Before I could tell her that it was, in fact, a wasp, she added, "Because, you know, Karl comes very quickly and we thought it would be nice to help Arienna's mum still get her big O."

I cringed. Gross. That was not the image I wanted in my head. Karl screaming and getting fined once he opened the box though... Now *that* was what I was here for.

"Ummm...oh..." Gerald said. "How...polite."

"Yep."

There was a moment of thick silence under all the buzzing.

"It accidentally got set off." Fabia raised her arm at the elbow and moved it horizontally back and forth, going really fast. "It's quite a powerful one. Very large, hence the size of the box." She raised her thumb, her arm still jackknifing away. "Good for both holes."

I was going to be sick. Dear gods, I needed to boil my eyes and then squash them.

"As you can see, it can last for quite a while, unlike Karl, and –"

"That's okay," Gerald blurted. "I don't need all the details." He took a step back. "I'll go find some tape so you can open the box and turn it off before the magic runs out" –he winced– "in case she wants to use it tonight."

Ugh. Yeah. That was always the worst. No, wait. The worst was thinking you had enough magic when you started, only to then have it slowly die on you. I mean, fair enough, a dead vibrator was just a dildo, but I did not have the arm strength to continue the pace.

Rounding on me, Fabia placed both hands on her hips. "I can't believe you brought a freaking bee to the wedding!" Her eyes were narrowed into such slithers, I could barely see them. "Do you have any idea how venomous they are?"

I lifted my chin. "It's not a bee."

"The only thing more venomous is a –"

"It's a –"

"Wasp!"

"Wa..." I trailed off, suddenly realising it might not be a good thing to admit that. She already looked really pissed. Like, way more than usual.

Her eyes narrowed. Her jaw ticked.

Drat. I was so screwed.

"I found some tape!"

Oh, thank the gods.

Placing Hyatt down on the table, I hurried past my scowling best friend. "Thank you, Gerald. We'll sort it out ourselves."

"Okay, but the first dance is nearly over and I was wondering if..."

"Not now, Gerald!" Fabia snapped.

Blushing a deep crimson, he pedalled backwards. I watched him go in sudden annoyance. If he'd been about to ask me to dance, then he would've been more susceptible to me taking him home, and I *really* wanted to get laid. "Dang it, Fabia. I'm pretty sure you just cockblocked me."

Ignoring the most important thing right now, she said, "Help me get rid of it before he comes back."

Spinning around, I raced towards the table. "What? No! He's a present." I spread my arms out wide, desperate to keep her from grabbing him. I'd raised the guy since he was a larva. I mean, yeah, he'd done nothing to show his appreciation of me. In fact, he'd chewed half my furniture and forced me to sleep outside, but he was still my baby. He still deserved to be protected.

"Arienna, it's a wasp. Hurting things is what they do. We have to get rid of it. They are pure evil."

"That's not true. They're just misunderstood bees."

"Also evil."

"Who are just misunderstood balls of fluff."

"That can kill you. Now help me 'set it free' before we're caught."

"But –"

"Wasps can't be pets, Arienna. Now come on before someone sees!"

"Fine!" Pouting, I dropped the protective barrier of my arms. "But we're releasing him somewhere nice."

Biting the inside of her lower lip, Fabia stared at Hyatt's nicely wrapped carrier. He'd settled down now. The paper was only a bit crinkled from my fingers having dug into it. Maybe if I rearranged the bow to hide the worst parts, no one would even notice.

And then I could find Hyatt a home and move on to helping his brothers and sisters.

A feeling of relief moved through me. They really were starting to get out of hand.

Fabia breathed out slowly. "We need to figure out a way to carry it. Maybe if we got a sheet and I grabbed one end and you grabbed the other with the box in the middle –"

Rolling my eyes, I picked it up. "Hyatt's not going to hurt me."

The need to yell at me and the need to move as fast as possible warred clearly in her eyes. The bright silver rings of annoyance were flecked with dark splashes of concern.

Gods, I needed to stay off the booze. What kind of

wishy-washy description was that? Though give me a couple more days without sex, and who knows. Fabia was quite hot. I was ridiculously hot. We'd make a cute couple. And let's face it, given how many times Fabia got into trouble, she probably knew a few things.

"Fine. But if you get stabbed, I am so rubbing it in your face. Then I'm carving it on your tombstone. Here be the biggest idiot."

I grinned. Sarcastic Fabia was my favourite. She was so much better than Annoyed Fabia.

"Right. Where to?" I asked, really hoping it was not far. I wanted to get back before Gerald went home with someone else. Probably Pram.

Ugh. Pram. Karl's ex-girlfriend and my biggest nemesis.

Maybe I could give her a wasp too.

And then there would only be sixteen left to go...

"At least to the Rivers of Wraith."

I nearly dropped Hyatt. "But that's going to take all night! I'll have to convince Gerald to come with us if I want to get laid today."

My best friend crossed her arms, unmoving in her stubbornness. "Fucking tough. You brought a wasp into Brownston. We have to get it far enough away it won't come back because if Hyatt is actually a female and lays eggs, we'll all have to migrate elsewhere."

Groaning, I asked, "Can I at least tell Gerald to head to my house after the wedding?"

"No."

"Why not?"

"Because he's a twat, for one, and two, we have a freaking *wasp* that's no longer asleep."

"Okay, fair." I shifted the box onto my hip. "But, now hear me out, Gerald has a dick, and that ticks *all* my boxes at the moment."

Rolling her eyes, Fabia gestured towards the flowerline. "Just get moving."

"You just don't like him because he keeps arresting you," I muttered as I dutifully made my way into the woods. As the flowers stretched high above us, I looked up to watch the beambugs fluttering between them, lighting up the dark of the night.

Gods, I wished I could fly.

Then I could make it to the rivers in no time, drop off the box, and come back here in time to get laid.

Instead, I would have to walk for *hours* there and *hours* back. In these blasted uncomfortable heels. In this stupid uncomfortable dress. With this annoying trip-hazard of a hem. Why did wasps have to be the size of our chests?

When my heel sank into the dirt for the second time, I put Hyatt on the ground, took off my shoes, and chucked them back towards the party. Next went the dress. Then the box. Turning to Fabia, standing in just my pale blue slip, I nodded. "Alright, I'm ready to go."

But her eyes weren't on me.

They were latched over my shoulder.

Where a particularly angry buzz was disrupting the air.

And numerous gasps were beginning to rise.

And the sounds of chaos were overtaking the funky music.

Puzzled, I looked over my shoulder. At the sight of Hyatt finally free of his box, I lifted my hand and waved.

THREE

A good brownie never screams.

Ever.

— Arienna

"Oh my gods, Fabia, *look*!" I squealed, clasping both hands over my cheeks. "Isn't he cute!"

The iridescent teal making up Hyatt's thorax was my favourite colour in the whole Seven Planes. The rich plums and pinks of his abdomen were a close second. But it was his large black eyes and dark blue fuzzy antennas that I loved the most. Hyatt was freaking cute.

He was going to get *all* the lady wasps.

Cursing, Fabia grabbed my arm. "Why is he already covered in blood?"

As she ran her hands over my arms and chest, I mourned the fact that she didn't linger on my boobs. What kind of friend was she?

"Are you hurt?"

"Well, I just stepped on my own foot and my vag–"

"From Hyatt." She shoved me away.

Ugh. Rude.

"No. I told you, Hyatt wouldn't hurt me."

"Where's all the blood from then?"

I waved my hand. "Oh that? It's probably Bo's."

"And who is that?"

"One of Hyatt's brothers." I cocked my head to the side. *Ugh. Cock. I could use one of those right about now...* "Ex-brother? Actually, you know what? I don't even know if they have the same mum. I found them all separately –"

"You did what? How many are there?"

"Brothers?" Dear gods, *brothers*! That's what I needed. Though not wasp brothers. Ew. Brownie brothers. Covered in mud as they wrestled. Wearing nothing but – No, no. That would take too long to wash off. And who was I kidding? I didn't need foreplay tonight. They could just –

Fabia snapped her fingers in front of my face.

"Hmm? Oh, at least six." *Six!* "Probably more though as most of them haven't hatched yet." *More!*

If it wasn't for Fabia, I would've combusted at the thought of six or more men drilling into me. But she looked like she wanted to slap me. And although a good brownie was never violent, Fabia *had* set Lief's house on fire. She'd claimed it had been an accident, but I was pretty sure the only accident was that he hadn't been in it. Wisely, I took a step back.

"So can I, like, go back to the party now that Hyatt's out of the box? We don't have to set him free anymore and –"

Fabia's glare caused my hope to die. At this rate, I was never getting laid, let alone by six god-like brothers. Maybe I should just jump in front of Hyatt now, saving myself from the misery of forever having my mum's butt on mine.

"No," Fabia growled. "And do you want to know why?"

Shoulders down, I nodded. Best to get this over with. She was unreasonably stubborn when it came to telling me off.

"Ask me why," she said, her tone more venomous than any wasp.

I sighed, itching to go find Gerald. "Why?"

"Because he's going to kill everyone!"

Oh yeah...

My eyes widened.

Drat.

Oh yeah!

Suddenly realising what I'd done, I spun around and faced the party.

There were thousands of brownies here.

It was basically the whole town.

The only town for miles.

If they all died, who would I have sex with? Some people might be into necrophilia, but I sure as hel wasn't.

I liked my men moving.

And warm.

And their penises actually erect.

And not smelling like –

"Hyatt!" Waving my arms, I ran out of the woods and rushed through the archway. The wedding party had dissolved into pure chaos. No one was dancing anymore. They all stood in a serpentine line in front of the venue's doors, waiting for their turn to enter. Even the musicians and clowns had joined them. The only ones that hadn't were town-drunk Freiser and goth-lady Lililana. Freiser was passed out behind the bar – or dead, it was hard to tell – and Lililana was sitting, nursing a gin and tonic, watching as Hyatt destroyed what remained of the cake.

My heart stuttered.

Drat.

Gerald was going to be working all night, fining everyone for ruining the party.

Worse, he'd be working with Pram.

As the head journalist of the *Broonie Toonie* crime section, she would be the one following him around, asking him questions, using every excuse to touch him. Normally, it was funny watching her dote around him like a lovesick butterfly, but dang it, he was my best chance of getting laid tonight without having to indulge in a lot of small talk.

And I *needed* to get laid.

Like, soon as.

Before the ambrosia wore off and I redeveloped – I shuddered – *standards.*

Heading for the bar, I nodded at Lililana and swiped a bottle of ambrosia. She ignored me, as was her thing. It wasn't rude. She might be a goth, but she was still a good brownie.

Popping off the cork of my bottle, I guzzled as much alcohol as I could. Hopefully, that would keep me going until Gerald was no longer busy.

Or I found someone else to replace him.

I wrinkled my nose as I eyed the rest of the bottle.

Nope.

Even if I drank all of it, it wouldn't be enough to sway me into necrophilia.

Shuddering, I drank some more to rid myself of such thoughts.

"You freaking idiots!" Fabia screamed as she cut through the line. "Just get inside!" Gasping, I raised my hand to my mouth. Burping against my palm, I shared a look with Lililana.

A good brownie never screamed.

And they never cut in line.

And they certainly never did both at once.

Looking around the crowd, I searched for Gerald. He would come hurrying over soon enough with his little notepad out and scribbling fines for her left and right. I wondered if those two would ever get along. If they didn't, double date nights would be *awkward.*

"That's so metal," Lililana said as she watched Fabia cut all the way to the front of the queue and dash inside.

Bringing the bottle back to my lips, I downed half of it, knowing I'd need at least that much to bail Fabia out of jail. Although most brownies could get out with a simple, "I promise not to do that again", which took two freaking seconds, she always made it difficult. We were there for bloody hours, arguing about dumb rules and being in cults and whatever else she talked about. Honestly, I didn't really pay attention.

"Bit rude though," I replied, squinting at the white venue doors, wondering if that was Gerald standing beside them, holding them open.

I groaned.

It was.

Forget him working all night.

He'd most definitely be dead. The door holders always died in events like this.

Dang it.

Sighing, I pulled out a chair beside Lililana and joined her.

"So Hyatt's pretty cute, isn't he?"

Scoffing, she ignored me.

I beamed. I'd always known we were friends.

Before I could engage with her again, Fabia came bursting out of the venue, two bottles of fresh mint spray in her hands.

"That's *so* metal," Lililana said as she sipped her drink.

I nodded along. "Wait until Hyatt smells it. He is not a fan of mint."

She glanced at me, her chin jutting out. "Hyatt is the wasp?"

I grinned with pride. "Yep."

"That's so metal."

My smile widened to the point of pain. Oh yeah, we were going to be besties.

"Get the fuck inside!" Fabia screamed as she ran towards the cake and Hyatt. Realising there was a threat in the area, or maybe just smelling the mint, Hyatt fluttered his wings and rose into the air. His buzz sent shivers down my spine. He was a right dick when he was annoyed – as Bo had quickly found out when he'd stolen his treat this morning.

I hoped, for Hyatt's sake, that he was more polite this time. Fabia was freaking scary when she was angry, especially when it came to dicks.

Just ask Lief.

Homeless, traumatised Lief.

I brought the bottle back to my lips just as Fabia reached the fountain I'd picked out a few weeks ago. Carved from stone, a man laid on his side in a pool of ambrosia. His arm propped up his chiselled jaw. Six delicious abs flowed down his body. And a jet of bubbly liquid shot out of his godly penis. I sighed. What I wouldn't give to find a man like that...

Diving into a roll, Fabia dodged Hyatt's first attack. She came back up on her feet and shoved away the brownie that had tried to give her a hand. Aiming a bottle at Hyatt, her eyes narrowing, she fired.

A stream of liquid mint arced beside him as he weaved

to the side. Buzzing angrily, he curled his bottom half, aiming his stinger right at her. As he flew in a straight line, Fabia held her position and raised both bottles.

My mouth dropped open in awe as she fired two streams directly at his face. He pulled up, his wings flapping wildly, his body twisting and bobbing through the air as he tried to shake off the mint. Diving onto the nearest brownie, he wrapped his legs around her head and stung her right in the mouth.

She fell, unable to gasp, her throat swelling up in an instant.

"You are all idiots!" Fabia screamed as Hyatt charged at her again. She ducked and dived and fought like a freaking badass. The line slowly moved behind her.

Figuring I should probably go help before it got out of hand, I left my bottle on the table and stood. The world tilted sharply. The floor came up and met my face.

"Why, hello there," I mumbled against the cold grass. Kissing it, I giggled, then pushed myself into a sitting position. Grabbing hold of a chair, I pulled myself up.

"Dear gods, there's three of them!" I gasped as I watched three Hyatts and three Fabias battle it out. The three women all held a smashed bottle in their hand. The three Hyatts buzzed angrily, swooping and diving over the crowd.

Running towards them with open arms, I shouted, "Stop!"

A flying shoe slammed into my nose, dropping me to the ground. Groaning, I mumbled, "So we meet again." Even in pain, I was a freaking polite brownie.

Clutching my face, I crawled onto my hand and knees. Looking up, I found that the three Hyatt's had disappeared. I really hoped they'd flown off.

But I didn't even get the chance to look around for

them before my vision was blocked by three Fabias. And they all looked pissed.

Climbing to my feet, I went on the defensive. That was always the best course of action. "Why did you never tell me you were a triplet?" I asked. "I thought we shared everything."

All three of them rolled their eyes. Oh yeah, they were definitely related. They had that down pat.

"Like you told me when you picked up all the wasps?"

Drat. This was not supposed to backfire. Time to use the 'can't be mad at me because I did it for a good reason' technique. "But I only did it so they wouldn't grow up like you." It broke my heart knowing she'd grown up thinking no one, not even her parents, had loved her. Having seen her pain, I couldn't let anyone or anything else go through that.

"Like me?"

Gods, they even all talked at the same time. That was rude. Now I didn't know which one to address.

"Yeah, like you. All orphaned and stuff with no one to love them."

They pursed their lips together.

I smiled. "But hey, it's cool that you've found your sisters. Isn't that nice? Group hug!"

Stumbling forward, I wrapped my arms around the one in the middle. She pressed her palm against my face and shoved hard. "Get off me, you twat!"

Ah, her expression of love was always so energised. This one was definitely the real Fabia.

"You're lucky no one important died today, but a lot of brownies will if those other wasps get out," she hissed.

I giggled. Oh, silly Fabia. She never believed in me. Waving my hand, I assured her, "Oh, don't worry about them. I've already got a plan!"

FOUR

A good brownie never starts a war.

Even if you didn't mean to.

— Arienna

Worst.
I groaned.
Idea.
I whimpered.
Ever.
I was never drinking again.

My head felt like it had a sword rammed through it. A fiery sword. One that had been cursed to inflict even more pain than was possible. A magical fiery pain that made me wish I was still drunk.

Groping around my queen-sized bed, I searched for a wayward bottle. There was usually one...or two cuddled up against me.

Nothing.

Poop.

"I am going to kill you," Fabia hissed.

Too late. I'm already dying.

Groaning, I waved my hand in my best friend's general direction. My head was absolutely killing me and I was not in the mood to plot out my fictional death in another one of her books.

"What happened?" I pressed my hand against my eyes, trying to block out the morning light.

Why did drunk me never remember to close the curtains? One job. I only ever asked her to do one job, and she always failed.

"What happened?" my best friend hissed. "What *happened*?" As Fabia's volume increased, I really wished she'd follow the rules more. Perhaps I should remind her that a good brownie never yelled.

"Rule number sixty—"

"*I am not yelling*!" she yelled.

Moving my hand away, I slowly opened my eyes. A blinding white light pierced my skull. Squinting, I tried to focus past it.

"We are in *jail*," she said as she started pacing on my left.

My brows furrowed. That was weird. No one ever stayed overnight in jail. The cells all had king-sized beds and the sheets were changed every day, but they were never actually used.

Throwing me a dark look, she added, "In Raza."

"What?" I jerked upright, grabbing my head in both hands. "That was a bad idea."

"Oh? Now you can tell if something is a bad idea? Where was that insightful ability last night?" Her words dripped with sarcasm. "Where was it when you snuck into Raza, ran through the human portal, and tried to bring back a colony of bats!"

"I did what!"

Shooting to my feet, I leaned against the wall for support. My heart hammered, and my eyes stung from the harsh light. I looked around the place, desperate to see something other than the three white walls and steel bars.

"Why didn't you stop me?" I very nearly yelled, panic starting to set in. The fairies were a monstrous race. They ate trespassing children. They tortured whomever they wished. They put the milk in before the cereal. We couldn't reason with these people. We were going to die and I hadn't even got laid! Well, I don't think I had. I furrowed my brows, trying to remember last night.

A sudden punch of electricity shot through me. Dark-violet eyes filled my mind, alongside an oversized nose and sharp cheeks. But the image was hazy and fleeting.

Blinking, I wondered if that had been a memory or a dream.

"Well, I didn't think you'd go into the human realm!" Fabia shouted in exasperation. "You've done a lot of stupid shit, but that?"

"Of course I would do it! Fabia, I'm an idiot! The last time I got drunk, I brought home Karl. And before that, I got a picture on my butt of –" I took a deep breath, struggling to keep my voice level.

"Yeah, well. Between owning up for the wasps at your house or coming here, I thought this would be the safer option."

"How? Our punishment is me saying, 'Sorry' and promising never to do it again. A fairy punishment is –" I broke off on a hard swallow. Remembering all the tales I'd heard, I shuddered. There wasn't even an ensuite in here. Just a toilet in the corner...which was directly in front of the bars. Anyone walking down the corridor would be able to see us.

That just wasn't humane.

Shaking her head, Fabia started pacing faster. She brought her hand to her lips, nibbling on her nails. "Well, I never made it a secret that I wanted to visit this place. I've talked about it for years. My books all take place here. What author wouldn't want to visit their books?"

I sighed. That was all true. Drunk me was too wonderfully clever for her own good.

"Okay," I said slowly, trying to think past my searing headache. "If you can just tell me everything that happened, maybe I can start to remember. Then I can tell them if I meant to do it or not." And if I hadn't, then they'd have to let us go. It wasn't nice to charge someone for something they didn't mean to do.

Fairies were barbarians, sure, but surely they weren't that backwards?

Fabia turned away, chewing faster. "I can't," she whispered. "We got separated. I thought you were right behind me when the guard came, but –" Her guilt cut through my heart.

Walking over to her, I put my hand on her shoulder. "It's okay," I assured her. I knew she'd never leave me on purpose. Fabia might break a lot of the rules, but she was a good person. A loyal friend. The kind of sister I always wished I'd had.

"I'm sure we can sort this out," I said with a nod of my head. "Queen Hurvan will help us. We have a treaty with them after all, and we're at peace, so she'll just ask nicely and..."

I trailed off as a movement on the other side of the bars caught my eye. A dark figure was coming down the stairs at the end of the hall.

Stepping past Fabia, I stuck an arm through the metal

bars and waved. "Hey, hey," I called in my most polite voice. "Can you come here, please?"

He didn't give any indication he'd heard me, but his feet carried him to our cell. When he stopped in front of me, his face finally out of the shadows, I stared at him in shock. I'd never seen a scar before and the entire half of his face was – "Ow!" Fabia elbowed me hard in the ribs.

"Are you in charge?" she asked all businesslike. "I would like to speak to Queen Hurvan and inform her –"

"We've already talked to her." The scarred man didn't glance at her, his eyes still locked on mine.

My cheeks heated as I realised I couldn't hold his gaze. My eyes kept wanting to roam over his face, to take in every detail. I wanted to ask him what had happened, but a good brownie never pried.

Looking down at my feet, I shuffled back a bit. Fabia instantly took my place.

"Well, *we* haven't. And I'm sure if we did, she'd be able to clear up this mess and –"

"Your queen agreed to sacrifice you to save everyone else. The treaty between our people is quite clear. If a brownie ever breaks one of our laws, the treaty is voided and we go to war. We have already breached your... territory."

Fabia shot me a pointed look. I pretended like I couldn't see her. Like I couldn't hear the memory of her arguing for us to build a wall around our kingdom. I mean, it's not like it would have worked anyway. The thing about fairies is they had wings. And the thing about brownies is we'd have let anyone in if they'd just asked nicely.

"The terms of our new agreement includes the handing over of any brownies that have committed a crime." He looked at Fabia. "Entering our lands is not a crime." His gaze turned to me. "But entering the human realm..." He paused.

Slowly, I lifted my gaze to his, trying not to cringe in preparation of his words.

"Is punishable by public execution."

I cringed.

"But she didn't mean to! She doesn't even remember doing it!"

His eyes bore deeply into hers. "And I don't remember what I did to piss off my wife, but I obviously did something to make her burn half my face off."

I gasped. Fabia turned pale.

"Did she say sorry?" I whispered. Sorry fixed everything. My stomach twisted as I studied the deep grooves cutting across his face. For the first time, I started to doubt the power of an apology. His own wife... I couldn't imagine being married to someone so cruel.

When Fabia didn't say anything more, he turned to me. I swallowed hard and dug my fingers into my thighs so I didn't take a step back.

"Do you know what a public execution entails?" he asked.

I glanced at Fabia. She grew paler by the second. "No," I squeaked.

"You will be smothered in honey to be feasted on by ants. Once they eat off all your skin, we will release pregnant wasps so they lay their eggs inside your body. You will be kept alive, force fed omini, until the maggots eat their way out. You'll scream the first few days, but eventually your vocal chords will snap. You will be cut open from shoulders to wrists, from thighs to ankles. And then your bones will be snapped inside you. Your ears will be cut off, as will your tongue. Your ribs will be cracked open and spread apart. And as you're struggling to breathe, your intestines will be pulled from your anus and strung around your neck. Only then will you be granted mercy."

My mouth opened and closed. I couldn't speak, couldn't think, couldn't focus on anything other than that gruesome picture. *Of my soon to be fate.*

Hunching forward, I vomited all over his shoes.

Whatever I'd eaten last night was chunky and red and looked like –

I vomited again.

Brains.

"Uhhh," I moaned as I spat out the lingering bits in my mouth. My heart pounded so loudly I barely heard the man's next words.

"Luckily for you, though," he said tightly as he shook his right foot, "King Morningstar is feeling generous today and would like to offer you a deal."

"What kind of deal?" Fabia asked warily. Her voice was small, nothing like her normal self.

I trembled as I wrapped my arms around my stomach, trying to hold myself together. They would do everything he'd said they would. I would be tortured for weeks, maybe a month. I would spend the last of my days crazed and in pain. I would be lucky if I remembered my own name, let alone Fabia, my dearest friend. I looked at her and she at me. I could see the worry in her eyes. The heartache and the guilt.

I couldn't let her suffer through my torture.

Taking a deep breath, I swallowed hard and then looked up into the man's cold plum coloured eyes.

Opening my mouth, I projectile vomited all over his tunic.

Oh my gods. I held eye contact!

FIVE

A good brownie never vomits on
someone.

Let alone twice!

— Arienna

I wanted to tell him sorry. I wanted to tell him to move
out of the way because once I got started, it was very hard
for me to stop. The smell. The acid burn. They both
worked to upheave my stomach. Still staring him in the
eye, I vomited again.

"For Hel's sake!" he shouted, his wings fluttering
behind him as he jumped back. Sagging against the bars, I
moaned. I'm never drinking again, I vowed. Never ever
again.

And given I might only live for a few more hours, this
time I might actually be able to honour that promise.

"You need to move us far enough away she can't smell
it," Fabia said from her position far off to the side.
"Otherwise, she's just going to vomit until she dies and

then whatever –"

I heaved, coughing and gagging as I struggled to keep what remained in my stomach down.

"– deal your king wanted to make would be over."

"Do you think I'm stupid? You'll try to escape as soon as I let you out."

"Oh, no, what's wrong, big man? Muscles only for show? Can't handle two freaking women? Two *brownies* who've never known combat?"

He glared at her. She scowled back.

My eyes watered. As I groaned, "Sorry," he moved further back.

Smart man. Last night's dinner missed him completely this time.

"Fine. Get her off the bars."

Pulling a wand from the pouch hanging at his side, he waved it in front of us. I stumbled forward as the bars disappeared. A sharp tug on my arm kept me from face-planting in my own vomit. Forever grateful, I tried to turn around to tell Fabia thanks.

"Don't look at me!" she snapped.

Moaning, I closed my eyes. I just wanted to go back to sleep and then wake up in my own bed.

"She needs water and some air," Fabia said as she walked me around the edge, "and you need to get changed so she can't smell you anymore."

"Prisoners don't give orders."

"I'm not a prisoner, remember? Entering here isn't a crime."

"But helping a fugitive escape is."

She snorted. "Does she look like she's going to run anywhere?"

I lifted my head and smiled reassuringly. He did not look pleased.

"Follow me." Turning on his heels, he led us down the hall. Fabia half-carried, half-dragged me behind him. The further away we got from the smell, the better I started to feel. When we made it to the bottom of the stairway, I lifted my head and froze.

The fairy had stopped, blocking us from going any further in the narrow corridor. Not facing us, he looked down at his chest and undid his belt. Peeling the straps of his tunic off his shoulders, he let the garment drop to the floor before strapping his belt back on.

"There are baths on the next floor," he said as he climbed the stairs.

Neither of us moved.

Taking in his well-defined muscles and godly physique, my nausea was instantly replaced by lust. Wicked, dirty lust that was heightened by every centimetre I looked down his body. Muscles bulged as he walked. His buttocks grew tight as he climbed. His wings, a dull translucent shine, did little to hide the perfection of his ass.

"Fuck me," Fabia breathed.

Oh baby...

The things I wanted him to do to me, I didn't even have names for.

But they most definitely involved more than four seconds of action...

When my gaze trailed down his thighs, I had to bite back a moan. Dear gods, were all fairy men this ripped? He looked like the statue from the wedding. *Oh, please let that apply to his penis too.*

"Are you coming or not?" he asked, his head never turning around to look at us.

"Not yet, but I'm −"

Fabia jabbed me hard in the ribs.

Rubbing my side, I glared at her. Before I could tell her

off for cockblocking me – something she was annoyingly good at – she pulled me forward at a ridiculous pace. With all my attention on climbing the stairs, I didn't even get to check out his ass. Talk about a horrible start to the day.

At the top, I jerked out of her grip. Strolling over to the fairy, I rolled my hips seductively. "So what should we call you other than Glorious Se–"

"You're expecting us to climb that?" Fabia cut in, pointing at a sheer stone wall.

When his attention shifted to her, I struggled not to scowl. Dear gods, what did a girl have to do to get laid? I'd already befriended a wasp and started a war. You would think that would get a girl at least *something*. It's not like I was asking to peg him. I just wanted a normal lay. Shucks, I would even be willing to negotiate on the four seconds.

"No," he said coldly. "Don't be stupid. You'll never make it."

Everything but my heart froze. *That* jerked hard and then started hammering like a toddler with a new drum kit. My eyes snapped to Fabia. *Please don't.*

"Oh? Think we're too weak? Not *fairy* enough?"

"No."

He'd said it as if she was a child wanting to stick her hand into a beehive. I winced, knowing full well what was about to happen. She always did struggle with keeping a cool head.

"They've been specifically smoothed down so nothing can traverse them without the aid of wings," he said.

"See, Fabia," I gushed, turning to her. "It wasn't a personal at–"

"But even if you had wings," he continued, speaking down his nose, "you aren't clever enough to navigate the tunnels.

She took a step towards him, or rather towards the wall behind him. "Chal–"

"You mentioned hot baths," I blurted, rushing between them, breaking their line of sight. That's what you did with aggressive wasps; I could only hope it was the same with people. The last thing I needed was to be the cause of Fabia's death. The dumb twat never could resist a challenge.

"Yes." He didn't look at me, his eyes locked over my shoulder. "Although you're looking a lot better."

He said suspiciously.

I pressed my hand to my head and groaned. "Not really. But a bath will fix me up the rest of the way, I'm sure." Rubbing my temples, I added, "Can't make decisions when you're hung over, right?"

Pursing his lips together, the fairy gave it a bit of thought.

Dear gods, Glorious Sex God, it's not like I've asked you to spell a wand...

Stepping back, I grabbed Fabia's arm and threw her forward. She sucked in a breath as she stumbled against him. Her hands pressed against his chest. His glorious naked chest, and for a moment, I regretted saving her from herself.

But I would do anything for my friend. Including cockblock myself from a guy dubbed the Glorious Sex God. She better bloody appreciate it.

"What in Hel's name, Arienna?" Fabia snapped as she turned her head, her eyes threatening a slow death.

"Take her first," I said, looking at the fairy. "I'll wait here and she won't leave without me."

I couldn't explain it because he didn't move a muscle, didn't shift at all, and yet...his entire demeanour changed.

Darkened. Sent shivers down my spine.

He's going to eat us!

Before I could launch myself at him so Fabia could get away, he growled, "I'm ugly, not stupid. Whatever trap you have planned, I'm not going to fall for it."

"Trap?" I blinked, then laughed loudly, only to instantly regret it as my head screamed with pain. "No, mate, seriously. I am doing your job. You have to get both of us up there, right? And you don't know who to take first? This is like the classic, a vampire has a wasp, a brownie, and a fairy that he needs to phase somewhere scenario. Except, you know, a lot easier. If you take Fabia, she won't run off because she loves me." *And she won't have the opportunity to try to climb the bloody wall.*

"And you don't love her?"

"What? No. Wait, yes." I rubbed my temples. It was way too early for this level of thinking. I needed another drink.

"If I take her up first..."

The world slowed as I suddenly realised the two of them were still pressed up against each other. Fabia's hands were still splayed across his chest. His glorious naked chest. And one of his arms had subconsciously wrapped around her middle. Fury and tension radiated between them, burning the non-existent gap separating their bodies, but I knew a good match when I saw one. I might be hopeless at a lot of things, but I was a freaking goddess when it came to matchmaking.

"And came back for you, that would give her time to search for a weapon and try to ambush me. She could grab one of the vases off the tables."

"Or the chair," I offered, my mind racing with date possibilities.

"They're side tables. There aren't any chairs."

"Oh."

"But thank you for admitting your plan."

Fabia groaned. I gasped. "What? No!" Stepping forward, I waved my hands out in front of me. "I was just showing you I was actively listening. That wasn't the plan at all! Right, Fabia?"

She didn't say a word.

Oh drat. That had been the plan.

"So I'll take you first and she" –he pulled her away from him– "can stop trying to frisk me for weapons."

I snorted. Yeah, that's exactly what she'd been doing. Frisking for weapons. Where would he even hide –

My eyes widened when he reached forward and snagged her wrist. She tried to jerk away, but he just pulled her against him and grabbed the knife that had been tucked in the back of her waistband. It was at least as long as her forearm.

"What? How? Where? When? What!"

Neither of the two acknowledged me. They just stared at each other, creating a tension so thick, not even that massive knife could cut it.

"Ugh. Just have sex already. I'll turn around."

Spinning around, I stared down the tunnel we'd come out of. Not even two seconds later, a rough hand grabbed my shoulder and an arm wrapped around my knees, scooping me up. "Wow. That was quick. Are you sure you don't need more time?" I craned my neck to look over his shoulder. "Fabia, did you fini–"

"Shut up, Arienna."

A low rumble vibrated from the fairy's chest, making my body go soft. "My brother is going to love you."

"Brother?"

With a spread of his wings, he launched us into the air. A small yelp escaped me. Wrapping my arms tight around his neck, I burrowed my eyes into the crook of his shoulder. *Don't look down. Don't look down. Don't look down.*

Peeking through a crack in my eyelids, I looked down.

Dang it, Arienna!

"Relax," he growled as he pulled at my arms. "If you strangle me, we'll both die."

"Oh yes. Let me just relax now after that visual." I squeezed my eyes shut. My stomach grumbled with warning.

"If you puke, aim down."

"Ah, but there's a huge flaw in that plan." I sucked in a trembling breath. "To do that, I would have to *look* down." Just the thought of doing that again made me queasy.

His wings fluttered quicker behind him. "If you puke on me again, I swear I'll drop you, king's orders be damned."

"Gods, you and Fabia are made for each other," I groaned. "Both of you suck at pep talks." Needing a distraction, I asked, "So the king is your brother, huh?"

"Yes."

"Older or younger?"

"Older."

"By how much?"

"You ask a lot of questions."

"But I'm relaxing, aren't I?"

He glanced down at me and shook his head. As he banked left to go through another tunnel, my fingers dug into his skin.

"So...uh...what's this deal you were talking about him wanting? You know, the one that doesn't end in my torturous death?"

He careened right, then left, then down, then right again. I pressed my eyes tight together, no longer taking note of the path he was taking.

"In order to sign a new law, he needs the signature of a queen."

"But I'm not...I'm not a queen," I managed to say once he started flying straight again. My entire body was shaking now, begging to meet the floor. Just not as a giant red splat. I shuddered. Why would I even think that?

"You will be once you marry him."

"Oh." My eyes snapped open. "Oh! Wait. Um..."

I struggled to bring my thoughts together into any sort of coherency. Me, queen? Of the fairies? I didn't have wings! I didn't want to eat children. But I also didn't want to die. Maybe I could only eat bad children?

My stomach twisted. My heart plummeted. I couldn't do it! Unless...

No!

But...maybe I could make eating children illegal? Unless that started a civil war because children were seen as a delicacy here? So maybe only eating them on certain days? Like at an annual festival? Would that be a compromise they'd be willing to accept? I shook my head. Faster and faster and faster.

"I can't be queen! I don't even know what I'm doing with my own life. Ask Fabia. I make horrible choices, especially when drunk. I mean, just look at where I am now!" I winced. "No offence."

"You won't be making any choices. We'd just need you to sign your name from time to time."

"On what?"

"On whatever Richard wants you to."

"But what if it's for something bad?"

"Worse than a public execution?" he not so subtly pointed out.

I thought about all the babies. Fairies only ate children

at the moment. "Yes?"

"Trust me, it won't be."

I wasn't sure. But before I could voice my doubts, he deposited me onto beautiful hard ground. Falling to my knees, then to my face, I hugged it as well as I could. I was never leaving the ground again.

"Think about it while I get your friend," he said, launching back into the air. "Because I assure you, Fabia will be forced to watch."

SIX

At times of war, there is no such thing
as a dirty trick.

AND WE'RE ALWAYS AT WAR.

— RICHARD

The ambience in the room was cold enough to store a dead body. Caroline pressed her lips tightly together. Petre sat as still as the calm before a storm. And the other ten women glared at me as if their looks really could kill.

Delight filled my bones.

Leaning forward, Caroline pressed both hands on the table. "You did what?" she demanded, her voice as icy as her gaze.

I looked straight at her, a smirk twitching at my lips. When the time finally came for me to plunge my sword into her stomach, I would do it with the utmost pleasure. "I've sent Nicholas to propose to a brownie on my behalf," I said evenly. My wings stretched out lazily behind me. Her mouth thinned into a slit.

"A brownie cannot be queen," she sneered.

"In which law is that defined?"

Her jaw ticked. Fury radiated off her in a blissful heat that warmed the iciness of the room.

"It's not," Petre cut in, glaring at Caroline. "We all know brownies are technically one of us. Just because they've lost their wings doesn't mean they are a different species."

"As unfortunate as that is," Bailey muttered.

Petre shot her a sharp look. The woman lowered her head. "Be that as it may, King Morningstar has every right to take one as queen."

"And I will," I clarified just to piss Caroline off even more.

She bit her tongue, her scowl deepening.

Turning my attention to Petre, I slid the file in front of me across the table. She stopped it with one delicate hand. Her long black nails dug into the first page. Holding my gaze, she asked, "What is this?"

I smiled. "That is the law my wife and I will be signing into existence as soon as she becomes queen. The positions of Court will no longer be inherited."

Murmurs of outrage bubbled up. I talked over the twelve of them, not raising my voice in the slightest. "Neither will the positions of king and queen. Each of us will be voted into place by an educated populace. I have listed a series of requirements that each voter must meet, as well as the rules of engagement between running parties."

Her lips twisting into a promise of pain, Petre flipped open the file. I waited patiently as she skimmed through it, my stomach clenching with nerves I refused to show.

For six years, I had spent every evening drafting this law. I had run numerous scenarios, gathered various opinions and research. I had revised and revised and revised again until I had a copy I was finally willing to approach the Court with. This was what our country needed to move forward. It might end with me no longer on the throne, but it would be progress.

"If you think we will allow this to pass –"

"You will," I cut in. "Thanks to Oyveni" – *the fucking bitch* – "the fairy queen can pass any law she chooses in times of war." My wings flickered behind me, their dull light reflecting in Petre's hazel eyes. "And we are at war. On numerous fronts, if you recall."

Her wings fluttered quickly behind her, their light flickering on the walls. Seething, she slammed the file shut. "Do not play us as fools, my lord. A little ant told me that the brownie you are proposing to is currently sitting in jail." She glanced around the table, a sneer twisting her lips. "With the charge of entering the human realm."

The angry murmurs instantly turned into sounds of triumph.

"That is punishable by death."

"I am well aware," I replied with a shrug. By the time the brownie would stand trial, her use to me would be over. "I am to marry her, not save her. Whatever you decide her punishment should be, so be it. I trust you to be fair."

Caroline's hand slipped into her robes. I shifted my legs under the table, ready to shove my chair back should she attack. Keeping my eyes focused on Petre, I watched Caroline – and the others – in my peripheral.

"We will not grant her lenience just because she is a brownie."

"I would expect no less."

Something akin to pride filled her silver and green eyes. They would be the first things I carved from her when the time came.

"You would subject the girl to a royal's death rather than let her die as a commoner?" she asked, arching a thin brow.

As a commoner, the brownie would die quickly and painlessly. But as a royal, she would be made into an example. She would be tortured for weeks, maybe a month or two. She would die in agony and all because I had use of her.

Smiling lazily, I shrugged. "She is a criminal. She will face whatever is her due."

My stomach clenched with guilt. I ignored it. I was too close to let a single woman, a brownie no less, come in the way of our future.

Pushing back from the table, I stood. My eyes scanned the twelve women, lingering on Caroline's cloaked hand before returning to Petre. "We will wed this evening. Her coronation will take place in three weeks."

Turning, I made my way to the door. I listened for the whisper of a flying blade. But only silence followed me out; I held no illusions that the room would remain that way after I was gone.

As the doorman closed the door behind me, my gaze locked onto Jace. He leaned against the wall, tossing a knife into the air. As our eyes connected, he caught the blade. Sliding it into the sheath up his sleeve, he pushed off the wall and followed me through the castle.

"I take it that went well," my head of security said, his eyes scanning my face.

I nodded. "No one tried to stab me this time. Have you heard from Nicholas?"

"No."

I frowned. How long did it take to propose to someone? He should have given me an answer before the meeting.

Now he was two hours late. A few years ago, I would have wondered if he was having sex with them. But after his ex-wife had destroyed his face...

It had been years since he'd known the intimacy of a woman.

"Is Nicholas seeing anyone?" I asked.

Jace shook his head. I'd asked him that question so many times over the years. And every time, it was a no.

The tension in my shoulders rippled up my wings. Perhaps once I was voted out of being king, I could finally find some peace. And then I could focus on helping my brother. The muscles in my neck knotted all the way up to my skull.

"Tell Nicholas to find me in my study after he gets my answer."

Jace raised a brow just to annoy me. He knew I hated the fucking gesture – and not simply because I couldn't do it like he kept saying.

"Don't you think you should at least meet her? Given everything you're going to put her through, it's only kind."

I glared at him. "What would be kind is if she never meets me before her death."

Unfazed by my tone, he waved a hand. "She'll have to at her coronation. You'll be the one putting the crown on her head."

"I am aware."

We stepped out onto this floor's balcony. Shafts of light cut through the leaves surrounding the city, basking us in a golden glow. As we took to the air, we caught the sound of metal clashing against metal alongside young warcries and yelps of pain. Looking over at the training fields, I watched as hundreds of children practised their sparring. Armed men and women walked between the masses, stopping here and there to give extra aid to those struggling with the lesson.

Landing on the balcony above, I headed inside.

"If you can convince her her death will have meaning," Jace continued as soon as he landed behind me, "perhaps she'll die in peace."

"Her entire kingdom has known nothing but peace for generations," I snapped. "She has no concept of pain. As soon as she sees the jars of honey to be slathered on her, she'll break. No 'believing in our cause' is going to help her through that."

Nor me as I applied it.

"We could intervene."

Stopping, I turned to look at him. Despite his duties to this kingdom and his unwavering loyalty, I knew the burden he hid upon his shoulders. He might try to pretend that he was no longer affected by all the deaths he dealt, but we'd grown up together. I'd watched him cry over a dead caterpillar he'd found. I'd watched him bury it in secret.

And I knew that the tattoos spreading across his back and chest weren't markers of heroic acts. They were reminders of every life he had taken. Of every man, woman, and child. They were burdens he would never forget.

He might kill without hesitation for the kingdom. He might be the boogeyman the Vylians, the Alzans, and the Okahi all feared. But beneath all that, he was still the bleeding heart of his youth.

And I couldn't have that. Not in this. Not with everything hanging on his silence.

"If you tell anyone what really happened last night –" I warned.

He looked away. "You know my loyalty is with you."

My jaw tightened. I forced my tone to soften. "That

was never in question. But I also know your heart is purer than anyone else's, Jace, and so I am begging you to leave her to her fate. The gods will smile kindly on her in the next life."

A blatant lie that we all couldn't help but believe.

Glancing back at me, he nodded.

We continued through my private chambers. I locked eyes with every single guard we passed, showing them my respect and thanks despite not wanting them here at all. Perhaps when I was no longer king, I would find out what it meant to have true privacy.

"Go find out what's taking my brother so long," I said as soon as I made it to my study.

Ignoring me, Jace followed me inside. He scoped out the room, making a point of walking around the desk sitting in the middle of the floor and then flying up to the mezzanine overlooking it. I barely bit back the urge to order him out. A quick glance would've done just as thorough a job.

But telling Jace to do anything only turned him into more of a nightmare.

My lips twitched. I did not smile.

"All clear," he said unnecessarily as he landed back in front of me.

When I simply stepped out of the way of the door, he smiled.

"Ever so subtle."

"Just see what's taking Nicholas so long. I have work to do."

I could see he still wanted to say something. My eyes narrowed, warning him not to open his mouth.

"You know that favour you owe me?"

My eyes narrowed further in disbelief. My body stilled as memories of that favour assaulted me. "*This* is what you're going to waste it on?" I breathed.

"She's innocent, my lord. And we are playing with her life like a —"

"Fine," I snapped, not wanting to hear any more. The things I had done...

Shoving past him, I strode down the hall. "I will go see her. I will even say a few words to her," I snarled. "But that is it, you understand? And you are never to bring this up again."

SEVEN

A male cannot inherit the crown unless
he proves himself capable.

Fuck you, Owen!

— Richard

"Will you do this for me, Jace? For her?"

His muscles completely relaxed. The air rippled with danger. Despite myself, my fingers grazed the hilt of my dagger.

"Why did you tell me?" he asked, his voice low and dangerous.

Clenching my jaw, I forced the memory down. But it lingered in the form of a bad taste, a tormented energy that needed to be expelled. My muscles twitched. The urge to pick a fight, any fight, coursed through my veins.

Tightening my hands into fists, I flexed them and then relaxed. I rolled my neck from side to side. Bit back the urge to throw a fist into the wall. Once we stepped out onto the balcony, I dove off the edge, hurdling straight down to the dungeons.

But not even the high speeds could rip the guilt off my shoulders.

The sharp twists and turns did nothing to expunge the energy eating me alive.

"Did you do it?"

Jace didn't look me in the eye. Barrelling past me, he was the epitome of a haunted man. A broken one.

Pulling up at the last second, I landed hard on the dungeon balcony. Sweat dripped down my face. My breath released in hard exhales. Jace landed softly behind me, his footsteps damn near silent.

I stopped at the top of the stairs. Frowning, I locked eyes onto my brother's discarded tunic.

Jace laughed, loud and carefree. "Zeus' ass. That bastard finally got laid."

I wanted to smile, but I didn't. Assaulted by the image of a pink-haired brownie in the arms of my brother, I was filled with an even bigger urge to hit something.

Ignoring the unwanted, and unreasonable, snake of jealousy, I turned around and faced the maze above us. "We'll leave them to it," I said.

With fast flutters of my wings, I took to the air. I flew just as hard going up as I had coming down. Except this time, it wasn't the guilt driving me.

It was the image of my fiancee getting her brains fucked out by my brother.

Which was completely. Fucking. Unreasonable.

She isn't mine, I told myself.

Even when she married me, she wouldn't be mine.

I touched down on the next floor up, needing to wash the guilt and the jealousy off my skin.

"Will you speak to her at the wedding then?" Jace asked.

Ignoring him, I headed inside.

The halls were wonderfully quiet, this morning's sparring session having not yet finished. As soon as it did, these corridors would be packed with sweaty warriors.

"Which one do you think Nicholas is with?" Jace asked, not taking the fucking hint that I didn't want to talk. Or rather, he'd taken the bloody hint and then thrown it out the godsdamn window.

Pretending as if I hadn't heard, I headed towards the back chambers, where only my elite guards were allowed to bathe. The sound of a moan cut my stride mid-step.

My chest tightened, and I knew without a doubt that the moan had been *hers*.

My fiancee's.

The brownie that wasn't mine.

"Dear gods, this feels *amazing*," she moaned, each word slamming into my heart, making it pound with a fervour I didn't desire.

Was she naked? Did she like it rough? Was she touching herself, sliding two fingers in as she–

Lunging to the right, I slammed Jace into the wall. My forearm pinned across his throat. My eyes narrowed in warning. The bastard had tried to sneak past me to take a look.

Cursing, I took a step back and dropped my arm.

Jace stared at me for a split second and then he laughed. "Jealousy looks good on you, my lord."

I played with the idea of cutting his tongue off and shoving it down his throat. Except, masochist that he was, he'd probably get a boner.

I turned away in disgust.

"Where are you going?" he shouted.

I froze, knowing damn well he'd said it loud enough for my brother to hear. A promise of death in my eyes, I turned back around.

Jace grinned, not a slither of fear in him. Out of the two of us, we both knew who'd win in a hand to hand fight.

"Richard?" Nicholas called from the other side of the door. Water splashed. Wet footsteps squelched across the floor.

Before he could open it, I strode inside. Jace trailed behind me, a shadow I'd long learned I couldn't shake.

"Did you get an answer?" I snapped, my voice a near guttural growl. The urge to look into the pool, at the pink-haired brownie relaxing in it, wrapped around every atom of my existence. My entire body was as attuned to her now as it had been last night when I'd held her in my arms.

But I refused to give in, to look. I was the master of my own body, and the pull of my lifemate could go fuck itself.

"Not yet. I've only just asked."

"You've been down here for hours, Nicholas," I growled.

My brother raised a brow in surprise, his eyes glancing to Jace. Picturing the bastard behind me smiling like a fool, I struggled to regain my control.

"It's you..." the brownie breathed, rising from the water like Aphrodite had all those years ago. "I'm happy you're not a dream."

I looked at her, about to ask what she was talking about considering she'd been passed out drunk when I'd found her. But with that one glance, my tongue became as useless as a male virgin to a woman wanting an orgasm.

She was naked.

And dripping wet.

And staring at me as if she wanted to have things done to her that would make even a grown man blush.

Feeling heat rising to my cheeks, I looked away from her gaze. Technically.

As my eyes latched onto her small breasts, I was irritated to discover she wasn't naked at all. Her bathing suit – or bra, rather – was just a close match to the colour of her skin.

Scowling, I looked at Nicholas. Jace snickered behind me.

"Is everything okay?" my brother asked slowly.

"I needed your answer before the meeting," I snapped. "What have you been doing?"

"And why did you need to take off your tunic?" Jace added.

I refused to react, to show my need to know. As Arienna moved again, stepping from the rock pool, I found myself watching her. Her legs, although short, captivated every inch of me. Beads of water slid down her tanned flesh, and I imagined licking them all up with my tongue. The V between her thighs was soaked, though not in the way I wanted. I wondered if she was a squirter. I cursed myself for never being able to find out.

If the Court discovered she was my lifemate, they would figure out a way to use her against me. They would make the torture even more vile, expecting me to break, to refuse to do my duty and execute her. It would be grounds for my 'dismissal' as king, something I refused to let happen.

Wrenching my gaze away from her gorgeous body, I focused back on my brother.

"Well?" I growled when it took him more than a second to respond. Fuck. I needed to get out of here, to get away from her.

"What in Hel's name is your problem?" The woman's voice was sharp and fiery. "Do you get off on throwing your weight around? No wonder you've never found a wife on your own. I bet Arienna isn't even the first you asked, is she? But they had all gladly chosen death rather than be shackled to you."

A smile pulled at my lips as I turned to the other brownie. It was not a friendly one. "If you want to stay in my kingdom, you'll go back to standing in the corner like you were." I was guessing here. I hadn't even realised she was in the room until she'd spoken.

"Hey! You don't talk to her like that."

I turned to Arienna before I'd even known what I was doing. "You don't talk to her like that, *my king*."

She stopped in her tracks, her brow furrowing in surprise.

My heart began to race. "You will address me with respect." I just wanted to hear her say it. *My king*. "Just as I will you." I paused, looking her in the eye. "My queen," I breathed.

She swallowed. My gaze followed the working of her throat. "Well...uh..." She glanced at her friend. "Respect is earned and um..." Her eyes pleaded with her friend to help her out. I turned my head to glare Fabia into silence, but Nicholas had already grabbed her from behind and wrapped one hand around her mouth. The corners of my lips twitched as I turned my attention back to my lifemate.

"To respect me, you have to respect her."

My eyes narrowed.

She started to fidget, playing with a tendril of hair as her cheeks heated. But she still held my gaze. Still held my breath in the palm of her hand. "My king."

Instantly, the tension in my chest relaxed. I glanced at Nicholas and nodded for him to let Fabia go. He did so slowly.

"Get her ready for the wedding," I said, taking a step

towards the door.

"But I didn't agree −"

My eyes snapped to hers, burrowing into the pale pinks of her irises. "You just did when you claimed me as your king. My queen."

Her cheeks flushed, making me want to go to her, to claim her as my queen in every sense of the word.

Instead, I forced myself to leave. She was a means to an end first and foremost. A figurehead queen second. And third...

And third, she was a dead woman walking.

She wasn't anything other than that.

EIGHT

A good brownie never lies.

Unless she really needs to help her

friend.

— Arienna

"Fabia," I asked as I watched the hottest man in the world walk away from us, "is my jaw on the floor? Because I feel like it's on the floor."

Dear gods, his back was fine. Corded muscles angled down to his pelvis. Black leather hugged long lean legs. His wings, greyish and glowing, were currently erect, leaving his ass open for blatant, undisturbed ogling. And dear *gods*, his *ass*...a girl could get lost in it. Preferably with her tongue.

I licked my lips, totally on board with this whole marriage thing. "So any chance we can get married tonight?" I asked as the door closed behind him. *My king.* Or like, right now? Or better yet, an hour ago so we could go ahead and consummate?

Fabia stepped in front of me with a scowl. "You have the *worst* taste in men," she said, shaking her head. "That guy's a total dick."

I peered around her, as if I could catch a glimpse of him through the wooden door. "But he's hot." I grabbed her arm with both hands. "And Fabia, I think he wants to have sex with me."

Scoffing, she shook me off. She opened her mouth to say something when a towel landed on her face.

"Get dressed. The wedding is set for tonight and we have a lot of work to do."

Excited, I grabbed the towel off Fabia's head and flung it around my shoulders. Rushing over to my clothes, I missed whatever she'd done, but the next thing I knew, there was a grunt and a hiss of pain.

I turned, the towel around my head, my hands drying my hair. "What the – Fabia! Seriously? *How?*"

Staring at the knife in her hand, which was pinned above her head as he pressed his hot wet body against her, I was bombarded by questions. So many questions. Where had she even hidden it? How did she get it? How long had she had it? How many knives did he have? Also, *where?* He was dressed in nothing but boxers! And seriously, could their faces get any closer without kissing?

"The next knife you try to use on me," he growled, "better well cut me."

Holding her gaze, he clawed the weapon from her hand. She breathed hard, her chin jutting out as she looked at him in defiance.

"The next knife, you won't see," she warned.

He laughed, but it sounded like a challenge.

And suddenly, I felt like the side character in a book.

But damn if I wasn't going to be the best side character to my bestie.

Slowly sneaking over to my discarded blue slip, I picked it up and headed for the door behind me. I wasn't sure where it led to, but it was away, so that was good enough for me. And them, I imagined. Unless...

He was an exhibitionist?

I froze. Crap. How did I know if I should stay or go now?

"Arienna," Fabia hissed. "Where are you going?"

Dang it! I'd just cockblocked my best mate. What kind of a side character was I? What kind of a friend? I cocked my head to the side. Actually, if this was a romance novel, that's exactly what a side character would've done.

They always had the worst timing.

"I was just giving you two lovelies some privacy," I said, turning back around. "You looked like you were about to go at it." I looked at Nicholas. "Quick question, are you into voyeurism?"

"Am I into −"

"We were *not* going to 'go at it'. We are never going to 'go at it'. Because unlike you, I have much better taste in men." She tugged on her long-sleeved button-up shirt in a way that suggested she was already suffering from sexual frustration.

I grinned.

This was going to be so much fun. Fabia hadn't crushed on a guy in...well, ever.

I glanced at Nicholas.

He wasn't looking at me. His eyes were glued on the floor. His shoulders were curved in ever so slightly. As if he sensed my gaze on him, he looked up. And then quickly away. "Just get dressed and meet me outside."

Spinning on his heels, he left the room.

Fabia tugged on her trousers as I stood there frowning.

"Come on." Wasting no time, she grabbed my arm and

yanked me towards the other door. She pulled it open, then cursed when she saw it was a closet.

Looking up, she craned her neck side to side. "There's a vent up there," she said. "If you give me a lift up, I can reach it."

Shaking my head, I pulled out of her grasp. "I don't want to escape."

"What? Why?"

"I'm tired and I've just had a bath. I'm clean. And –" I paused, thinking everything through. "I think this could work."

"You're still drunk. Great."

"No. Fabia." I stepped away. "Listen."

She looked at me, giving me her undivided attention despite her obvious thoughts about it.

"You burned down Lief's house. I just watched my mum marry the man I thought I would. Sure, I'll have to figure out a way to bring–" I stopped just before I said, 'over all the wasps'. "Over all my stuff, but I'll be a queen. That'll most likely be a non-issue, really."

"But he's a monster. You've heard all the stories. They eat *children*."

"But they don't eat babies."

She shook her head.

"Okay, fair. But I could try to change that as queen."

"Arienna –"

"We had a connection."

She just barely stopped from rolling her eyes. "You thought the same about Karl. And Jack. And Simon. And Patrick. And –"

"Not like this." I took a deep breath, wringing my hands out in front of me. "I think he might be my lifemate."

She snorted. "Again. Karl. Jack. Simon –"

"Fabia!"

"Arienna!" she said, exasperated. This time, she did roll her eyes. "Look. I love you. I will follow you into the dumbest of places, like here, because I know I can always get you out. But this is not Brownston. You can't just say sorry. You're going to be shackled to a madman who eats children and has massacred numerous towns and villages. He is the boogeyman, the most devilish of devils. There is no one worse than him, and I will *not* see you whittle away over time, snuffed out by his darkness."

I swallowed. My pulse hammered under the emotion in her eyes. "I love you too," I murmured. "But maybe I can change him."

"You can't. Men like that don't change." She let out a slow exhale, then offered out her hand. "So please, Arienna, just give me a leg up."

I looked at the door Nicholas had just exited. The one *my king* had left through too. A pull in my chest wanted me to follow him. It was a primal need I couldn't ignore, and I just *knew* I was right this time. He was my lifemate. The literal other half of my soul.

I looked at Fabia.

But she was my best friend.

Nodding, I dropped the towel and headed towards her. Overlapping my fingers, I locked them together and stood directly below the vent.

Fabia stared at me for a second, a lifetime of feelings passing through that look. I smiled softly. So did she. Then she placed one hand on my shoulder and her foot in my hands. With a deep breath, she stepped up and reached for the vent.

Digging a hand in her trouser pocket, she pulled out the multi-gadget she always carried with her. After a few seconds, she lifted the vent off, stepped down, placed it on the floor, and then went right back up. She hauled herself through the hole until only her legs were sticking out. I watched as she shimmied forward and then stopped.

"Mmhmmffmph."

I tilted my head, trying to make out her words. "I'm sorry, what?"

More muffled noises reached my ears.

"I didn't get that."

Her legs kicked against the wall, saying what her mouth could not. *Oh.*

Oh!

Goosebumps broke out across my skin. I looked around the room, my heart racing. I needed to find something to barricade the door. If Nicholas came in and caught Fabia trying to escape... I shuddered, not even wanting to think about what punishment that would bring.

"Just hold on," I said as I rushed over to the closet and started pulling things out. Robes. Towels. Mats. Slippers. All of little use. Ugh. Where was the fun stuff? Like a couple of chairs or the crate of toys one could use while having a bath? Did these fairies have no sense of fun?

Stepping back, I placed my hands on my hips and scowled at the pile before me. *Think, think, think. How can I use any of this?*

A knock sounded on the door. I jumped a good few centimetres in the air. My heart followed suit, lodging in my throat.

"Are you two done yet?"

"No!" I said loud enough to be heard but not too loud to count as a yell. Grabbing a few towels, I ran over to the door and started silently shoving two under the gap, wedging them in tight. "Don't come in. I'm only half dressed. Needing to get dry and all that."

"I'm sure you're fine as is."

"No, no." I twisted the last towel into a cord, then looped it around the middle hook hanging on the door. With luck, they made things properly here. Holding my breath, I gave it a slow hard tug. The hook didn't budge. Smiling, I wrapped the other end of the towel around the door handle and tied the two ends together. "Don't want to get my clothes wet," I said with pride as I surveyed my handiwork. It wasn't the prettiest, but given what I had, it would do. He'd eventually be able to force the handle down and shove the door open, but the towels would buy us some time.

"It'll be fine. You'll be changing as soon as we're in the royal chambers anyway."

Ah! Why was he making this so difficult? A good brownie was never difficult. "Yes, but..." I said, reaching for something that would stop him from entering. "I'm wearing a slip. It'll cling to me when wet, and in that case, I might as well walk around in my underwear."

"That's also fine. We have no issues with near nudity. Or full –"

"No, it is not!" A pool of heat blossomed in my belly, shooting straight down to my most sensitive part. I clenched my thighs together as I thought about half-naked fairies. One fairy hunk in particular. "But just, uh, out of curiosity," I said, ignoring the fact that my friend was still stuck behind me, "does Richard often walk around nude? Or with a semi – er, I mean semi-nude?"

There was a heavy pause. "You have one minute to finish changing."

I wasn't sure if I was annoyed or relieved by his answer. When Fabia kicked the wall, I froze.

"What was that?"

Panicking, I blurted, "Fabia's on her period! That was a clot –" *Idiot! That wouldn't make a noise!* "Er, that dropped onto...my foot! And caused me to jump..." *Ah! I need a thumping noise!* "And, um...uh...um...my...my arm smacked her in the face! Because I was shocked....and grossed out." *But how would it possibly have hit my foot?* "It was my fault," I continued quickly, having just figured out the answer. "I shouldn't have stuck my bare foot in between her legs, but I didn't want her blood all over the floor. She bleeds a lot, you know? It was a very big clot. Absolutely massive. And letting it drop to the floor wouldn't have been polite, and we're guests and – Well, prisoners, well, ex-prisoners. Well, I'm the only ex-prisoner. I'm not sure what Fabia is. But anyway, we are polite guests slash ex-prisoners..." I trailed off, really hoping that was enough information. Lying did not settle well in my stomach. A good brownie never lied and I'd just thrown out a lot of them.

The echoing silence frayed my nerves. I twisted my hands, waiting anxiously for him to answer.

Just as I was about to ask if he believed me, there was a massive thud against the door. My eyes widened as I scrambled back.

This is why you should never lie!

"Fabia, we have a problem!" I nearly shouted.

The thud came again. The door groaned on its hinges, but the towels held it in place. A flood of relief washed through me, only to be quickly dammed as the door came crashing down on the third round.

My jaw dropped to the floor as he lowered his foot and stepped inside. His eyes instantly rose to Fabia's body, her legs still sticking out of the vent.

"She jumped up there out of sheer embarrassment," I croaked. "She's not trying to escape, I swear."

Dear gods, I was going to Niflhel. A good brownie never lied and I'd just gone and done it again.

Ignoring me, Nicholas spread his wings and rose into the air. He hovered behind her. But when she kicked out at him, he swerved to the side. "If you hit me," he growled, "you will stay up here until you starve enough to slide out yourself."

I gulped.

Fabia was bloody stubborn. When he touched her hip and she kicked again, I called up, "I won't get married without her!"

He glared at me but didn't comment. I think he got the message though given he tried again.

"Do not make me gas the fucking vent," he said as he dodged another kick.

Her legs started to shake and I was pretty sure she was getting tired. Maybe in an hour or so, she'd let him grab her. I looked around the room. "Shall I get some oil?" I asked, not seeing any. *Or maybe a book to read.*

I was absolutely certain this was going to take a while.

Glancing at me, he scowled. His face twisted into an ugly mess, and I instinctively took a step back. Feeling the burn of my cheeks, I raised my hands to my face to cool them down.

"Sorry," I whispered but it was drowned out by his curse.

"For fuck's sake. We don't have time for this." Ignoring the sharp kick of her legs, he grabbed one ankle and then the other. His wings flapping fast behind him, he powered back and pulled.

She slipped straight out. He fumbled in the air, clearly not having expected it to be so easy. As she swung low, her head aiming straight for the ground, he tossed her up by her feet. Wrapping his arms around the back of her knees, he held her tightly against him.

Fabia glared at me from between his legs.

Grinning broadly, I took a step back.

Without a word, Nicholas swung her in his arms so he could cradle her against his chest. She refused to put her arms around his neck. She didn't tell him thank you either when he put her on the ground.

Rude.

Swinging my arms awkwardly at my sides, I decided to break the tension. "So...period pains, am I right? They can make even the sanest person do crazy things."

"She's not on her period!" "I'm not on my period!" they yelled at the same time.

Holding my hands up, I backed away. "Thank gods for that. You two are crazy enough."

She spun on me, but before she could say anything, Nicholas cut in, "Walk. No more wasting time."

"Okay. Okay..."

Clenching his teeth, Nicholas gestured towards the door. I grabbed my slip as I walked past and pulled it over my head. Stepping into the hall, I turned around to ask Fabia if she'd be my maid of honour. She'd already agreed fourteen years ago, but I was excited to ask again.

I was going to get *married.*

To a hot hunk of a man.

And then we were going to have *sex.*

Yes, please!

NINE

A fairy never goes back on their word.

Even if it takes multiple lifetimes

to uphold.

— Richard

"Are you really not going to go to your own wedding?" Jace pestered for the umpteenth time. If I hadn't owed him my life, I would've killed him for this.

Glaring at the document in my hand, I tried to focus on its contents. Contents that outlined the Vylian surrender and would see peace brought to our northern lines. And yet, all I could damn well see was the way Arienna had risen out of the water, the droplets sliding down her skin, the lust clear in her rose-pink eyes, her lips parted in desire.

The pen snapped in my hand.

Cursing, I lowered it to the desk.

Refused to meet Jace's knowing eyes.

"You know, it's brownie custom to kiss at weddings."

My gaze flew to his. Scowling at his disrespectful grin, I replied, "There won't be any kissing."

"I don't know. She's pretty hot and Nicholas seemed –"

He dodged the first half of the pen I threw at him. The second one too. The fucking bastard had the reflexes of a snake.

Placing both pieces back down on the desk – a move I had absolutely no idea how he managed given I'd watched them both fly past him – he grinned. "If Nicholas is going to be your stand in, he will kiss her. A brownie marriage is not recognised otherwise."

"Bullshit."

"Maybe. But are you willing to take the chance? I saw the way you looked at her..." He paused.

My sixth sense didn't like the glint in his eyes.

"She's your lifemate, I take it?"

I didn't answer, knowing it would be pointless.

"Fuck. Fate hates you, do they not? To show you your lifemate only to have you torture her to death?" Sitting on the edge of my desk, he whistled.

My glare hardened.

"Don't you want to know what it's like to kiss her?"

I glanced at the sharp half of the pen. If I was quick, I might be able to stab him now that he wasn't standing...

Grabbing that half of the pen, he twiddled it between his fingers.

The dull half would still work if I shoved it hard enough...

Laughing, Jace tossed the pen back on the desk. "Alright, alright, I'll drop it before you sprain that muscle ticking away at your temple."

When he leaned forward to poke it, I swatted his hand away. "One of these days, I'm going to call my debt done," I growled.

He smiled with all the confidence of a viper having cornered a mouse. "No you won't. Your guilt will push you to pay me back across multiple lifetimes."

"Did you do it?"

I ignored the haunted look he'd cast at me that day. The weeks of silence. The year he'd disappeared.

"Although..." Jace said as he stood. "If you attend your own wedding as the groom, I will count one of those lifetimes paid."

I pushed away from the desk, not even pretending to study the bilateral agreement anymore. "Why do you even care?" I demanded.

He headed for the door, his smile long gone. Under his breath, he murmured. "Because Aurelia would've."

My heart stopped.

Glancing at the only photo in my study, I curled my hand into a fist. After all these years...

Her bright smile, radiant and pure, looked back at me, frozen on a day I would never forget. A day neither of us would ever forget.

"Did you do it?"

He didn't look me in the eye. Barrelling past me, he was the epitome of a haunted man. A broken one.

"Jace!"

A knife buried itself into the door behind me. And then he'd said the only words he would utter for weeks.

"You owe me."

Jerking my gaze away, I pushed the memories aside. "Fine," I called over my shoulder. Not turning. Not being able to see the pain in his eyes. "I'll be there." Yanking open a drawer for a new pen, I resisted the urge to grab the bottle of whiskey in the drawer beneath. "But there'll be no kissing."

He chuckled with a sincerity that irritated my sixth

sense. Ears straining for the slightest of sounds, I slipped out my wristband of throwing knives.

"Got it," Jace said, projecting his voice across the room, closer to me, as he moved closer to the door.

He glanced at me when he was a step away. Nodding, I rose to my feet, ready for whatever attack the Court was planning this time. Not that they would get past Jace. There was a reason they always waited until he wasn't around.

Opening the door, he grabbed whoever was behind it, jerked her inside, and shoved her against the wall. The door slammed shut from his kick, and his foot pinned it there fully.

Leaning in to whoever it was, he murmured, "Hello, sexy."

Annoyed, I put my knives away.

"Careful, Jace," Nicholas called through the door. "This one bites."

"I also stab," Fabia growled.

Jace's head dipped as he glanced between their bodies. "You'll need a bigger blade than that to cut through him."

"Just the tip, right?"

He laughed as he leaned in. The smell of blood pierced the air. "Marry me," Jace begged.

"What in Hel's name is wrong with you?"

"A lot." Striding over to them, I ordered, "Let Nicholas in."

Taking his time, all the while staring into Fabia's irritated eyes, Jace leaned back and lowered his foot from the door. He held up a small, familiar knife in his hand. "Nicholas." He grinned. "Stop letting women play with your knives."

My brother swore as he barged in. He swiped for the knife, but Jace held it out of reach. It disappeared from his hand a moment later.

"Cut the magic shit," I growled, thankful yet again that he didn't have actual magic. He'd be unbearable if he knew even the simplest spell. And dead. Very very dead.

"That wasn't me," Jace said, dropping to his knees in front of Fabia. Looking up at her in adoration, he begged again. "Please marry me. I cook. I clean. I do the laundry. I'm all up for knifeplay and my cock is –"

"Bleeding," she cut in coldly, but there was a smile tugging at her lips.

"Well, now you know I have no issue with it being covered in blood. I hear sex on one's period is more stimulating anyway."

"Gods, Jace! Learn to have a fucking filter."

"Why, when I get to see a beautiful goddess blush?"

Nicholas looked at me, but I refused to get involved. "Where is she?" I asked, turning the conversation to actual important matters.

"In the royal suite. She's with Lorton, getting her hair done. Ajax will be here in two hours with a range of dresses. There are three guards on her door."

"Who?"

"Saragese, Marrabel, and Irin."

I nodded. They were all good women. Trusted women. But still... "If Evangeline was back, she'd get past all of them."

"But she's not. She's in Gretadal on assignment." He glanced at Fabia. "And I'm heading back there now. I just came up to drop off the new maid of honour."

"Irin is her maid of honour," I reminded him.

He held up his hands. "Trust me. This is not a hill you want to die on."

His lack of faith in me was irritating. "Get Irin in here and take this one back."

"*This one* has a name," Fabia snarled. "And I'm her maid of honour. We swore it to each other years ago."

"I don't care what you pinkie swore to each other when you were children. A fairy maid of honour's duties are too important for you to fuck up."

"Oh, I'm sorry." She crossed her arms. "I didn't realise this *Irin* knew Arienna enough to know how to calm her down when she starts panicking and second guessing herself."

"Why would she second guess herself? It's between me or death."

"Well, if it was me, I would've chosen death."

My jaw ticked. I glanced at Nicholas, but all he did was grin. The bastard.

"Enjoy." With a short wave, he stepped into the hall and closed the door behind him. The click was annoyingly final.

Looking at Jace, I gave a sharp nod.

Shooting to his feet, he wrapped his arms around Fabia's waist and hoisted her into the air. He grabbed her throat with one hand and slammed her towards the ground.

Her body bucked. Her legs curled up between them and corded around Jace's neck. As he leaned forward, his momentum unstoppable, she grabbed the back of his head with both hands and pulled.

They slammed into the ground. Jace grabbed one of her legs, twisted free, and then rolled her onto her stomach. As soon as he did, he jumped to his feet and stepped back. "Gods, you have to marry me."

Following him, she aimed a kick at his balls. Grabbing her ankle, he spun her around and pinned her against the wall. "Easy," he murmured. "It was just a test."

"What the fuck?" she seethed.

"You have quite the mouth for a brownie." Studying her, I walked forward and leaned against the wall beside her. Jace nodded at me, letting me know he had her, not that I'd doubted him for a second. I'd been locked in his grip enough times to know there was no way she was getting free.

Her lips pursed. Jace cupped her mouth with his hand before she could carry through. "I would be honoured if you spat in my palm, my goddess."

Fabia rolled her eyes. And the way he'd said 'my goddess' brought out a dry glare from me. When he winked, I knew he'd been taking the piss about how I'd called Arienna my queen.

I was never going to live that down.

And a part of me didn't want to.

Clamping that dangerous thought down, I looked into Fabia's eyes. "A fairy maid of honour needs to be able to protect the groom from being kidnapped. Stay behind Jace and don't get in his way."

"What happens if I don't?" she mumbled against Jace's palm.

"Arienna dies." A bit of an exaggeration but not much of one. The tradition of kidnapping the groom would invite every idiot in my kingdom to try their hand given my bride would have to pay to get me back. And if she couldn't, the date of her execution would come well before our wedding.

"Your culture is messed up."

"At least it's not a cult."

Her eyes softened the tiniest bit. When she pushed against the wall, I nodded at Jace to let her go. Stepping back, he pulled out a knife as big as his forearm and offered it to her hilt first. "Don't do anything stupid," he said. "I would hate to have to bury my goddess."

Her lips moved wordlessly before she could choke out, "How serious is this kidnapping business?"

"Normally, not much. Those doing the kidnapping are often friends and family having fun, and if they manage to kidnap the groom, they only ever ask for tokens of payment." He grinned. "But Richard has pissed off a lot of people, and weapons aren't explicitly banned."

"Shocking." Grabbing the knife, she swung it around a bit, testing its weight. Her nimble fingers moved it in every direction, impressing me more than I'd ever admit.

"Now where would a good brownie learn that?"

Stilling the blade, she lowered it to her side. Her eyes bounced between us. Her voice lowered. "I taught myself."

Jace whistled. "I'd like to see you on the training field."

Her eyes lit up as bright as beambugs before dulling into a hard, suspicious line. "You can't buy me that easily."

I smiled in amusement. "You're assuming you're worth buying? Cute."

Had Jace not stepped between us and grabbed her arm, she would've tried to stab me. "I'll take that back, thank you very much," he said as he relieved her of her weapon. Turning to me, he shoved me back. "Go get on with your boring paperwork. I have a protege to train and a goddess to convince to marry me."

Grinning, he shooed me over to my desk.

If he'd been anyone else, I would've fired him a long time ago.

Instead, I did as he'd requested. Settling in my chair, I watched the door close behind them. Then I turned my attention to the agreement in front of me. Picking up the thick stack of paper, I checked over all the terms and conditions. My mind stayed focused. Sharp. It didn't wander to a certain brownie getting dressed on the floor below me.

It didn't wish I could see through the rock beneath my feet.

And it most certainly didn't imagine the dresses sliding down her skin, then pooling on the mosaic floor.

Fuck.

TEN

A good brownie always strives for peace.

Especially in times of war.

— Arienna

"So does your brother like being pegged?"

Nicholas coughed into his glass behind me, his drink spraying out of his mouth and nose. "What – where –"

"In his ass." I tilted my head as I stared at myself in the three full-length mirrors. Swaying side to side, making my wedding dress swoosh, I added, "Normally, anyway. But I guess it could go in his mouth." I winced. "I don't want to know about the urethra." Though I was certain someone somewhere had tried it. Shuddering, I ran my hands down my thighs, smoothing the silky material.

"No." Nicholas coughed some more. "I know what... pegging is." His eyes refused to meet mine in the mirror. "Where did that come from?"

"Fabia said all fairies like being pegged. She researched

all about you for her books. I've never done it, though, so if you have any pointers –"

"Ajax!" Nicholas hollered. "Bring over another dress."

"What? Why?" I asked, trying not to sound irritated. "I like this one."

I looked down at the gods-awful dress. Dirt coloured, it bunched at my waist and sagged over my boobs. But I didn't care anymore. I was tired of trying on dresses. I was tired of being poked and prodded. I wanted to explore the castle. I wanted to find Fabia. I wanted to accidentally run into Richard and see if he had a semi.

"No fucking duh," Ajax answered as he came striding over with a dress in his hands. "That one is hideous." He shot me a look of pity. "You look like you have the chest of a man." Glancing at Nicholas, he added, "And you are not picking any more."

"I know my brother's tastes."

"Your brother doesn't have any taste. Wearing black armour with pockets is not taste. This" –he held up the dress in his hands– "is taste."

And oh baby did I agree.

Feather-white with black and silver embroidered thorns snaking up the hems, the dress took my breath away. The bodice was made up of tiny feathers arcing from the waistline to over the breasts. I had no idea how it would possibly stay up as there didn't seem to be any straps, but it falling down in front of Richard would be no bad thing...

"It's white," Nicholas scoffed.

"It's *pearl*." Gesturing to me, he said, "Come here, love."

Lifting the hem of my hideous skirt in both hands, I stepped off the dais.

And froze.

My breath caught in my throat.

My chest tightened to the point of pain.

My palms grew damp.

And a shrill ring sounded in my head.

Holy crap. I'm getting married!

To a man I don't know.

A tyrant.

A monster.

A warmonger.

Who ate children.

And murdered babies.

And who probably put the toilet paper on backwards.

I gasped for breath.

I closed my eyes.

"Arienna?"

Ah! What am I doing?

I couldn't do this. I couldn't marry a man who was known for the massacre of entire families. He'd killed his sister. Probably his parents too.

And I was going to let him kiss me?

Sleep with me?

Marry me?

Oh gods, no.

Hoisting my skirt high in the air, I took off on a run.

The door of the suite loomed far ahead of me. Too far. I could hear Nicholas running after me. Questions were thrown into the air that I couldn't answer. I could barely hear them over the pounding in my skull. I needed to get out. I needed to escape. I needed –

One foot banged into the other. My arms flew into the air. The skirt twisted around my legs. Flailing, I watched as the ground came crashing up to meet my face.

Strong hands grabbed my waist. They yanked me up a split second before I busted my nose. Planting me on my feet, they spun me around.

Looking at Nicholas, I gaped at him like a dying fish. "I can't marry him."

"The alternative is death, Arienna. You don't want that."

I shuddered. "But that just drives my point home. It's between him and death? How can I marry someone like that? How did you –" I swallowed as my eyes scanned the scars on his face.

A coldness washed over his features. "Richie is nothing like Dorothy. If he wasn't forced into this position, he wouldn't be marrying you. But he found a way to save you. And him." He paused. "And all of his people."

"What?" My eyes searched his, begging for something I could hold on to in the chaos of my mind.

"Richard is fighting for change," he murmured. "Good change that will hopefully see us at peace – a life we have not known for generations, for thousands of years. He has sacrificed so much to get us here, and all he needs now is you. You have to marry him, Arienna. For us. For peace."

My mouth floundered for oxygen I couldn't seem able to grab. I knew it was flowing through my lungs. I knew I was still breathing. But that part of my body felt tight and foreign.

Peace? My marriage would create peace?

How could he throw that on me? How could he think that more expectations and an overwhelming weight of responsibility would be a good thing?

"I need Fabia," I croaked.

"She's unavailable."

"But she's my maid of honour. She needs to be here. I need her here." My hands twisted in my skirt. I sucked in a ragged breath, trying to calm the panic drowning out all thought and rationality. "I need her –"

"Not to be that guy," Ajax cut in, "but we're running

out of time. So if you could have your panic attack while changing, that would be great."

I gulped.

Grabbing my hand, Nicholas gave it a small squeeze. "You're going to be fine," he said, looking me in the eyes. "And if you ever think you won't be, just look at me, okay? I'll be standing right behind Richard, so you'll be able to compare my face and his and know you got the right brother."

My laugh came out flustered and weak. It was a horrible joke, but a good brownie always laughed at one's joke.

And I was a good brownie.

And good brownies never stood in the way of peace.

But... but...

"I need to talk to Fabia," I croaked.

He stared at me for a long moment. My breaths came out faster and faster. My hands grew clammier. Wet. Ushering me over to a chair, he sat me down and gave my hand another squeeze.

"Okay. I'll go get her. You just wait here and take deep breaths, okay?"

I nodded as I struggled to do as he'd requested. A big breath in. And out. In. And out.

Oh gods. What was I doing?

I squeezed my eyes shut as I dug my fingers into my lap.

I couldn't marry him.

But I had to marry him.

But I didn't want to marry a monster.

But –

Oh gods, Fabia, where are you?

Ignoring the loud commotion behind me, trusting Jace entirely, I watched as Fabia wrestled with her opponent on the ground. She'd kept up a lot better than I'd thought she would. Six kidnappings she'd defended me from so far, two of which had been instigated by my own guards. Granted, with those, Jace had allowed only the weakest member to get past him, but still. My guards trained day and night, had since they were children.

And with the amount of gold on the line, I knew they'd given it their all.

Which begged the question: where in Hel's name had Fabia learned to defend herself?

My eyes narrowing, I watched her every move. I didn't like puzzles. I didn't like unanswered questions. Especially when they could ruin the plans I'd spent the last six years making. Had the Court planted her with Arienna? Was she an agent of Evangeline's, a member of FI9 who'd give up her life to the cause? A cause that did not swear loyalty to the crown but to the kingdom itself. A kingdom I wanted to flip upside down...

I would be a fool to trust her.

Jace appeared beside me. After sharing a glance to let me know everyone else was taken care of, he tilted his head at Fabia. The same concerns were obviously on his mind. I nodded. A lifetime of working together, of truly knowing each other, allowed a whole conversation to pass wordlessly between us.

Raising a hand to his lips, he took a bite of a gosberry. The gods only knew where he'd got it. "Lock your legs around her neck, my goddess. She'll pass out faster."

Fabia shot him a dry look even as she did as he'd

suggested. Kristist clawed at her ankles but couldn't stop them from squeezing the air out of her lungs. After a few seconds, the young warrior in training tapped out and Fabia released her as she rolled to her feet. Reaching down, she offered the girl her hand with a smile. "You'll have to teach me how you did that jumping kick earlier."

"Only if you show me that thing you did with my blade."

"Deal."

Grinning, Kristist climbed to her feet. She hobbled around, looking for her blade.

Taking another bite of the berry, Jace pulled a sheathed bronze knife out of his tunic. He offered it to the girl hilt first. "Looking for this, my lady?"

Glancing at me, she smiled wryly. Glancing at Jace, she blushed madly. "N-no," she squeaked. "You can keep it."

"When did you have time to get food?" Fabia asked as she pushed her lilac bangs out of her face.

"When you were taking your sweet time with this young lady."

Kristist turned as red as his fruit. When he pressed it to his lips, I thought she was going to swoon. *So much for her training to be a tough-ass warrior.*

Making a note to have Echo pit the girls up against the older males, I grabbed her knife from Jace's hand. "You did well, Kristist," I said as I walked towards her. "But next time, aim for me, not one of my guards. I'm your target and you always take out your targets as soon as you get the chance." I held out the blade. She took it with steady fingers.

"Y-yes, my lord."

"Now back to the training field. I'm sure Echo is looking for you."

She grinned devilishly. Scooting past me, she went to

help her team. Words of encouragement in the form of taunts and teasing sounded behind me.

A warmth seeped through my chest at the sounds. It was because of her that I was doing all this. Because of them – the young that had not yet experienced the cruel horrors of war.

"We should head to your rooms, my lord," Jace said, finishing the last of his berry. "We only have an hour left for you to get ready."

Nodding, I headed for my rooms with Fabia and Jace flanking me. Had Irin been here, she would have taken point, but I wasn't about to let a civilian be the first to enter potential danger – even if I had my suspicions that Fabia wasn't a civilian at all.

When we arrived at my quarters, though, Jace was the first one at the door. Standing off to the side, he opened it, then strolled in.

I stood with my back to the wall, facing down the hall, one eye on Fabia, the other scouting for danger. The Court hadn't attacked yet, and with every passing second, my unease strengthened.

Just yesterday, Josie had tried to kill me – under orders from her mum, no doubt. It didn't make sense for them to leave this golden opportunity untouched.

"Clear," Jace said as he appeared back at the door. Stepping out, he gestured me in.

Midstep, I heard someone shouting my name. I turned just as Jace shoved me inside the room. He grunted in pain, then erupted into laugher. And I knew that whoever had hurt him would not be alive by the time I turned around.

Fabia screamed as she was shoved in behind me. I caught her in my arms, backpedaling fast to counter her momentum. As the window shattered behind me, I cursed.

Shoving Fabia back towards the door, I grabbed the two knives sheathed on my forearms. Pulling them out, I turned.

A shuriken cut across my cheek. Another hit my left shoulder. The third sailed overhead as I dropped to the ground and threw one of my knives into the stomach of a woman with blue hair.

As she fell to her knees, I rolled towards the assassin to my left. My fingers grabbed the shuriken embedded in my flesh mid-roll. Pulling it out, I flung it at the assassin on my right.

Shooting to my feet beneath my last target, I jerked my hand up. My knife sank deep into her stomach. Grabbing her arm that had arced towards me with another blade, I leaned back until I hit the ground. Flipping over my shoulders, I jerked the knife all the way up to her throat. She gurgled in the last seconds of consciousness as I tossed her across the room.

Back on my feet, I turned to face the other two I had wounded but not incapacitated.

Fabia stood over them. Shaking. Bloodied. But strong. One of the assassins laid on her back, unmoving. The other was sitting on the floor, her hands pressed to her stomach, trying to hold in her intestines.

Walking over to them, I squatted in front of the gutless woman. "Who are you working for?" I asked softly.

Lifting her chin, she refused to answer. I wasn't surprised. I wasn't exactly known for my mercy.

Nodding at her, respecting her loyalty even though it wasn't for me, I turned to the woman passed out on the ground. Without a word, I slit her throat.

Ignoring Fabia's shout, I swivelled and buried my dagger into the loyal assassin's heart. She held my gaze until the last of her life escaped her lips.

"Why did you do that?" Fabia shrieked as she pointed Jace's knife at me. "They were down. They'd surrendered. They'd –"

"Committed an act of treason. If I let them live, they will only try again."

Her hand shook feverishly. "You could imprison them. You could –"

"Let them rot away for the rest of their lives?"

"Yes!"

Her innocence made me smile. What I wouldn't give to believe that death was the worst thing that could befall a person.

Her eyes widening in disgust and fear, she backed away. Right into Nicholas' hard chest. His arms wrapped around her, and he disarmed her in the same second. As the knife cluttered to the floor, he pulled her away from me.

"Let me go!"

He murmured something in her ear. It didn't seem to calm her any.

Turning from her, I looked at Jace as he entered the room. My eyes latched onto the wound in his arm. A massive hole requiring immediate attention according to anyone else. A flesh wound according to Jace.

"How many?" I asked.

"A dozen, including these three."

"You know any?"

He nodded. "Francesca, Lei, Delilah, Prione." Gesturing at the one I'd thrown across the room, he murmured, "Jennifer." He looked at the one whose heart I had pierced. "And that's Ashley. I'll get the identities of the rest."

"Any of them have ties to the Court?"

"All of them. Francesca and Jennifer are Caroline's nieces."

I cursed. Wiping my blade on my bloodstained tunic, I scowled. "Move the wedding up to fifteen minutes. I'm going to get changed. Make sure my bride's ready at the altar."

"Yeah... about that..." Nicholas said from over Fabia's shoulder. He still held her wrapped in his arms. Her hands still grabbed at his wrists, but at least she was quiet now.

"What?" I snapped.

"She's having second thoughts."

My eyes locked on to Fabia. "You said you know how to talk her out of second guessing herself?"

Shaking her head, she gasped. "No. I won't do it. I won't let her marry a monster."

Her eyes flicked to the women at her feet.

"She can either marry me or she can join these women on the floor."

Fabia's face paled. Her lips wavered. But she didn't cower. "No."

"You will," I said softly, "or I will kill you first and make her watch. I suspect that will hurt her more than any blade."

A single tear slipped down her cheek. "You monster."

"Fabia!" Jumping to my feet, I launched myself against her chest. I'd expected her to try to shove me away, but her arms just hung loosely at her sides. Grabbing her shoulders, I held her at arm's length. My own needs faded away under the paleness of her features. "What's wrong?"

"I'm sorry," she whispered. "But you have to marry –" She swallowed hard, her pulse hammering at the base of her throat.

I frowned. "There's blood on you..." My grip tightened

as my eyes scanned her body. "Did he hurt you? Are you in pain? I'll tell him off. I'll –"

"No." She pulled me into a hug. "I'm okay. It's you I'm worried about."

"Me?"

Pulling me down onto the seat, she held me in her arms. My stomach twisted in concern. My pulse started to beat rapidly again as I waited for her to speak. This was so unlike her. If Richard had hurt her...

"The wedding has been moved up to now. Nicholas is standing outside. As soon as we've spoken, we'll head to the hall."

"But I don't even know if I want to get married! I need to talk to you about –"

She grabbed my shoulders and gripped them hard. "You don't have a choice, Arienna. You *have* to marry him."

"Because of the peace thing, right? But I was thin–"

"No." Her fingers dug into my skin, shutting me up. "Because he'll kill you if you don't. And I've seen... He'll do it, Arienna, and I can't... You can't let him..."

It was the first time I'd ever seen her cry.

Shocked, I could only stare in silence.

Then I was pulling her into my arms and holding her close.

As she sobbed against me, fury lit up my insides. I was going to tell him off. I was so mad at him for hurting her, I wanted to...I wanted to...I wanted to *scream.*

When the door to the suite banged open and Nicholas strode in, I snapped, "We're not ready. You can tell him to bloody well wait."

He opened his mouth, then closed it again. After a few seconds, he asked, "For how long?"

"Until Fabia stops crying."

"And how long will that take?"

I narrowed my eyes at him, for once not caring that I was being difficult. His brother had hurt my best friend. He was related to the bastard. Snarling, I answered, "However long it flippin' takes."

ELEVEN

A wedding is not recognised unless all parties are willing to get married.

EVEN THE OYVENI LAWS I AGREE

WITH ARE FUCKING ANNOYING

– RICHARD

It'd been thirty minutes so far. One more and I was bursting the door down and dragging her out of there, Oyeeni's laws be damned.

"Relax, brother. I'm sure she'll be out soon."

"You said that twenty-five minutes ago. How long does it take a brownie to cry?"

Nicholas shrugged. Jace shook his head. "At least we know she's not an agent of Evangeline's."

"Unless she's faking it and is using this time to kill Arienna." Jace had meant it as a joke. I knew that, and yet, it didn't stop my heart from tightening so hard in my chest, I wanted to rip it out to relieve myself of the pain.

"My Grace –"

Ignoring his protests, I shoved into the suite. The door

banged hard against the wall. The two women looked up at me. Fabia flinched, but Arienna glowered as if she really hoped she could skewer me with just a look.

Wisely, Ajax disappeared into the shadows.

Marching over to them, I ripped Fabia out of my fiancee's embrace.

"Hey!" Arienna gasped. "You can't just do that."

Shoving Fabia into Nicholas' arms, I then reached down for Arienna's wrists. Hauling her to her feet, I dragged her from the room. She tried to stop me. Her attempts at digging her heels into the mosaic floor were laughable. Her fingers grasping at mine almost made me smile.

Scanning the corridor as I headed for the great hall, I waited for the next attack. The Court wouldn't have sent just one.

When we made it all the way to the altar without trouble, I tensed, not liking the ease of this one bit. I looked behind me at Jace as he barred the doors to the great hall shut. With the place to ourselves, I relaxed. Slightly.

There were still windows in this room. And shadows that hadn't been checked.

As Jace, Nicholas, and the three other guards we'd picked up along the way swept the area, I turned my head to Arienna. Her eyes were still sharp with fury. Her lips were still tight with disgust.

"Don't you wonder what it'd be like to kiss her?"

Wrenching my eyes back up to hers, I finally let her go.

And immediately wished I hadn't. The loss of her heat against mine, having it no longer pressed against my palm did unwanted things to my stomach.

Things I did not have the luxury to feel.

"When Jace asks you if you wish to marry me, you will

say –"

"Go to Niflhel." Her eyes widened as she clasped a hand over her mouth.

Her fierceness was annoyingly cute.

"I'm sure I will once I die, but until then, you're stuck with me."

I grabbed her bicep, telling myself it was so she didn't bolt rather than the need to just feel her against me.

"So when Jace asks you, you will say yes."

"No."

"*Yes.*"

"*No.*"

I stared at her, my jaw ticking. How I wished I could gag her and force her to nod her head. But the marriage wouldn't be recognised then. Her title as queen wouldn't be recognised. And her signature, her very important signature, wouldn't be recognised.

Exhaling sharply, I looked at Jace. It was his fault I was here dealing with this shit.

Standing at the altar, he grinned at me. The bastard.

"I will only say this one more time –"

"Great. Then I'll only have to say 'no' one more time."

Narrowing my eyes, I tightened my hold on her arm. Her skin burned into me, marking my soul, making me want this marriage for more than just her signature.

Which was stupid. And dumb. And maddening.

My lifemate or not, she would die as soon as her sentence came down from the Court. The best thing I could do for her, for both of us, was to ignore the pull between us.

My eyes landed on her lips as she mouthed the word, "No."

Leaning down, I placed my lips against her neck. Felt her shiver despite her anger. Felt her lean against me despite her fury. Nipping her neck, not above using the information my brother had given me, I said, "Say yes and I will let you peg me in a month's time."

She sucked in a sharp breath. I watched as her silver gaze grew hooded. "Tell me what you did to Fabia."

"What?"

"Tell me why she's crying."

Straightening, I frowned. *That's* what all this was about? For fuck's sake, I could've sorted this ages ago. "I was attacked. She saved my life. But we don't accept apologies for crimes here."

"What does that mean?"

"It means I slit one's throat and stabbed another in the heart in front of her. Their heads were then cut off so they could not heal. They died for their treason."

She paled. Swayed against me.

Raising my other hand to her bicep, I held her steady.

Arienna looked at me – really looked at me – and I had to fight the urge to glance away. I didn't like the judgment in her eyes. The horror. The disgust. The *fear.*

The fear punched a hole in my gut right up to my heart and gripped it with strong fingers.

"And I will keep getting attacked until we get married, so if we could hurry this up –"

"Tell me something about yourself."

"What?"

"Tell me a secret no one knows." She grabbed the front of my waistcoat, desperation in her eyes.

"Arienna –"

"Please."

I started to shake her off me.

"Please." It was barely more than a whisper. A silent prayer that only I could hear.

Exhaling roughly, I pulled her to a corner of the room.

Knowing Jace had the hearing of a fucking bat, I leaned down so my lips touched her ear. Fighting the urge to grab it in between my teeth, I whispered, "I've always wanted a pet dog."

She turned her head to look at me. The brush of her cheek across my lips was almost too much. Digging my fingers into her wrist, I waited for her to say something.

"A dog? They're flippin' massive. They'll eat you. Not to mention, you have to go through the portal to Earth, which is a crime."

"I know." I smiled. "Which is why I don't have one. Doesn't mean I don't want one though."

After a heavy moment of silence, a small smile pulled at her lips and sucker-punched me right in the solar plexus.

"Don't you want to know what it's like to kiss her?"
"Okay."

Dear gods. I leaned in, my eyes fastened on her lips. My heart pounding. My desire pooling in my cock, making it rise to attention despite the restriction of my trousers.

"I'll say yes."

Fuck.

Pulling back, I cleared my throat and willed my cock to go back down before she noticed. "Thank you."

She nodded. Her eyes widened as they met mine. Then her head ducked back down and she sucked in a harsh breath, her eyes locked onto my waist.

My blood heated. My fingers on her wrist tightened. I fought the urge to guide her hand to where I wanted it most. Fought the urge to give the Court any ammunition against me.

But then her eyes snapped up to mine, heavy and half-lidded with desire. Her lips parted and her tongue – dear gods, her tongue – ran along her upper lip.

"If we could hurry this up before the second team gets here," Jace interrupted, "that would be good. As much as I love a good fight, Fabia looks like she's going to be sick."

Her eyes darted over my shoulder, fastening on what I was certain was her friend. Straightening, I released her wrist and stepped back, allowing her to walk to the altar. After taking a moment to collect myself, of reminding myself why anything between us would be a bad idea, I followed suit.

The wedding ceremony passed quickly due to Jace only mentioning the legally required parts. Within thirteen minutes, he'd made it to the end.

"Do you, Richard Morningstar, enter this marriage willingly?"

"Yes."

"And do you, Arienna Neath, enter this marriage willingly?"

My chest tightened in apprehension of her answer. Despite her reassurance earlier, I wasn't sure if she'd actually go through with it. She looked clammy and off balance. Her breaths came out all too quick.

She glanced at me, then Fabia, then me again. I willed her to say yes.

Opening her mouth, she froze.

Then closed it.

Then opened it again.

Jace glanced at me. Another few seconds of hesitation and he'd be forced to cancel the wedding. Oyveni's law was clear: any pause longer than ten seconds after the question counted as a sign of duress.

"Yes," she breathed, releasing the tightness in my chest.

"Then I pronounce you wife and husband."

With the ceremony over, I started to turn around to

leave. I was half way around, facing Arienna, when Jace stopped me cold.

"You may now kiss the groom."

As soon as those words poisoned the air, Arienna threw herself into my arms. She wrapped her hands around my neck and yanked me down, moving me out of surprise rather than from her strength. Her lips touched mine, and the curse I'd been about to hurl at Jace was drowned out by the wet slop of her mouth. The glare I'd been about to pin him with was now redirected to her. Lifting my hands, I went to rip hers off me.

But instead, they landed on her face, cupping both her cheeks. Tilting her head, I went over every possible reason why I should put a stop to this. I was going to be the one executing her. The one torturing her. The Court would use her against me.

And yet, none of that stopped my fingers from holding her still when she tried to move back. Didn't stop my tongue from pushing past her lips and claiming every part of her mouth. Didn't stop me from running a hand down her face to her neck. Her pulse beat rapidly against my palm as I curled my fingers around her throat. A breathy sigh escaped her as she pressed against my hand.

Testing me.

My grip tightened. My cock jumped upright, begging to be used with the same fervour she was.

Moving my other hand into her hair, I grabbed her pink locks and pulled. Her lips were ripped from mine, giving me the reprieve I didn't want but desperately needed.

As she opened her eyes, staring at me under lashes heavy with lust, I was nearly overcome with the urge to taste her again. To claim her soft lips as mine.

But I didn't need to kiss her in order to seal our marriage.

And I sure as Hel didn't need to see her again until the coronation.

Dropping my hands, I shot a hard glare at Jace, turned on my heels, and strode from the hall.

For fuck's sake, I never should've come.

TWELVE

A good brownie...

Never eats children.

That should be a rule, right?

— Arienna

Oh.

Dear.

Gods.

That man could kiss.

Raising a hand to my lips, I wondered how I'd made it twenty-seven years without ever having been kissed like *that*. Karl's idea had been all tongue and no lips. And he definitely had never done that hand thing.

I trailed my fingers down to my neck and swallowed, feeling my pulse against the tips. Feeling the ghost of his touch still branding my throat.

My eyes landed on his ass as he walked away. Between his wasp-like wings and his pitch-black waistcoat, my eyes couldn't see much of it, but my mind didn't seem to have the same issue.

Hot.

Damn.

That man was fine.

All the things I would do to him. All the things he would do –

"Ow!" I flinched away, rubbing my ribs where Fabia had elbowed me.

"He's a warmonger, remember?" she hissed.

My brain said yes. My heart said no. And my pussy said, "Oh, baby," as it imagined him destroying me like he had so many villages. Oh gods, I wanted him.

"Arienna!" She tugged on my arm.

"*What?*" I asked in exasperation.

"He's a mass murderer," she reminded me. "And a child killer. Remember the Massacre of Yanaho? Not even the newborns survived. He gutted them all himself. And all because he couldn't be bothered listening to them cry for their mothers and fathers – people *he* had killed."

I winced. The heat in my blood started to cool.

"And then there was the Feast of Kulther. They lined up all the orphaned children and he picked which ones he wanted to eat. It's said he preferred the younger ones for their more tender meat. Which means he deliberately killed more than necessary to make up the difference in food."

"More than necessary?" Nicholas asked dryly.

"It's simple maths," she snapped, "something I'm sure your brain would struggle with."

"Fabia!" I gasped. "That's rude. You should apologise."

"Rude? What's rude is killing unarmed people without giving them a trial." Her voice broke on that sentence, but she didn't look away from the cold eyes of the fairy. "And in case you haven't noticed, Arienna, we're no longer in

Brownston. The rules don't apply anymore."

"Yes, they do. They're the rules regardless of where −"

"A good brownie always fights for peace." Ripping her eyes away from Nicholas, she grabbed both of my arms. "You are queen of the fairies now, Arienna. They're the most vicious monsters out there, worse than centipedes. Their king is a tyrant, who is hated so much by his own people they want to kill him. What do you think he wants with you? You think he needs you to sign a peace treaty? Are you really that naive?"

Ignoring the sting of her words, I shrugged out of her hold. "Naivety is just something pessimists say to crush the souls of the good." Stepping back, I added, "Also, he's not as toxic as some of the men you write about. At least he hasn't taken a knife to my −"

"That's fiction, Arienna." She rolled her eyes, then quickly glanced at Nicholas. "Just because I write about it doesn't mean I actually want it. Just like you reading about it doesn't mean you actually want it, right?"

Well, maybe not the knife and blood stuff. But... My hand feathered to my neck again. *Maybe the rest?*

She groaned. "You are hopeless." Sighing, she shoved my shoulder. "Just don't give him your heart, okay? He doesn't deserve it."

Before I could respond, Nicholas pulled me back and gestured to the two guards. "Take Fabia to her chambers." Glancing at me, he ushered me towards the door. "I'll show you to yours."

"For the consummation?" I grinned. A shiver slid down my body as I followed him down the hall, to this floor's balcony. I wondered what *my king* would taste like. Touch like. Thrust like.

But then I imagined his sword thrusting into a woman.

"I slit one's throat and stabbed another in the heart."

"He's a mass murderer and a child killer."

"You think he needs you to sign a peace treaty? Are you really that naive?"

As we touched down on the next floor up, I blurted, "What does Richard want with me?"

Two guards stood at attention opposite us, their miens fierce. Nerves fluttered through me at their coldness, but I found the courage to smile at them anyway. They didn't smile back nor acknowledge me at all. And Nicholas didn't answer as he guided me between them, then down the hall they were guarding.

The silence stretched until it became unbearable. Was Fabia right? Had I just helped a tyrant commit another act of madness? Was I too naive? Was it really that *wrong* to believe there was good in someone? Even a supposed monster?

As my thoughts consumed me, Nicholas stopped in front of two more guards. They stood on either side of an ornate door. The carvings in the wood were beautiful, and had I had the heart, I would've studied them in great detail.

Instead, I faced my new brother-in-law. My chin up. My back straight.

I tried to ignore the hammering of my heart.

I swallowed past my suddenly dry throat.

What if Richard was, in fact, a monster?

But before I could speak, he pulled me inside and shut the door behind us.

"We don't eat children," he said as he walked around the room, glancing behind the furniture as if he was looking for something.

Relief flooded me. Then I shook my head, remembering all the nightmarish tales whispered throughout our city. "Yes, you do. Everyone knows –"

"No. We really don't." He poked his head through the open door of the bathroom.

"But everyone says –"

"They're just stories. Morbid exaggerations told by our enemies. Some spread by us as a fear tactic." He passed under the archway leading into the bedroom. "If people are too afraid to fight, that's better for us. Less deaths."

I frowned as I followed him, not sure what to believe. Fabia had seemed absolutely convinced he was a monster. And she was my best friend. She'd always been there for me. She'd always done what was best for me. She might not be a perfect brownie and, truth be told, she frustrated me from time to time, but she was a good person. With a good heart. I trusted her completely.

"So what happened at the Feast of Kulther then if you didn't eat them? It's said you could smell burning flesh for miles."

After checking under the bed, he turned to face me. "Yeah...no, we burned them. We just didn't eat them."

My mouth fell open. My brain scrambled. "How is that any better?"

"Well, eating them would make us cannibals. There are a few that dabble in that, but most of us don't."

"Dabble? How do you dabble in cannibalism?"

He shrugged. "Same way you dabble in gay sex. If it's just the tip, you're still straight."

I blinked, not knowing what to say to that.

"But we only burned them because they were infected with zombie fungus. There was no saving them by the time we got there. So this is your suite," he said, gesturing around us. "As you saw, there's a bathroom, bedroom, and lounge area. If you want food, just ring the bell by the door. If you want to go anywhere, one of the guards outside will accompany you."

He walked past me, leaving me standing there as my mind struggled to catch up. Turning, I chased after him. "Wait! What about the Massacre of Yanaho? Did Richard really kill all the children?

He paused with one hand on the door. "Of course not."

I exhaled in relief.

"That would've been a waste of good labour."

Stepping outside, he closed the door behind him.

THIRTEEN

To kill a member of the Court is to commit an act of treason.

FUCK SEMANTICS.

— RICHARD

"You killed my nieces."

Reviewing the last page of the Vyli-Raza agreement, I didn't bother glancing up at her. Josie stood beside her mother, both armed to the teeth no doubt, but Jace was behind them. By the time they drew any weapon, they'd be gurgling through the new holes in their necks.

"Your nieces committed treason," I said as I made a note on the last article. I would not be able to sway the Court to give up even a centimetre of the land they deemed as ours – land that was well into Vylian territory.

"They partook in a tradition of marriage."

"While armed."

"Against you and Jace. They were teenage girls barely through their training. It would've been suicide for them to try to assassinate you."

Finished with the agreement, I put my pen down and looked up. "If they'd been on their own, perhaps I could believe that. But they were with eleven others, many of whom were not, as you say, teenage girls. Lei and Prione trained with Jace as children."

"They were friends and there was a kingdom's worth of gold on the line. Who wouldn't be tempted? Even split between thirteen people, they'd be able to buy a city."

I glanced over at Josie, ignoring her flirtatious smile. "Your daughter was nowhere to be seen." Pulling the top pile off the stack of petitions I had to get through tonight, I started to read.

Another request to deny citizenship to an enemy of war. Great. My evening couldn't get any worse.

For the last decade, I had been fighting to keep our borders open. It had been hard enough trying to convince them to accept people from the countries we were no longer at war with. Getting them to accept those from places we were actively at war with was going to be a ball-ache. But it wasn't something I was willing to go back on. A veteran – of any war, of any country – deserved to find peace wherever they could. And as the cause of their unrest, the least I could do was help.

Fighting the urge to chuck the petition in the bin, I started to read the reasoning.

"Regardless of whether or not you believe my nieces' innocence," Caroline sneered, "they are members of the Court and killing them is punishable by death."

I stilled. Looking up, I caught her gaze. "There are only twelve members of the Court, each of whom have one vice member that steps in should they be needed. Josie is yours."

Her smile cut across her cheeks, chilling me down to

my bones.

"If you're aware of the exact wording of the law, it says, 'to kill a *member* of the Court is to commit an act of treason'."

My fingers tightened on the pen in my hand. When I got close to snapping it, my grip loosened. The tension in my shoulders did not.

"A member is a term that can be used to describe any and all family members."

My chest tightened. I refused to give in to the urge to look at Jace. "That's fucking bullshit, Caroline. A family member has never been shortened to just 'member'. It is always followed or preceded by 'family'."

"We'll just have to let the Court decide that." Her smile was full on feral. "Now who was it that killed them? So I know whose name to put on the form."

"Get out."

"You are legally obligated –"

"I have three days to get you that information. Now get the fuck out of my study."

Jace stepped forward behind them.

Turning towards him, Caroline's smile twisted into a sneer. "I know it was you, and I cannot wait to watch Richard skin you alive."

Nodding at her daughter, she headed for the door. As the two left, the pen finally snapped in my hand.

"Careful, my lord. If you break any more pens, you're going to bleed the treasury dry."

Glaring at him, I threw the two halves at the bin. Ink flicked through the air, staining the petition I was working on. *For fuck's sake.*

"She has a good argument, Jace."

"Caroline always has an argument. She never stops arguing."

"The Court will rule in her favour. They've been trying to get rid of you almost as long as they have me."

His smile made me want to smile and I hated him for it.

"I do believe they tried to kill me first." He pulled aside one half of his tunic to stare at the tattoo on his stomach. "Yep, says right here: 16 Moqui 1992. Evangeline stabbed me when I was three years old."

"We were playing," I scoffed. "She wasn't even head of the FI then, and it was an accident. That doesn't count."

"She's always been a wily one. Knew the threat I would be when I got older. Also, who has that sort of an accident with a pencil? It's statistically impossible." He ran a finger along the scar cutting across the left half of his stomach.

Rising from my chair, I started to pace. "If the Court accepts Caroline's definition, you will be charged with treason. I will be forced to publicly execute you."

"Ah, I see now why you're upset." His eyes twinkled as they tracked me across the room.

"Don't –"

"You're worried I'll get a boner 'cause I'm a masochist. But if you just start with my cock –"

"Dammit, Jace! For once, try to stay serious."

"You're right. Sorry. If you started with my cock, I'd definitely get a boner." He grinned. "Don't look, but I'm getting one now just thinking about it."

Striding back to my desk, I pulled out another pen, a piece of paper, and the royal stamp. "I'm sending you to Urabel on assignment. You'll leave tonigh–"

"The hel I will." He retrieved a green berry from his tunic and sat down on the edge of my desk. "They've tried to assassinate you twice in two days. I'm not going more than five metres from you, let alone to the most northern reach of our kingdom." Pulling out a knife, he cut into his snack.

Ignoring him, I started to write down his orders. The pen disappeared from my hand.

Snap.

I looked up just as the pieces went flying through the air. A bit of ink splashed on my cheek. "I'm not killing you," I ground out.

"Will you at least do the whole knifeplay thing? I haven't had sex in –" He twirled his knife in the air as he counted. "Ten, eleven hours?" Cutting another slice off his berry, he added, "Besides, you need me to help you dig through all the paperwork so we can mount a defence."

"I have a whole team of scholars –"

"That you trust?"

I didn't bother answering. It was no secret that I didn't.

"It'll be fine," he assured me, "and if not, I'll get to have your sexy hands all over me. That's pretty much a win-win."

Exhaling sharply, I bit back everything I wanted to say. The only person more stubborn than Jace was Nicholas. Getting either of them to look after themselves was more pointless than an old man's weiner. I grabbed the last pen out of the drawer. "Fine. Then start mounting a defence while I get through these damn petitions."

"Will do." Finishing off his berry, he licked his knife clean. Spreading his wings, he flew to the mezzanine, grabbed the spare chair, and landed back in front of me. Opening the door, he said something to one of the guards, then sat down and pulled out another berry. One of these days, I was going to figure out where he kept the damn things.

Twirling the pen in between my fingers, I pretended not to notice the feel of his stare. I concentrated on the petition in front of me, writing counters to the reasons they'd given.

1. They could be spies wanting to create discord in the kingdom. *There will be intense background checks and* ~~*interrogations*~~ *interviews beforehand.*

2. They would commit more crimes.

I pinched the bridge of my nose as I thought it over. Spouting statistics wouldn't sway these people. This was an emotional matter, not a factual one. All it would take was one drunk at the bar and there would be another assassination attempt on me by some idiot trying to put a stop to immigration.

Flipping to the back of the petition, I ripped all the pages off holding the signatures. Passing them to Jace, I said, "Figure out who all these people are. I want to know if they're going to be a threat to any citizens immigrating over."

Folding the pages, he slid them into his tunic. "Is this a hitlist?"

"Potentially."

He grinned. I didn't.

"Well, if you want to impress Arienna, I would suggest it isn't."

"And I would care about impressing her because?" I shouldn't have asked. I knew I shouldn't have. And yet, I hadn't been able to stop.

Raising a brow, he grinned. "I saw the way you kissed her."

"It was a simple kiss."

"You grabbed her throat, pretending it was something else, I imagine."

Well, fuck. Now I was imagining it. My hands on her ass. Her breast. Her hair as she kneeled before me, her mouth –

"Careful with that pen there, my lord."

"I told you there would be no kissing. To defy a direct order –"

He shrugged. "So charge me. I'll be dead by the time of my hearing, I suspect."

My eyes narrowed.

His grin widened.

"So when's the last time you had sex? Because it might be worth jacking off beforehand. Don't want to let down our whole gender by coming too soon."

Sliding one of the throwing knives free from my wrist, I threw it at him. He dodged it with a nimble backflip. Spreading his wings, he landed on the wooden edge of the mezzanine, another berry in his hand. The knife cut into the chair he'd been sitting in.

A knock at the door caused him to laugh. "Saved by work."

Flying down, he opened the door and took a tome from the guard. Pulling my knife free, he placed it on the desk, then settled in his chair, his back against one arm of it, one leg hanging over the other. With that stupid smile still on his face, he began to read.

I looked down at my own work, focusing on the words.

But all I could think about was my hand on her throat. Her breasts. Her ass.

Her moaning beneath me. Above me.

Her legs spread.

Her mouth full.

My name on her lips.

My king...

The pen snapped in my hand.

FOURTEEN

A good brownie never has sex with bad
people.

But is killing infected children

really that bad?

— Arienna

I paced the suite in my blue slip: bedroom, sitting
room, bathroom. Bathroom, sitting room, bedroom. The
floorboards stayed silent beneath my feet. The thoughts in
my head wouldn't stop screaming.

I was married.

To the fairy king.

A warmonger.

A potential cannibal...

Who supposedly wanted peace.

And a puppy...

And who kissed like he couldn't exist without tasting
me...

Confusion and confliction ruled inside me. I wanted to
believe he was good. I wanted to believe he wasn't a child-

eating monster.

What I really wanted, though, was to have sex without my stupid conscious getting in the way. I could practically hear Fabia's eyes rolling around in her head at that.

"He's a warmonger, remember?"

That just meant he had extensive experience ravaging people.

Also a cannibal –

So he knows how to eat.

– who eats babies.

He could eat *this* babe.

There's something seriously wrong with you...

Uh, yeah, duh – I wasn't currently getting my insides rearranged by my husband.

I winced.

Rearranged in the good way, obviously. Not in the "your intestines will be pulled out of your anus" way. Ew.

And who had even thought of that, anyways? Whoever it was – *they* were the ones who had something wrong with them. Not me.

I was just a simple girl who wanted to get laid. What was so wrong with that?

Besides, I was 99% certain Nicholas had been joking about the whole child slave labour stuff. I mean, really, who would want to use children as slaves? They started off puny and weak, and then when they finally hit puberty and were capable of packing on muscle, they became, well, *teenagers*.

No.

No one in their right mind would ever think that was a good idea. Groups of teenagers were scary at the best of times. Give them all a reason to hate you and I'm pretty sure your death would be counted as a suicide.

After all, there was a reason no one wanted to foster

them – even when money was offered.

Walking back into the bedroom, I stopped at the foot of the bed. My cheeks heated as I imagined firm abs and hard hands crawling all up my body. My fingers trailed across my throat. My pussy clenched with need.

It had been days since I'd been laid. Almost a year since I'd experienced an orgasm through someone else's doing. Surely, that justified sleeping with a potential mass murderer?

I mean, the men in Fabia's romance books weren't exactly honourable either. In fact, they were even worse than Richard. They didn't just burn babies; they knew how many dead ones it took to fill a bathtub. Thirty-four. As well as the amount needed if the babies were blended first. Fifty-two and a half. They had killed and ravaged and done so many unspeakable things all just to get their woman back. And she hadn't even been in that much of a danger considering the woman that had kidnapped her had ended up in her harem a dozen chapters later.

So really, when compared to the love interests in her books, Richard was a flippin' saint.

And if he was a saint, was it not my duty as a good brownie to worship him?

Preferably with my tongue?

I licked my lips.

Bit back a groan.

Oh yeah, that's definitely what I should be doing.

I'd run my lips down his chest, making my way to his glorious, sexy cock – it would be long and thick, but not too long or thick. Nothing scary. Or ugly. Gah, so many of them were ugly. Why couldn't the gods have given men something that had an appeal equal to boobs? I mean, those were nice.

But instead, they'd given us veiny dicks.

And hairy balls.

How was that fair?

Men got to suck on freaking heaven – big or small, it didn't matter; all boobs were great.

But balls?

There wasn't a single ballsack in existence that was nice to look at. They were wrinkly and hairy and were only ever put in our mouths out of kindness.

Man, the gods had really messed up there. If they'd just made balls and cocks nicer to play with, we'd do it more often rather than only when we felt super loving. Like on their birthdays and special occasions.

I cocked my head to the side, a new business idea coming to mind. Make-up for ball sacks. Or masks. Fabia would love that. I took a step towards the door, wanting to go tell her, before remembering Richard was coming soon.

I grinned. *Coming soon. Oh yeah, he will be.*

Shimmying out of my bra and panties, I stood in just my blue slip. It wasn't the prettiest piece, but it was sexier than my plain tan underwear. At least this had a bit of lace...even if that lace was stained from my adventures.

I frowned.

Licked my finger and rubbed at a stain.

When it didn't come out, I swallowed nervously.

Richard was a king.

He had his whole pick of women.

He was also a warrior.

Had his whole pick of villagers.

Whereas all I'd had was Simon. And Karl. And I hadn't even managed to keep them!

"Oh no, no, no, no." Pacing, I rubbed at my blue slip harder. What if I embarrassed myself? What if he wasn't here because I wasn't attractive enough? Knowledgeable enough? What if –

I stopped, my heart in my throat.

What if he wasn't already here because he didn't want to be here? It had been nearly an hour since Nicholas had left, and Richard hadn't arrived.

He might never be coming.

I flinched, thoughts of Karl swarming my mind.

Memories of him not coming home on time.

Learning he'd been with my sister.

Then my mum.

What if Richard was with someone else?

What if on our wedding night, he was...

I shook my head. Took a deep breath. Tried to control the shakes trembling throughout my body.

No. He wouldn't do that. He was my lifemate...wasn't he?

"Are you really that naive?"

Rushing to the door, I yanked it open. "Where is he?" I demanded, not sure if I wanted to know, but unwilling to take it back. I couldn't stay ignorant again. I couldn't be the joke of everyone's glances. Their hushed whispers.

The guard on the right turned to me, her gold eyes full of pity. She glanced down my body, taking in all the stains. I crossed my arms over my chest, trying to hide the worst of it. My cheeks heating, I glanced at my feet.

"Who?" she asked.

I looked up at her, blinking rapidly as I struggled to keep my feelings in check. "Richard. King Morningstar."

"I am not privy to his schedule."

My fingers dug into my arms. The doubts clawed at my mind. Flashes of a woman that wasn't me rolled through it, wrapped up in the arms of my lifemate.

"But I would imagine he's in his study. He spends most nights there."

A chill ran through me. Did I really want to voice the

next words?

Trembling, I murmured, "Can you take me to him, please?"

Without a word, she walked forward. I followed her, my eyes on my feet, my heart in my throat. With every step, my doubts strengthened. He was a king.

And I was just a commoner.

What could he possibly want with me?

"Keep your chin up," she said as we rounded a corner. "Richard doesn't like weakness."

My eyes darted to her, taking in her black leather armour, the decorative sword at her waist. Her muscles were perfectly defined – a clear testament to her strength. Whereas I didn't have a muscle on me that was of any use. I spent my days reading and drinking. Gods, I could use a drink right now.

Reaching over, she nudged my chin. "Look up," she said, "and breathe. He's not as scary as he looks."

Scary? I blinked. He looked scary? I just thought he looked delicious. Too delicious. Ridiculously delicious. So delicious he had to constantly fend off women wanting to get in his pants. "Is he kind?" I blurted. *Kind enough not to cheat?*

She snorted. "No."

My chest deflated.

"But he respects your boundaries. If you don't want to do something, just say so."

"What if I don't want *him* to do something?"

Her eyes flicked to me. A knowing grin pulled at her lips. "Trust me. You'll want him to do everything."

My mouth opened as my eyes widened. "Wait, what? What are we talking about?" But my pussy already knew, growing damp again with expectation.

"Him in bed...aren't we?"

No, but we sure are now.

"How many women has he had?"

She shook her head. "Ask me something you actually want to know." She leaned over. "Like where else is he pierced."

I stumbled over my own feet.

She laughed, carefree and teasing.

"His nipples?" I breathed, picturing it in my mind.

She shook her head again.

My eyes widened. I swallowed. *Hard.* And imagined something else sliding down my throat. A cold piece of metal hitting my tonsils.

Dear gods, I could not wait to feel it.

"Does he last longer than four seconds?"

It was her turn to stumble. "Oh, you poor little thing. Seconds? No. Minutes? No. Hours... I've heard he's gone for days before."

My mind melted from the heat coursing through my body.

"And given how long it's been for him...suspected, of course." She grinned. "We take bets. Ajax said Irin said that Revna said that no one has gained entrance to his bedroom in almost six months."

My feet banged into each other again. I reached a hand out to the wall to find my balance. "Six months?"

"Suspected. My sister reckons it's been longer."

"How much longer?"

"A year? But that's just crazy." She stopped before we turned the corner. Lowering her voice, she leaned in. "Do me a favour and keep track of how long he lasts the first time, will you?"

"The first..." I blinked, the rest of her words sinking in. "What, no? I'm not –"

She laughed. "Yeah, you're right. There's no way you'll

be in a mind to count." Shrugging, she stepped around the corner. "But with a week of latrine duty on the line, I had to ask."

Before I could say anything, she stopped in front of a black door. Two guards were stationed outside it: one raven-haired male, one blonde female. Curved decorative swords hung at their sides. Leather adorned their toned bodies.

"She's here to see King Morningstar."

Nodding, the woman knocked on the door.

I twisted my fingers in my slip, my nerves coming back in a rush. Would my guard have brought me here if she had known there was another woman inside? Had she purposely distracted me from my thoughts on the way over so I would embarrass myself in this moment for her own entertainment?

Brownies could be cruel despite all the rules.

Fairies were worse.

I shivered as the door opened from the inside.

Jace poked his head out, his mien easy, relaxing some of the tension in my shoulders. A grin spread across his lips as his eyes landed on mine. "Come in."

I glanced at my guard before taking the first step. My chest squeezed all of the air from my lungs as I took in *my king*. Sat at his desk, his head bent over some paper, he looked regal. Untouchable. Way out of my league.

Maybe this was a mistake. Maybe I should've stayed in my chambers.

"Your wife is here to see you." Walking past me, Jace settled himself beside Richard. He smiled encouragingly and I grabbed on to that like the last slice of cake.

Lifting my chin, taking solace in the fact that he was alone, I blurted, "I would like you to...to join me in my chambers. For our wedding night."

Flipping a page, Richard kept his eyes on his desk. "No." He jotted something down. "You're dismissed."

FIFTEEN

A good brownie never screams.

Ever. Ever.

— Arienna

"What?" I stared at him, certain I'd misheard. As my fingers dug into my thin blue slip, I wished I was wearing something thicker, something that could guard me against the harsh cut of his words, the embarrassment piercing my soul. I wished with all my being that I was at least wearing underwear. I'd taken it off to be sexy and now all I felt like was a fool.

"I won't join you in your chambers." He flipped the page he was reading, his eyes never once looking up. "I'm not interested in having sex with you."

"But why?"

"Frankly?" He jotted something down with one half of a pen. Ink stained his fingers. They were a bright red, the only colour on him. "You're not my type."

"What? Hot women aren't your type?"

Another jot. "You're sounding a bit desperate."

No freaking duh, I wanted to say, *I'm as horny as Zeus on a Wednesday, and I just want my marriage to be better than my engagement.* I glanced over at Jace, hoping he'd somehow help me, but all he did was keep his eyes on the door behind me. And I'd thought he was the nice one.

Exhaling strongly, trying hard to ignore the pain of rejection from my own husband, I said, "I know you didn't really want a wife and I didn't really want a husband." I shook my head as I thought about Karl. "Well, I did. But not you, and –"

He finally looked up.

Only it wasn't at me. And that hurt.

Staring at Jace, he said, "Escort my wife back to her chambers and imprison whoever brought her here."

My mouth fell open in utter shock and horror. "You can't do that."

His eyes flicked to mine, holding me down as good as chains. "You'll find, my queen," he murmured, "that I can do a great number of things."

And just like that, he stole all my breath. All my fear. All my thoughts about not being good enough.

My throat suddenly dry, I was acutely aware of the wetness pooling between my legs. It was like he had fucked me with his words, like he was still fucking me with his eyes. I swayed on my feet, unsure if I should move forwards or back.

"Jace."

That short command broke the spell. The flippancy of it caused a fountain of anger to explode inside me. It was such a new feeling, a powerful feeling that it left me momentarily shaken. A good brownie was never angry. A good brownie never screamed. But in this moment, I was tired of being a good frickin' brownie.

I just wanted my marriage to be better than my engagement. I wanted him to look at me as if I was more than a signature he needed on whatever it was he wanted. I *wanted* to get Karl's stupid frickin' dick off my skin.

Ignoring Jace as he approached me, keeping my eyes solely on Richard, I reached up and yanked a strap of my slip down.

Awareness instantly hit me. His eyes dipped to my chest. Heated and burning, they scorched a path down to my nipple. I could feel his hands there, his lips, his tongue, and my breath started to come out faster.

"Have sex with me," I demanded. Trying my hardest to pretend Jace was no longer here, I reached up to pull down the other strap.

Crack.

Something snapped and I wondered, briefly, if it was me. My sanity. But then I saw the ink pooling across his desk.

"Leave us."

Tears burned my eyes at the newest round of rejection. I yanked the other strap down in defiance.

"Jace," he snapped.

I tensed, waiting to be dragged out of here, but Jace simply walked past me. I thought I caught a glimpse of a smile on his face, but I couldn't move my eyes from Richard's to check. He held me captivated. Beholden. Enslaved.

The door clicked closed behind me. My heart pounded in my chest. Beneath my naked flesh.

My eyes widened.

My naked flesh.

My senses coming back to me, I yanked one of my straps back up. I was way out of my league. What the heck had I been thinking?

He wasn't going to be a gentleman like Simon. He wasn't going to be predictable like Karl. He was going to be –

My thoughts spasmed as he unfolded himself from his chair, his eyes never leaving mine.

I took a step back. And another. "Ah. Yes. No. You did say no and it would be rude of me to push. So...I'll just go now." I glanced behind me at the door, my feet shuffling me back. When I turned around to excuse myself one last time, I sucked in a sharp breath.

He was there, right there in front of me. Barely a tongue's length away. His eyes glued on mine.

Squeezing my thighs together, I was acutely aware of my breast hanging free between us. I raised my hand to cover myself, but he grabbed it before I could lift the strap.

His fingers like a cuff on my wrist, he walked me back against the door. One step. Two. Then the wood was hard against my back. And he was hard against me. And the air was nowhere to be found.

He pinned my arm to the wall. Staring into my eyes, he raised his other hand to the strap I had put back in place. His fingers grazed my shoulder, sending chills down to my very core. Ever so slowly, he pulled it down, letting the fabric slide across my skin. My tight little bud.

My thighs clenched.

My lips parted.

And his hand slid up my arm to cup my naked breast.

Leaning in, his breath hitting my neck, he asked, "And what did you have in mind for our wedding night, my queen?"

I swallowed, unable to speak.

"Did you imagine my hands sliding across your body? Cupping your breasts before claiming your nipples as mine?" He rolled my bud between his fingers, causing me to arch in expectancy. My lashes lowered. A moan built up in my throat. "Did you imagine my lips here, licking and sucking as I trailed my hand lower?" His fingers glided down my stomach, pushing my slip to the floor. "Did you imagine me here?"

He cupped me as if he owned me. I sagged against the door, my breaths laboured and hard.

"You must've," he murmured, his lips against my neck, "because you're already so wet."

My head fell to the side as my groan finally escaped, but he grabbed my chin and forced it back upright. His eyes bore into mine. "I asked you a question, *my queen.*"

My tongue became way too tied to speak.

His finger dipped between the lips of my pussy.

I whimpered – an actual bloody whimper – as I bucked my hips against him. His hand left my centre and grabbed my hip, pinning me to the wall.

"Don't make me ask again."

"Yes," I gasped. "I imagined your lips on my breasts." I leaned forward to kiss him, to relieve some of the pressure inside me, but he turned his head. Lowering it, he clasped his teeth around my nipple.

I jerked into his mouth, crying out in pleasure.

He released me before the pleasure could properly build. Turning me around, he pushed me tight against the door. He kicked my legs apart. His hand slipped between my thighs. His palm resting on my ass, he pushed a finger inside me.

I bucked against the door. Closing my eyes, I moaned in pleasure as his finger fucked me fast and hard.

His other hand wrapped around my throat.

Lifting my ass to him, I silently begged him to go faster. Harder.

He pressed his thumb against my butthole.

My eyes popped open.

My fingers grabbed his wrist, but he released my neck to pull my hand away.

The pressure against my back hole felt too tight. Sharp and painful like a dozen little tears were popping up.

And then he was pushing inside and I was closing my eyes and moaning.

"*Richard.*"

He slapped my ass.

"I told you to call me 'my king'."

As he slammed his hand into me, his fingers filling both holes, I struggled to stay standing. He wrapped an arm around me as my moans intensified. Pressing his fingers against my clit, he rubbed it slowly, lovingly, in a powerful contrast to the hard thrust of his other hand. My orgasm built until I was clawing at the door. Banging on it. Twisting against it. Rubbing myself against the wood and his hands. Chasing that specific outside stimulation that would send me over the edge. Gasping, so close, I shamelessly whimpered, "*My king.*"

And then I screamed.

And I didn't even care that a good brownie never did.

My orgasm ripped through me, stronger than it had ever been. My pussy and ass clenched around his fingers, squeezing them in erotic pulses that left my legs trembling and my chest heaving. I wanted to feel his cock inside me, rubbing against my inner walls as I rode out the end of this ecstasy.

But when his hand slipped from my grip, it was to grab my hair and pull me back. He forced me to my knees, and while I was still struggling to breathe, he shoved his cock inside my mouth. Rough. Hard. All the way. So deep.

My pussy clenched under the show of his desire.

My lungs struggled, needing air.

I reared back, gagging and coughing, but he had such a strong grip on my hair. Holding me still, he rammed his cock down the very back of my throat.

Again.

And again.

And again.

My eyes watered. My hips bucked. I wanted to reach down and touch myself, but my hands wouldn't leave his hips. My fingers dug into his skin. I wanted all of him.

He pummelled into my mouth, fucking it like some dirty little hole. I thought about biting him, causing him to jerk, making him mine as he was making me his, but I was struggling so much just to breathe that I didn't have the chance.

His hand tightened in my hair.

My throat gripped the end of his cock as I gagged and choked. My reflex kicked in. Vomit came up, but with nowhere to go, I was forced to swallow it.

I gagged again.

Tears streamed down my cheeks.

I wanted to look up, to peer into his eyes and know that I wasn't *just* some thing for him to use, but he was too blurry through my tears.

"Is he kind?"

"No."

I squirmed beneath his thrusts, heat building despite the pain in my mouth from the cut of his piercing.

"What if I don't want him to do something?"

"Trust me. You'll want him to do everything."

And dear gods, she was right. Grabbing both sides of my face, he picked up the pace. My teeth scraped against his cock. Cold metal caught on my cheek every so often, but he didn't seem to care. Pummelling into me, he stayed deep on the last thrust.

His balls felt so tight against my chin.

The underside of his cock pulsed against my lips.

Pulling out, he came all over my face, his cum mixing with my tears.

I panted for the air that I desperately needed. My pussy pulsed in the same tempo, wanting him, needing him to fill me.

Placing two fingers under my chin, he lifted until I met his gaze. "There's your wedding night. *Wife," he said.* "Now get the fuck out of my study and don't bother me again."

When I didn't move, too frozen with confusion, he bent down to yank up my slip. Not even bothering to pull my arms through the straps, he opened the door and shoved me out.

SIXTEEN

The welfare of the kingdom always comes first.

ONE OF THE FEW LAWS I AGREE WITH.

— RICHARD

"Classy," Jace said as soon as he re-entered, his eyes hard and full of judgement. "I can't believe it's taken you all this time to find a wife given your gentlemanly traits."

"Don't."

He took up position by the door, leaning right next to the spot where I'd finger-fucked her senseless, where I'd claimed her mouth as mine.

"I should let the Court know her torture sentence has already been served," he said.

I exhaled roughly. Tried not to recall the tears that had streamed down her face.

Fuck.

I yanked another petition off the stack.

"So what do you call that technique? Get her to divorce

you ASAP?"

"I can't have her dreaming up some fairy tale about us," I snapped. *I can't have her looking at me as if she sees something I'm not. Something good. Something worth fighting for.*

Glaring at the petition, this one about having at least one sex toy listed as an essential item for when declaring bankruptcy, I cursed.

Now all I could think about was having her at the mercy of a toy.

A good thing then, that I'd made sure she would never want to see me again.

SEVENTEEN

A good brownie does not curse.

Unless the situation really, really

calls for it.

— Arienna

Hot.

Flippin'.

Damn.

I couldn't wait to see him again.

That had been the best sex I'd had in a while – even if he hadn't actually put it in me. I'd been hurt when he had thrown me out half-way through, but I was willing to risk that pain again just to come that hard.

Stretching slowly, I sat up in bed, a goofy smile on my face. Desire formed at the mere thought of him. Flashes of me down on my knees, of him pushing inside my mouth, filled my mind. I could hear the grunts and growls of his arousal, taste his precum on my lips.

Reaching between my legs, I started to stroke myself. I

closed my eyes, imagining the hard push of his fingers, the rough taking of my mouth. Leaning back against the headrest, I ran my other hand down my throat to my breasts, then gave them each a squeeze.

"My king," I breathed, building myself up, thinking about all the things he could do to me.

Karl had always been a two-pumps man, and Simon had never wanted to do anything other than missionary. But Richard would try everything. I just knew it.

My hips bucking, I stroked myself faster, rubbing my sensitive bud.

Squeezing my breast, I arched on the bed and came all over my fingers.

I lowered myself back down, breathing heavily, and opened my eyes.

Dear gods, I was looking forward to seeing him this morning. Perhaps if he refused to let me leave the castle like I wanted, I could 'convince him with my wily ways'.

Giggling, I scooted off the bed and padded towards the bathroom. My blue slip sat crumpled in a heap where I'd left it by the sofa. Dirty. Used. *Delicious.*

Remembering all the glorious details about last night, I grinned as I passed it. Two steps later, I was hit hard with hindsight and regret: the slip was the only thing I had to wear.

But I'd used it as a rag last night, wiping all the cum off my face.

I wrinkled my nose. It was going to be dried and crusty now. Scratchy and gross.

And still I would be forced to wear it. My eyes lingered on my wedding dress. Nope. Out of the two of them, the cum-covered slip was still the prettier option. Nicholas' taste really was awful.

After washing up in the bathroom, I tugged on the slip

and tried my best to ignore all the parts where it stuck together. It's not like I'd left Richard's study very sneakily. Crusty clothes or not, everyone would know. And if I was being honest, a part of me liked them knowing.

Back off, people. He's mine.

I grinned as I opened the door of the suite.

"Gods, you look awful," Ajax said as he barged in past me. "I hope this isn't your default setting."

My mouth dropped open as I followed him. "What are you doing? I'm about to go see Richard."

Turning, he looked me up and down. "To do what? Ask for payment for your services?" His lips pursed. "No, that can't be it. Even prostitutes have better style than" –he waved a hand at me– "whatever this is."

"Hey! I'm –" My attention was snagged by a young girl wheeling a full-length mirror and a railing of clothes past me. She settled them in the middle of the room, causing me to groan.

"Please tell me I only have to try on one thing. I have to get home today to...uh, pick up some belongings." That technically wasn't a lie. Wasps were sort of belongings – if anyone could really own a ball of angry, violent, do-their-own-thing fluff. That didn't listen to a word you said, ever.

"If it's the right thing, then yes." Ajax turned to the girl. "Ella, step aside and let her choose. We'll see what her taste is and go from there." He pursed his lips. "She can't exactly choose worse."

"Hey! My dress was pretty. I just took it off because it was too restricting."

"Well, luckily, everything here is designed for ease of movement because restrictions can get you killed." He flicked through the rack and grabbed a purple jumpsuit. "For instance, this. The legs are loose, allowing full kicks to the face. The skirt is reinforced woven spider thread, making it virtually stab proof, and the belt has a wire underline, allowing it to be used as a garrotte should the need arise." Pulling it off, he wrapped it around his throat.

I cringed, deciding against this piece immediately.

"The cape sleeve is brilliant for hiding your knives and other weapons, and most importantly," he said, digging his hand into the trousers, "it has pockets."

I forced a smile. "Well, uh, it's very pretty and I really love that it has pockets, but is there anything that's less... lethal?"

He blinked. Then shrugged. "I guess you don't need any weaponised clothing given you'll always have a guard on you. And you know, the whole, being executed thing." He nodded as he rummaged through the rack again. "It'll probably be kinder to let someone kill you now."

"Oh no," I assured him, "I'm not being executed."

He glanced at me over his shoulder, a dry look in his eyes. "King Morningstar doesn't share anything, sweetie, least of all his crown. You can ask his sisters that. Wait, no you can't because they're dead." Grabbing a short black dress with silver embroidery crawling across its hem, he held it up to me. "This has concealment straps for about a dozen weapons but nothing built in."

I shook my head, still stuck on the whole 'I might be executed thing'. "But Richard said if I married him, they'd stop the execution."

"Did he? Because our king is many things, but he's not a liar. The Court decides executions, not him."

"But, he –" I trailed off, realising that he hadn't ever actually said I wouldn't be killed. He'd said I wouldn't be tortured.

My breath caught.

My mind screamed.

The mother flippin'.
Frecken'.
Bloody.
Poopface.

No. I hesitated, a pressure building in my chest. A good brownie never cursed. But...

"The mother *fucker.*"

And gods did that feel good to say even if it had been muttered under my breath so softly I hadn't heard it.

Louder, I asked, "But why marry me at all then?" My throat tightened. My thoughts spun.

"Let's go with this one," he said. "I think it'll bring out your eyes nicely, and knowing King Morningstar, he'll be dressed all in black. You'll match."

Bewilderment covered my face. "I don't want to match with him! You just said he's still going to kill me."

"Well, aren't you lucky then. I would kill to die right now."

"What?"

Shaking his head, he gestured to his assistant. "I'm done for the day. Deal with this while I go get a drink. If you can get her to pick out a few more outfits, I'll give you a raise."

My mouth fell open when he actually left. Fairies were the worst! How could he drop a thing like that and then leave me to deal with it on my own?

My breathing came out faster.

Anger built in my chest.

The world started closing in.

My hands clenched.

I was going to be sick.

Or faint.

Knowing my luck, I'd do both.

Breaking through my haze, the girl said, "I'm sorry to

bother you when you're clearly going through something, but can you just pick a few outfits at random? I could really use the extra cash, and Dad's a stickler for raises."

I looked at her, blinking rapidly. "What am I going to do?"

"Well," she said slowly, "you could pick out a few extra outfits." Smiling cheerfully, she added, "maybe even the one you'll die in, hmm?" Holding up a red jumpsuit, she waved it in the air. "For instance, this. You wouldn't even be able to see any of the stains."

My mouth fell open. Horror grabbed hold of my heart and squeezed.

"Or..." she said, dragging the word out as she grabbed a black jumpsuit, "this one will hide not just the blood but also your piss and shit. That's pretty good, right? Dying in style."

I shook my head frantically. "But I don't want to die in style! I don't want to die at all!"

"Well," she said in frustration, "you don't really get to choose that, now do you?" Forcing another smile, she added, "But what you can choose are a few outfits. So what do you say?" She held up a dark plum-coloured dress and a black three-piece suit with a purple shirt. "These are sexy and queen-like, hmm?"

A good brownie would've said yes. A good brownie would've helped her get that raise.

But if I was going to die by my own husband, then screw the rules. Where had they ever gotten me anyways? Here. Dying. That's where they'd gotten me.

Well, I wasn't quite dying yet, but I would be soon.

"Get out."

"What?" Shock laced her words, alongside annoyance and disappointment, but I didn't care.

"Get. Out."

If these were the last moments or days of my life, I wanted to enjoy them. And she was not enjoyment. She was depression and punch-her-in-the-face-ion. I'd never punched anyone in the face before, but I was pretty sure that's what this feeling was.

Scoffing, she shook her head and left, and then I was on my own with my thoughts and I didn't know if that was worse.

"He's executing me." I couldn't believe it. Didn't want to. "He's *executing* me!"

No, wait. I could believe it. Quite easily, actually. He was a fairy, and everything was starting to make sense now. Why he hadn't asked me to marry him himself. Why he hadn't come to see me on our wedding night. Why bother getting to know someone, getting attached when you were just going to kill them, amirite?

"That's why he came on my face too! Why make love when you can just fuck it, huh?"

Throwing my hands in the air as I paced, I disliked how much sense everything was making. More so, I disliked that Fabia was right. She was never going to let me live this down.

Live.

I snorted.

At least my death would have one nice outcome.

My feet grinding to a halt, I thought about all the things I'd planned on doing with my life. All the dreams I'd made that had yet to come to fruition. And okay, most of them I could've already done had I not kept putting them off, but, like, that was different. That was before I knew I was actually going to die. There was nothing better for stopping one's procrastination than the approach of death. Right?

A little voice said I was lazy enough for the answer to

be no.

Ignoring it, I started to pace again. I needed to find out how much time I had left. Then I could start planning for all the things I wanted to do, like –

My eyes widened as I remembered the wasps. I ran to the door. Although I had separated them all before the wedding, the buggers liked chewing through my walls despite me having bought them perfectly good, fairly expensive chew toys. And if they got out, they'd kill each other, just like Hyatt had Bo.

Just like Richard was going to do to me...

But it didn't matter how I felt about him anymore. I had to do right by my pets. Opening the door, I demanded to see my executioner.

For them.

For me.

But mostly for them.

EIGHTEEN

A good brownie always does right by her pets.

Even if that means she has to

deal with a ~~hot~~ jerk.

— Arienna

Dear gods, had I made a mistake.

I should've stayed far away from him.

Because my body was a flippin' traitor that was very much not connected to my mind.

Staring at Richard as he stood half-naked in front of me, his arms crossed, his lips in a thin line, I remembered the feel of him pressed against me, his breath on my neck, his fingers inside me. I felt his cock pushing past my lips. The best orgasm I'd ever had.

My mouth suddenly dry, I ran my eyes over his body, taking in every line of his muscled torso. He wasn't as big as his brother. His shape was more athletic, less gained from the gym – a slender, toned god of beauty. Faint abs angled down into a sharp V, which disappeared beneath his waistline.

A whimper built in my throat.

Dear gods, why did I always have such crappy taste in men? First Patrick, then Simon, then Jack, then Karl. And now the biggest douche of them all: a man that wanted me dead. *My king.*

"Well, I'll leave you two lovebirds to it," Jace said.

"Jace –"

Flipping off the balcony, he spread his wings. My eyes widening, I scrambled towards him. "Don't leave!"

An arm wrapped around my waist, hauling me back from the edge. I tried not to think who that arm was attached to. Tried not to feel the chest pressed against my back. But it was freaking impossible when his morning wood poked heavily against my spine.

Closing my eyes, I struggled to control my breathing.

The door clicked closed behind Jace – just as solidly as it had last night.

My mouth watered.

So did my pussy.

I tugged against him, trying to free myself. Thankfully, he released me and stepped back. Craving his body or not, I had to keep my mind in check. Because otherwise, I'd be in his arms in a split second with my panties around my ankles and his cock in whichever hole he wanted it.

I winced, ashamed at how easy I was.

Though really, I thought, *this is Karl's fault. If he'd just been a better lover, then I wouldn't be so sex starved.*

Slowly, I turned to face him. My eyes dipped down his chest to his clearly defined cock.

"If you keep looking at it, I'll have you down on your knees again."

My cheeks hot, I jerked my gaze to his.

But dear me, that was a flippin' mistake.

His violet eyes bore into mine with a heat that left me shaken.

"What do you want?" he asked, his voice smooth and low and tempting.

You. I swallowed. Breathed deep. "I want to go home." *And make sure the wasps haven't all killed each other.* That was why I was here, wasn't it? My eyes fastened onto his chest...

His gaze narrowed. "This is your home now."

"I know. I just want to get some belongings. This slip is starting to..." I trailed off as his eyes roamed down my body. Did he remember sliding it off me? Baring my breasts to his view? Did he see the cum dried on the front and bask in the knowledge that it was his?

Flustered, I crossed my arms in front of me, using them as a shield against his piercing gaze. Only to be acutely aware that all I'd done was lift my breasts to the top of my slip. They moved up and down with the fast pace of my breathing. My lips parted as I struggled to take in air.

The wasps. Think of the wasps. And the fact that he's trying to kill me.

But look at those abs, my pussy said. *Remember those fingers?*

His eyes slowly moved up to mine. "Hasn't Ajax already brought you some clothes?"

"Yes," I stammered, "but I want my stuff. My books and trinkets and –"

"Sentimental crap?"

My flair of annoyance helped battle my arousal, and for that I was grateful.

"Yes," I bit out. "Everything is different here. I just want something to make it feel more like home." *You know, a bit of comfort on my deathbed.*

He regarded me for a few seconds, making me twitch

under the heavy silence. "Fine," he finally said. "I'll have someone go collect it for you."

"No," I blurted, taking a step forward. If they found the wasps, they'd kill them. Fair enough killing me, but my babies? "I want to do it. I –"

"It's too dangerous for you to leave the castle until your coronation."

"So send a guard with me."

"I don't have the women to spare."

My eyes dipped to his chest. I yanked them back up as I shook my head. "Please. I need to go home. I need to say goodbye to all my friends and sort my house out and –" My gaze lowered again. Gods, why did he have to look so flippin' delicious? "Can you put on a tunic or something?"

"I already put on trousers for you."

A gasp escaped me as I imagined him naked, sleeping soundly, the blankets only half-covering his ass. My pulse raced beneath my skin. My pussy clenched with need.

"Well, um." I cleared my throat, telling myself to look away, to regain control, but I couldn't. "Thank you," I breathed, eyeing the V of his hips. His cock twitched, making me wet, making me nearly whimper.

"Come here."

Like a dumbie I went to him. *Ugh, is this what men feel like, always being led by their cock? But am I not better than this? Am I not a woman?*

Stopping a breath away, I craned my neck to look up at him. Oh gods, yeah, I was a woman and he was a man and there was very little space between us.

Raising his hand to my mouth, he stroked my lower lip with his thumb. "You're cut."

My tongue darted out to lick the tear he'd given me last night. It touched his finger – a sensation I felt all the way to my core. "Yeah. It got caught on your piercing."

And that was *not* an image I needed in my head right now. But he was shirtless and delicious, and my body remembered all too clearly how he'd made it feel a mere few hours ago. It didn't help that with every inhale, I breathed him in until he filled my lungs, my body, my heart, leaving me craving and wet.

Dropping his hand, he stepped back. "I'll go with you."

I blinked. "What?"

He stared at me.

I shook my head, his words sinking in. *Oh no. No, no, no, no, no.* My last moments, however long that was, were not going to be filled with him. Life couldn't be that cruel.

I opened my mouth, then closed it again. "You?"

His hot stare turned dry. "I do not take pleasure in repeating myself."

"But..."

Turning from me, he walked towards the dresser. "I can take the time to re-cement our peace treaty with King Openhei while we're there." He opened the drawer and pulled out a tunic. After wrapping it around his back, under his wings, he slipped his arms into the sleeves and tied it at the front.

"But he doesn't live there," I pointed out in desperation. "He's a couple towns away."

"I'll have him meet us there."

"But –"

He turned around to face me, holding a black leather belt folded in half. "We will leave in an hour. Tell Fabia if she wants any of her belongings collected, to make us a list."

"Can't she come with?" And then we could escape and I wouldn't have to die and –

He smiled softly. "No. She'll stay here as collateral." The belt uncoiled, its length reaching to the floor.

Snagged, my eyes followed it. Thoughts of him using it on me... Of me using it on him...

In a bad way, I assured myself. Not in a good, tie his hands down and use him way.

Dear gods, I need therapy.

"Was there anything else you wanted?" he asked softly, dangerously.

My pussy screamed for me to say yes.

Luckily, my brain spoke first. "N-no."

"Then you're dismissed."

NINETEEN

A good brownie never commits murder.

But withholding information isn't

really murder...is it?

— Arienna

Richard was coming to my house.

My wasp-infected house.

My *venomous, aggressive* wasp-infected house.

As I pulled on a dark plum-coloured jumpsuit with a silver cape sleeve, my skin broke out in hives. I should tell him what he was going to be walking into, but...

A little voice told me not to. Kings and queens were killed all the time, it said, and in many cases, their murderers became crowned and got immunity. All I had to do to fix my current predicament was to just withhold a bit of information.

I mean, it wasn't as if there was anything in the rulebook that said we couldn't keep secrets. In fact, rule two hundred and five said, 'A good brownie always keeps another's secrets when asked'.

And the wasps would probably ask me if they could speak considering most people wanted to kill them on discovery...

So really, I would be a bad brownie if I *did* warn him about them.

Not to mention, by staying silent, I was actively trying to stop someone from committing a murder, my murder. So...according to the rules...I would be a bad brownie if I didn't try to 'accidental death' him before I died.

Yeah, that sounded like legit reasoning.

Finished dressing, I checked myself out in the mirror, making sure not to look at my guilt-ridden face. But I could still feel it there inside me. A good brownie never committed murder. Ever, ever.

But then again, that little voice countered, I had already screamed and cursed and cried. So really, what was breaking one more rule? I mean, it wasn't like it was a big one. Reincarnation existed. And if you thought about it, which I was, I assure you, I'd actually be doing him a favour. Fairy life wasn't exactly kind, so if I just hit the restart button on his life...

And you know, opened a charity in his name...

Something to do with rehoming rat babies. They were kind of like dogs, which he wanted.

He probably wouldn't even be mad.

Nodding to myself, I twirled in front of the mirror. The opening of the door stopped me mid-spin. My feet banged together. My arms flapped uselessly, and I crashed to the floor with a not very graceful, "Umph."

Slowly lifting my head, I ran my eyes up heavy boots to leather trousers to a black tunic that wrapped around a body I knew looked absolutely delicious. I gulped as I stared into Richard's dark purple eyes.

They were hot and dangerous, scrolling over my body to linger on my ass.

Blushing, I scrambled to my feet and smoothed down my jumpsuit. "What are you doing here?"

"I came to collect you for our journey. Did you get a list from Fabia?"

I shook my head. "I couldn't find her."

"We'll just bring everything back then." He held out his arm, but I didn't take it, confused as to why he'd said that. If he was planning on having me executed soon, why bother with so much work? Fabia definitely wouldn't stay here after my death; surely, he'd know that. Unless...

My stomach sank.

Does he like her? Will he make her queen after me? Then kill her when he was done? My eyes widened. *What if I wasn't the first?*

"Are you not ready?" he asked, his arm still extended.

"Were you ever married before?" I blurted.

His arm fell to his side. "No."

"Engaged?"

His eyes narrowed. "Why the interrogation?"

I forced a smile. It wasn't that hard considering a good brownie had to smile at so many things – such as lame jokes and people they didn't like and kings that wanted them dead. "Just trying to get to know you," I said. "But no matter, we should go."

Silence stretched between us.

He didn't move.

Just studied me with his violet eyes.

Starting to panic, I wondered if he knew.

But that would be impossible, I assured myself. Fairies couldn't read minds.

Finally, he broke the tension. "Yes, we should," he said. Not waiting for me to reply, he turned on his heels and walked out the door.

Exhaling heavily, I followed him. This was going to work. I just had to keep my cool and he wouldn't expect a thing and then –

Wham!

No more Richard. No more wife-executing husband.

Guilt crept into my heart. I ignored it. *This is for the greater good*, I told myself. I'd be a much better ruler than he. I'd be a kind one. A generous one.

At the balcony, I took a deep breath and tried to hide my jitters. Forget the whole 'causing an accidental death thing'; I really didn't like flying. But I had to. For me. For my pets.

Expecting Jace to lift me in his arms, I reached for him.

But it was Richard who grabbed me.

With a small yelp as he took off, I wrapped my arms around him and held on tight. My heart beat so loudly I could barely hear the wind whistling past my ears. The higher he flew, the more I started to panic, until I was certain I was going to die of a heart attack.

"Relax," he murmured.

"Oh, yes, I'll just do that because you commanded it." My voice wavered. My pulse went wild.

Holding me tighter, he flew faster.

I was going to be sick.

But then a floor was under me and I was swaying on my feet with his hands on my shoulders. Tipping my chin up with two fingers, he gazed into my eyes. I'm sure I looked as wild and panicked as I felt.

"You don't like flying, do you?"

I shook my head.

"I take it you've never been on a bird then."

Before I could reply, he released my chin and placed his fingers against his mouth. The sharp whistle made me flinch. The answering caw and the flap of heavy wings made all the blood rush out of my head. Feeling dizzy, I swayed on my feet.

An arm was around me in an instant, holding me upright, pinning me to him.

I tried to push away, but his arm only tightened. And then I was clutching at him, trembling and shaking my head. "No. No, no, no, no, no," I begged, my eyes fastened on the massive raven that had landed beside us.

"You'll be fine. She's a gentle girl."

My body chilled. My vision narrowed.

"Hey, look at me." Violet eyes snagged me, holding my gaze hostage as two strong arms kept me standing. They were soft and gentle, so they couldn't possibly be his. "It'll be fine. Riding a bird is more stable than riding a rat." He clicked his tongue. The bird walked right up to us, pushing its beak between our bodies. If it opened its mouth, I was certain it could swallow my head whole. Perhaps I could get it to try; then I wouldn't have to ride it.

I moved my head, trying to mimic a worm.

All that did was make me dizzier.

"This is Maeve," he said, grabbing my hand and lifting it. He raised it to the bird's head and forced me to pet her. "She likes it when you rub her here."

He guided my fingers in a circular motion. I tried to snatch my hand away, but he held it still. Pressing his body against mine, his other hand rested on my hip. His breath feathered against my ear. His chest rose and fell against my back – even and calm. Soothing. "Just like that," he murmured.

Focusing on the movement of my hand, I tried so hard to relax. "I can't do this," I whispered.

And for the life of me, I didn't know if I was talking about getting on Maeve or causing Richard to die.

Perhaps both.

"Of course you can." Lifting me easily, he placed me on top of the bird. After settling in behind me, he clicked his tongue. Her wings opened, and I tilted forward, clutching at her feathers. She tossed her head with an angry caw.

Pulling my fingers free of their hold, Richard held them in his hands. "Relax," he ordered. "You're not going to fall. And if you do, I've got you." His arms tightened around me.

I stiffened, but as Maeve launched into the air, I was grateful for his presence. I liked his strong body against mine, his embrace holding me steady. I liked the fact that he had wings of his own and that his heartbeat pulsing against my back was calm and collected. Relaxed against my panic.

Dipping his head to my ear, his lips brushed my skin. "Close your eyes."

Already on it.

Looking into the blackness behind my eyelids, I tried to control my breathing.

It didn't work.

"Just concentrate on me." His words feathered through the darkness, and I latched onto them like a hot babe to her sugar daddy. "Focus on my hands."

They were strong and sturdy against mine. Squeezing my fingers. Holding me tight. When he released one of my hands, I started to panic over the loss of sensation. But his fingers feathered across the back of my knuckles, soft and light and soothing.

They traced their way up my wrist to my elbow. I sucked in a shaky breath as I focused on the gentle path they were creating.

A peace in the panic.

A straight line in the chaos of my mind.

"I thought about you all night." He nuzzled my hair as his fingers continued their slow exploration. "Having you against the wall." His tongue flicked out against my lobe. The new sensation rocked me, causing my lips to part. "On my desk." He sucked my ear in between his teeth. "In my bed," he growled around it.

Heart hammering, I couldn't stop the images from forming. In the darkness of my panic, I was completely at his mercy.

My hand that he still held, he placed it on my knee. Moving it slowly up, he trailed his lips to my neck. "I thought about you in that blue slip of yours, down on your knees as I knelt behind you."

I swallowed hard. Breathed harder.

"I thought about you sitting on my desk with your legs spread as you clutched at my hair."

My hand reached my thigh under his command.

"I thought about licking my way up your legs to *here*" –he pressed my palm to my pussy– "and eating you out until you screamed. I thought a good brownie never screamed..."

He pushed two of my fingers against the fabric. My hips bucked. My head lolled back, and I trembled against his hard chest.

"But you screamed last night and in my dreams. Over." He released my hand as he yanked one of my sleeves down. "And over." Down came the other one. "And over again." Shoving the cloth down to my waist, he freed my breasts to the air.

And I recalled all too suddenly that we were flying. The rush of the air against my chest left me frozen. My hand stilled. My breathing stopped.

Reaching up, Richard grabbed my chin and forced me to turn my head. Electricity arced between us, shooting through me and restarting my lungs with strong bolts of desire. Breathing hard against his lips, I sucked in gasps of air. His tongue swept inside, claiming mine, making me forget where we were. How high.

"That's it," he murmured. "Focus on me." He kissed me deeply, and I concentrated on the touch of his tongue, the hot moan vibrating against my mouth. My hand started moving again as he cupped my breasts and squeezed. He pinched the tight bud, rolling it between his fingers. As I sagged forward, my mouth left his.

But I kept my mind on his hands as he brushed my hair back. His lips were on my neck then, licking and sucking, and giving the gentlest bite. I jerked against him. Rooted myself in the sensations. His hand slipped down my stomach, beneath the fabric, my fingers.

I panted with expectation. As his hand on my breast moved to the other one, he licked his way up to my ear. Snagging it in between his teeth, he growled, "I thought about you riding my hand again. I licked it clean after you left."

Two fingers pushed inside me. A scream erupted from my lips, but it was ripped away by the wind. I turned my head, reaching for his lips, pushing against his hand when I found them.

He claimed me at both ends, his fingers moving so gently, his lips pressing against me so hard. The stark contrast left me shaken, unable to decide if I should be riding his hand faster or kissing him slower. As he took over every one of my senses – his taste of desire, his scent of masculinity, his soft growls of pleasure. And his touch. Dear gods, his touch – I raced to the edge of orgasm.

My hips bucking, my chest heaving, my hand slipping inside to join his, I flew apart on another scream.

He squeezed my breast hard as he swallowed my cries

of pleasure. Pinched my nipple to the point of pain. Then he was yanking my arm out of my jumpsuit and pressing down on my overly sensitive clit until I was jerking around in front of him. Spasming from the near painful pleasure, I struggled to find the words to make him stop. To beg for mercy. But all I managed was, "*Please.*"

"Please, my king," he murmured in my ear, causing my whole body to shiver.

"Please...*my king.*" And just like that he was inside me again, building me up as he pumped in and out. In and out. In and out. So fast I couldn't keep track. And then his hand was grabbing my breasts. His fingers were curling inside me, knocking against that sweet spot that caused me to see stars.

As my arousal dripped down my legs and soaked my ass, I squirmed against him.

"Stop," I breathed. "You're going to stain my clothes."

Relentless, he didn't listen.

Arching against him, I screamed.

Ever so slowly, he pulled his fingers out of me. My hips rose, still chasing those last little tremors.

I could feel the heat of his hand as it rose towards my face, then past it to his. The wet slurp of his mouth caused my lips to part as I envisioned him sucking on his fingers. On me.

Lowering his hand, he slipped it back inside my suit. Running his fingers against my wet thighs, he scooped up my desire and brought it to his lips. A moan escaped him this time. "I'm thinking about how wet you'll be when you sit on my face."

A pressure started to build again as his hand dipped south. He slid a finger between my labia, cleaning me thoroughly. My hips bucked. My groan matched his. After licking his fingers, he pulled my sleeves back up to my shoulders.

"Good girl. You did so well."

My body flushed. My chest expanded, and I half-turned to reach for him. *So does this mean I get the prize now?*

With strong fingers, he grabbed my hands before they could do any exploring of their own. Amusement lined his voice when he leaned towards me and whispered, "You can open your eyes now. Maeve's landed."

My brows furrowed in disappointment, then confusion, then horror as reality came crashing back down on me. Raising a hand to my lips, I wondered how in Hel's name that had happened. A few hours ago, I'd been planning his death. Still was, I assured myself.

Because despite how he made my body feel, I really didn't want to die.

My gaze flicked to him as he lifted me off Maeve.

When he smirked at me, the urge to warn him about the wasps bubbled up my throat.

But I swallowed it down.

Swallowed it like the good little brownie I was.

Oh gods, I was going to Niflhel.

Perhaps. But not today.

TWENTY

A good brownie never sics wasps on another.

Although, technically that's not an

actual rule...

— Arienna

My nerves were all over the place as we approached the mushroom-shaped house I called my home. Or had called. Or still called. Whatever. This was no time to get hung up on grammar.

Because inside there were who knew how many wasps. Poisonous little bastards that hated being caged.

And outside was Jace, who was reaching forward to open the door.

My mouth ran dry.

My heart squeezed.

As my hands clenched and unclenched at my sides, I tried to open my mouth to warn him, but I couldn't speak over the hard lump in my throat. Oh gods, I was about to commit murder and it wasn't even going to be on the right person!

A small noise escaped me, barely loud enough for me to hear. My face grew hot. I think I was going to faint.

Maybe none of my babies had escaped?

Maybe when Jace opened that door, he wouldn't be jumped by a dozen angry, starving wasps.

Maybe I could somehow convince Richard to go in first still, but how?

A movement by one of the windows caught my gaze. My heart felt like it was going to explode as I tried to see who it was. I prayed that it wasn't Gionova. She was a drama queen who went crazy if I was even one minute late feeding her. And it had been... I tried to do a quick calculation, but my brain wouldn't work. A bloody long time, whatever it was.

"Wait," Richard called out from in front of me. "There's something inside."

I raised a hand to my lips as I watched Jace move to the side, a hand on his waist.

Oh gods, I'm never going to try murder again. This is way too stressful.

And then the pin dropped, and I realised what would happen as soon as he looked through the window. Wasps were killed first, befriended later. Scrambling forward, I made it two steps before Richard yanked me back.

"Don't go in!" I shouted. My thoughts racing, I snagged at the bits of truth that wouldn't make me sound like I'd just tried to kill him. That would give my pets the best chance of survival despite being venomous bastards. "I think they might've got out!"

"What might have?"

I tried not to sound too guilty. "My wasps," I croaked, knowing how he would take it. Everyone hated them, feared them. They were things to be killed, not loved. But that was just because no one ever gave them a chance.

And okay, even after that chance, they were still kind of dicks. But they were cute dicks. And they meant well. And I loved them. I couldn't let him – He couldn't...

"Wasps?"

Murmurs erupted behind me – the guards' voices mixing with the hundreds of brownies that had gathered to watch.

"We have to move."

"Only grab the necessities."

"I'll grab the statue."

"I'll pack the gold clubs."

"The kids, Harold!"

A hard lump in my throat, I could only nod.

"How many?" Richard demanded.

I struggled to breathe, desperate to think of something that would make the number not seem so high. That wouldn't just make him want to burn the whole house down. I was supposed to protect them and now...now I might very well get them killed. My stomach churned.

"Don't make me ask again," he warned, a hard note to his voice that made me flinch.

"I – I don't know. A couple days ago, there were only six that had hatched and about eleven larvae. I separated them all before the wedding, but..."

As the hundreds of brownies dispersed to their own homes, Richard looked at me with unreadable eyes. "You do know wasps are venomous, right?"

I nodded, silently asking him to see them as something other than that.

"And yet you're living with seventeen of them?"

"Well, it was nineteen," I babbled, "but Hyatt is gone now and he killed Bo, so – Ow!"

His grip was like iron on my arm as he dragged me

away from my house. His fingers loosened the slightest bit, but they didn't give any illusion that I'd be able to free myself.

"Are you telling me you've been living with murderous wasps?"

His dark tone and the weight of his eyes told me to say no.

I moved my tongue around in my mouth, trying to wet it enough to speak. "No-ah." Coughing, I tried again. "No?"

He glanced up, looking over my head. His violent violet eyes narrowed. "I can see at least two of them."

"Well, technically...Hyatt was the only one that killed someone, and he flew off after the wedding, so..."

Shaking his head, he called out, "Burn the house down."

"No!" I lurched against him, clutching his tunic. "Please don't. They're my pets. I've raised them since they were larvae."

"I'm not risking my women for wasps."

"But what about all my stuff?" I asked, reaching.

"I'll buy you new things."

Frantic, I tried to kick him. He didn't even bother dodging, just looked at me dryly. I soon found out why when pain shot all the way up my leg. "Ow!" He held me upright as I hobbled, clutching my toes. "What are you made out of? Steel?"

There was a small twitch at the corner of his lips. Then they flattened again as he redirected his attention over my head.

As I turned, still fastened to him, all the blood drained from my face. Jace held a black ball of something in his hand; it soon went up in flames.

"Stop, please! I can get them out safely!" I struggled,

pulling with all my might to go to them. I couldn't watch them die. My lungs were being crushed. Gasping, I prayed for mercy.

They were just misunderstood balls of fluff. Delilah liked to sit in front of the window, deaf to the world, and Samson would follow me around the house. He didn't like being looked at or acknowledged in any way, but he liked my presence. Even Gionova wasn't so bad. She had only tried to kill me a handful of times. How could Richard give the order to kill them so flippantly?

"You're not going in." His words were emotionless.

Tears ran down my face as Jace took a step forward.

"You can drug them!" I screamed. "You can drug them, please!" I fell to my knees. "Please."

Jace turned to me. His eyes lingered on my face before lifting to Richard's.

I prayed in the absence of time. In that moment when life stopped moving. *Please.*

"Are you certain it will work?"

I collapsed, my shoulders dropping to the ground as I caved in on myself. One arm was held above me, tight in Richard's hand. I trembled as I nodded. "Yes. It'll be long enough for them to be moved, taken somewhere safely, and released. Please, just let me do it."

"No."

A sob broke me in two. They were my babies. How could he force me to watch them die?

"I'll do it."

My heart stopped, certain I hadn't heard him right.

"My lord –" Jace began.

"I'm not risking anyone else for these damn wasps."

"With all do respect, it is our job to give our lives –"

"Not over this, Jace. Not over a personal matter that doesn't benefit the kingdom."

I lifted my eyes to him. He was blurry through my tears, but I could see the honesty on his face. A shaky breath exhaled from my lungs. His thumb swept against the pulse in my wrist, slowly, gently. Easing it with every pass of his finger.

Sniffling, I licked the tears off my lips. How could he possibly be both this and the monster planning my execution?

"What do you use?" he asked, crouching down beside me.

I wiped at my eyes with my palm, then my mouth and nose with the back of it. Swallowing down the snot in my throat, I rasped, "Ambrosia."

His lips twitched. "The alcohol?"

Another sniffle. "They like it. They'll eat it until they pass out."

He leaned forward and kissed me, a quick peck on the lips, and I wasn't sure who was surprised more. With wide eyes, I stared at him. He held my gaze for a second, then glanced away.

"Someone get me some ambrosia," he said as he rose, pulling me to my feet alongside him.

Jace approached us as the women scattered. Leaning close, he whispered, "What are you doing?"

Letting me go, Richard gestured his head to the side. I watched as they walked away a bit, watched them talk, a heated discussion clear in their gestures. Jace waved his arms while Richard stood solidly, his arms crossed, his face saying he didn't give a fuck about whatever Jace was saying. His eyes latched on me...

They studied me, his violet eyes soft and hard all at once – an enigma. Everything about him was an enigma.

I raised a hand to my lips, feeling the ghost of that peck. It had been lighter than any of the previous kisses, and yet the heaviest of them all. I'd seen his eyes, the softness, his surprise. He hadn't meant to do it. Which meant he hadn't been able to stop himself, and that knowledge of his lack of control floored me.

He'd kissed me not for a role or a political gain. He'd kissed me for me.

And now he was about to risk his life to go save some wasps.

What kind of monster did that?

It didn't make sense.

But then again, *he* didn't make sense.

Turning towards my house, I hurried towards the door, seeking comfort in the familiar, in the predictable.

"Take another step," Richard called out behind me, his voice flat and even, "and I'll burn the whole place down myself."

My feet ground to a halt. "But –"

"Does Jace need to take you away from here?"

I shook my head quickly, hearing footsteps behind me. "I'll be good."

His lips pressed against my ear as he ran the back of his fingers down the side of my neck. "I know you will be because otherwise, I'd have to punish you." His fingers tightened around my throat, holding in the hot gasp that wanted to escape. "*My queen.*"

I shuddered, having the sudden urge to do something bad. Something naughty.

"The ambrosia, My Grace."

When his presence vanished behind me, I sucked in a ragged breath. It did little to bring order to the chaotic thoughts running free in my mind.

Walking over to one of the windows, Jace banged on it with a fist, drawing any free wasps to him.

Richard approached the door.

Opened it and stepped inside.

My breath caught in my throat. I wanted to call him back. I wanted to give myself time to think about what I actually wanted.

But that little voice in my head, that whisper of reason, told me to stay quiet.

You want to live, don't you?

I nodded even as I started to tremble. Excitement and fear swirled inside me. I latched onto the former until it took over everything else, until I stood here waiting in anticipation of his scream.

I wanted to live.

Above everything else, I wanted to live.

That little voice started to laugh. And then it cooed, *We might as well break all the rules then. Can't exactly go to Niflhel twice.*

TWENTY-ONE

There's never an easy solution to a political problem.

And if it seems like there is,

you're blind.

— Richard

She had fucking wasps — as pets.

Seventeen of them.

It was a good thing she was going to be executed then. Otherwise, she'd be the death of me.

My lips twitched as I walked through the house, but it wasn't in the smile gallows humour normally brought on. Jace was right. I was getting too attached.

But the idea of backing off, of not knowing her at all before her death...

Somehow that seemed worse.

A harsh buzz pulled my attention to my right. Jumping back, I hit the release mechanism on the knife strapped to my forearm. It shot forward smoothly, flawlessly, and I grabbed hold of its hilt before it could pass my hand.

Flying on the other side of a well-chewed door was a wasp the size of my chest. It was covered in blood and about to squeeze through one of the holes. Popping the lid off the bottle of ambrosia, I poured a bit on the floor.

The house near vibrated as soon as the sweet scent hit the air. Thunderous buzzing filled the back of the house. The wasp on the door crawled all the way through, and I raised my knife in preparation for a fight to the death.

Ignoring me completely, it landed on the ground and started to drink. I gripped my knife tightly, but it never even looked at me. Cautiously, I stepped around it and made my way further inside.

I passed through a kitchen and a sitting room, each with makeshift walls separating them. Seven dead wasps were littered in pieces across the floor. At least I thought it was just seven; that was how many heads I saw.

Glancing behind me, making sure Wasp One was still feeding, I climbed the spiral stairs to the second floor. Four closed doors greeted me and at each one there was buzzing. Through the holes of each door, I poured a bit of ambrosia into their rooms.

The buzzing instantly stopped as they drank. Making my way back downstairs, I did the same wherever there was noise until I was back at the front of the house. Wasp One was stumbling around as it continued to drink. Its little mandibles twitched back and forth as its fuzzy black antennas moved every so often.

How my wife had a heart big enough to care for this ugly thing, I didn't know. I twirled the knife in my hand. Studied the critter for a few more seconds. Yep, still ugly. And its stinger was massive. Forget dying of poison; it'd just skewer someone her size in half.

Shaking my head, I poured the rest of the bottle out by the door and exited the house.

"How long does it take for the ambrosia to kick in?" I asked, walking towards her.

"A couple minutes," she said, worry in her voice and eyes. "You didn't hurt any of them, did you?"

"No, but a few of them managed to get out and kill each other."

She paled and I shook my head. No wonder she'd come back after how I'd treated her last night. She befriended wasps. In comparison, I was a fucking treat.

"Arienna, love!" My blood chilled at the sound of a man's voice. Pulling her against my side, I turned to face the obnoxious asshole.

He was taller than me. Blond hair. Blue eyes. Not a piercing on him. He looked exactly like a man I would've pictured her with had I not already claimed her.

Reaching up to her neck, I brushed her pink hair back, revealing the mark I'd left on her. My lips. My teeth. My claim. My fingers brushed across it, forcing him to notice.

A scowl hid behind his tight smile.

Mine was out on the forefront.

"That's close enough," Jace said as he stepped between us.

It wasn't close enough. The douche wasn't quite within punching distance.

I shook the thoughts away. Doubled down on my control. But then she angled her body towards me. Her hand reached around my waist, and I knew in that moment that the two had done more than just fucked.

Glancing down, I saw it all over her face. She was going to use me to make him jealous.

Which meant she still had feelings for him.

Might even love him.

He was not going to see the next sunrise.

"Karl!" She gasped his name, her breath heady with

nerves. "What are you doing here? I thought you moved to the other side of town. You know, with my mother."

Her mother? I studied him some more. Perhaps he was older than he looked and he was actually her step-father, someone she wanted to show me off to? I relaxed a little, the urge to kill him dwindling.

"Yes, but once I heard all the buzz, I just had to come see for myself." He looked at me, trying to intimidate me but failing. "I see you've moved on, and so fast too."

"Fast?" She tried to take a step forward, but I held her by my side. "You moved on while we were still together!" Her voice wavered.

Mine came out on a growl.

He'd hurt her.

And so I would hurt him in return.

His eyes darting to mine, he took a quick step back. Glancing around, as if my guards would save him, he shook his head. "Wow. You got a temper on you. Raising your voice at me like that. Any higher and that would've been a scream. You all heard it. I'm lucky our wedding didn't go through."

"Your wedding?" I asked softly. Looking down at her for an answer, I was irritated when she wasn't already staring at me. Her eyes were still locked on this dumbass.

"It didn't go through," she said through clenched teeth, "because you were too busy banging my mum. And my sister!"

Dear fucking gods. Forget the wasps making me look like a treat. Her fiance was a piece of work. Oddly, that didn't make me feel any better. Her bar was so low, it wasn't exactly a compliment for her to want to be with me.

Irritation lined her eyes, and I hated knowing that it was because of him. That he had enough power over her to make her feel something other than the goodie toodie feelings brownies were supposed to feel.

I fingered the blade at my waist. Jace stepped closer to me, no doubt guessing as to the thoughts going through my mind. He always had been a killjoy.

"I only started banging your sister because you didn't care enough about me to stop eating donuts. You gained three grams since I met you."

Pulling the knife free of its sheath, I flipped it in the air, then threw it at his feet.

He jumped back with a squeal.

Shaking his head, Jace stepped out of the way. "You just dug your own hole, you moron."

Removing Arienna's arm from around me, I stepped forward. "By insulting my wife, you insulted me. You insulted the Raza kingdom because she is now our queen."

He paled. The smell of urine permeated the air and it was still a better addition to life than he was.

"And so I challenge you, Karl the Dumbass, to face me inside a fairy ring."

His eyes rolled back in his head and he collapsed.

Leaving him to sleep in his piss, I turned to Jace. "Load him up with the cargo. He comes back with us."

Small hands grabbed my arm. "You can't do this. He would've apologised. You can't kill him for it."

I turned to her, hating the fear in her eyes. For him. The bastard that had hurt her. "The challenge has been issued."

"So retract it."

My jaw tightened. "It doesn't work like that." And even if it did, I wouldn't.

"Why not?"

"Because it's tradition to settle such insults in the ring." And I was fucking looking forward to carving him to pieces.

"But it won't even be a fair fight! You'll just kill him."

I shrugged. "So I'll give him a blade and fight him unarmed."

"That's not the point!"

Ducking my head, I grabbed the back of her neck and hauled her close until we were nose to nose. "Why do you care?"

Her throat worked, and I had to struggle to stop myself from tightening my grip into a fist.

"He was my fiance..."

"Do you love him?"

"No!" She glanced away, looking at *him*. "But you can't just kill everyone you don't like," she said desperately. "I thought you wanted peace."

"His death won't change my treaty with the Vylians, I assure you. And I'll just apologise to the brownies."

Tears wetting her eyes, she tried to lean over to look at Jace. My hand tightened, causing her to flinch. Her gaze flew back to mine. My grip eased again. "Tell me why you want to save him," I demanded again, needing to know the truth.

"Because..." She glanced side to side. Her gaze dropped to her feet.

"Every second you don't answer is another punishment I will give you."

Her pulse beat rapidly against my fingers.

One second.

Two.

"Because he's not a monster like you!"

Time stopped.

My blood chilled.

Everything froze.

Then I blinked once and straightened. Looking down at

her, I murmured, "No. You're right. No one's quite like me."

Turning, I stopped at Jace's side. "Box up all the wasps and take them somewhere far away to be released. Only then is she allowed inside to collect her belongings."

Spreading my wings, I took to the air. Jace's curse reached me, but I ignored it. Speeding away, I searched for the gold and white chariot of the brownie royals.

I spotted it a few streets over. Landing on top of it, I rolled off the side and through the window.

Two gasps sounded as I settled on the empty seat facing them. The carriage lurched as the driver struggled to keep the four mice pulling it in line.

"We're in the middle of a peace talk with the Vylians," I said, cutting straight to the point. I wanted this over and done with. I didn't have the time nor the desire to suffer through any small talk. "I would like to open trade routes between the three of us."

"Hello, King Morningstar," King Openhai greeted. "It's nice to see you again. I hope you're enjoying this pleasant weather."

I bit my tongue as I waited for him to get through all the niceties. Fifteen minutes later, Queen Hurvan began hers.

Finally, they were done.

"You have a wasp infestation," I began, not wasting any more time. "I'm in the middle of sorting it for you as a gesture of goodwill between our kingdoms. In return, I want you to give Vylians and Razians full access to your markets. Our people will be allowed to trade here, as yours will be allowed to trade in ours – provided they have the required licenses, of course."

They shared a look. Leaning out the window, King Openhai asked the driver to circle the town. As he settled back down, he said, "We will pay for the wasp removal. We'd prefer a different...gesture of goodwill, if you will."

I stilled, knowing that tone of voice. People were always asking me to do the things they didn't want to do. "What is it?"

"As you know, our kingdom runs on a very strict set of rules. We are generous and kind."

"I'm not in the mood to listen to whatever crap you teach in your schools. Spit it out."

Queen Hurvan cleared her throat. "There are a number of people, immigrants mostly, that have come over here and taken advantage of our system. They break the rules repeatedly, but because they say sorry..."

"We can't do anything," her husband finished.

"Surprising," I mocked. "Who would have thought that people would take advantage of others in a cult?"

"This isn't a cult."

"That's what every cult says."

"I realise we have our differences, King Morningstar," Queen Hurvan said, leaning forward, "but we have less crimes committed than in Raza. The last murder to take place here was over two centuries ago. We have peace, something that your 'non-cult' kingdom does not."

"I thought you wanted peace... a monster like you."

Shoving her words down, I studied the two before me. "So you want me to kill these people for you?"

"No. Well..."

"No," King Openhai confirmed, glancing at his wife. "We just want you to take them away with you."

Scoffing, I leaned back. "You want me to take known criminals into my kingdom? What did they do?"

"Well...one of them pressures women into having sex with him."

"A rapist."

"No. Because they all said yes in the end and there wasn't any vio–"

"That's still rape and you know it. Otherwise, you wouldn't be pushing for me to take him." To kill him, even though they wouldn't say that. No, they needed to keep their hands clean. They needed me to get mine dirty for them.

"Because he's not a monster like you!"

"And the rest?" I asked.

"One creates a lot of...accidents that lead to people's deaths."

"For fuck's sake, just say he's a murderer."

"She."

I smiled coldly. "She. So you have a murderer and a rapist for me. Anyone else?"

Another glance passed between them. "There's a list," King Openhai said.

"How many?"

"Twenty-seven."

Tilting my head, I studied them. I let the silence stretch between us until they started to squirm. "That's a fair amount of people."

"What you're asking for is a big thing. Your kingdom is made up of –"

"Murderers and rapists?" I asked all too politely. *And ruled by a monster.*

"What my husband is trying to say is –"

"Your little 'paradise' here doesn't work."

A flush crept over her cheeks. "On the contrary. There are tens of thousands of people living here. Twenty-seven out of that is miniscule. Whereas the vast majority of your people are murderers."

"But not rapists," I said deadpanned.

Her thin brow furrowed. "Murderers are worse than

rapists."

Leaning forward, I braced my hands on my knees. "You *would* think that death is the worst a person could suffer." Standing before they could reply, I added, "I accept your deal. Give me a list of these twenty-seven 'accident causers' and 'a bit too forward men' and I'll take care of them by the week's end."

When they agreed, I exited the carriage the same way I'd come in. Spreading my wings, I flew back to my wife's house.

Ex-house, I told myself.

Whatever life she had here was over. I'd taken it.

And soon, I would take her new one too.

Landing beside her, I grabbed her arm, then hauled her onto Maeve. She yelped as she struggled to get back down, but I held her in place as we launched into the air. My hand slipped around to her front, causing her to still in an instant. My lips met her ear. Her breathing turned ragged.

Hearing her words over and over again, I pulled down her sleeves and shoved my fingers inside her.

Monster or not, it seemed I could still make her want me.

"Why do you care?"

"Because he's not like you."

TWENTY-TWO

A good brownie never plans a murder.

Is that a hard and fast rule or one
of the ones that are okay to break?

— Arienna

Ugh. My body was a traitor. It had come not once, not twice, but three flippin' times on the ride back to Raza. Seriously, what was wrong with it? My mind said no. My heart said no. But my body?

It rolled over for him anytime he got near it. It was driving me insane.

And messing with my feelings.

I wanted to kill him, not fuck him.

Unless... those two could somehow be combined?

I shook my head, ridding myself of the thought. That might sound like a good idea, get him when he's least expecting it, but I just *knew* that would not work out as well as I hoped. Maybe as a last resort...

A knock sounded on my suite's door and I hurried over

to it, really hoping it was Fabia. I'd called for her as soon as we had returned, but it had been over an hour now. Anyone could be behind that door. Knowing my luck, it would be Richard wanting to ravish me.

Moaning, I took a step back.

The idea to hide popped into existence right as the door opened.

My breath caught.

Then released.

"Fabia, thank the gods." Grabbing her arm, I pulled her into my bedroom. "I need to talk to you."

She looked at me, breathing heavily, her hands locked behind her head. Sweat glistened her brow and she was dressed in leather armour.

My eyes widened as I took her all in. "Have you been training with them?"

A sheepish, guilty smile curved her lips.

"Was it fun?" I asked, genuinely happy for her. She'd dreamed of training as a warrior for years.

She nodded, her small smile turning into a full on grin. "There are so many things to learn. You should see what even the little kids can do with a blade. And I figured if we're going to live here, I need to be able to protect you. Nicholas said he had to train for years before he was good enough to join the king's guard. Can you imagine?"

I bit my cheek to stop from blurting out the question I'd rung her for: *how do I kill my husband?* Instead, I listened intently, watched as her eyes lit up with glee. She looked so happy...the happiest I'd ever seen her.

And that made me truly hate Richard for the first time. With all my being.

Learning he was still planning on killing me had hurt. Hearing he had wanted to come to my house had made my survival instincts kick in – a crime of opportunity, really. I hadn't hated him, not like I did now.

But he was going to destroy Fabia's happiness. He was going to crush that smile and elation on her face. Even worse? He was going to force me to live my last moments of life, however long that was, distant from my best friend. I couldn't tell her my plans. I couldn't ruin this happiness for her, and so I would die alone.

My fingers bit into my thighs. Hatred built up inside me, wanting release. I would never forgive him for this. In this life or the next. Lifemate be damned.

"I knocked one of the soldiers down today. She'd been training for years. It was a lucky round though." Fabia rotated her arm, her face twisting in gleeful pain. "I don't think she was expecting me to know much. After that, though, she pummelled me good."

I forced a smile, pushing my troubles down. "You've been there all day, haven't you?"

"Yep! Echo said I could have an hour to come see you and then I have to head back for night training. She thinks she can fast track me to be a guard, so it'll only be, like, two years before I can join your service."

I made sure none of the sadness inside me leaked out as she talked about a future I would never be a part of. The hatred built inside me, propped up by pain and regrets and grief. I didn't even know you could grieve a living thing, but I did. And it hurt so fucking much.

I wanted to pull her into a hug and just hold her, but she would know then that something was wrong. And I couldn't take this from her when I knew deep down that it would be me dying, not Richard.

"That's amazing," I said. "What about Richard though? Won't you be guarding him too if you join?"

She wiggled her head in a way that said both yes and no. "I'll be following Echo's orders. She's the head of the

Royal Guard, and although she gets her rules from King Morningstar, he leaves her pretty much alone except for in times of civil war."

"And do civil wars happen a lot here?" I asked, a plan forming before being quickly dismissed. I didn't want to be responsible for anyone else's death other than *my king's*.

She sat down on the bed and cracked her neck from side to side. Given the amount of energy bursting from her, I was surprised she wasn't running in place. "There's been three during his reign – the most ever, and there's talk of another one."

"Why?"

"The first one was because he killed his sister to take the throne." She waved a hand. "Although that was done all honourably in a fairy ring, some people accused him of not actually killing her because they never saw a body."

Confusion pulled my brows together. "Aren't the losers consumed by the fairy ring itself?"

"Yeah, but some people, you know? They'll disregard anything to make their narrative fit." She shrugged. "The second was during that famine from a decade ago."

I nodded, remembering it well. It had affected all of us, many having died from starvation. "And the third?"

"Because he opened the borders, believe it or not." She laid back on the bed and looked at the ceiling, her arms behind her head. "You know, when I got here...and when I saw him kill those two girls last night..." She trailed off for a long moment before continuing. "I thought he was a monster."

My breath hitched. I didn't want to hear this. I needed to keep thinking of him as evil, as a man whose death would be for the best, not just for me but for everyone. Recalling Karl's screams and begs for mercy as we'd landed in the aviary, I tried to block out her words.

"But he's actually striving towards peace. Everything he's done – and I'm not saying they have all been good things, but –" She looked at me and I struggled not to look away. "He really cares about his people."

Fuck.

"He challenged Karl to step inside a fairy ring," I blurted, needing to change the subject, needing to hold on to his cruelty.

"What?" She bolted upright, her eyes locked on mine. "Karl's here?"

"Yeah. He came to my house when we went to Brownston –"

"You were at Brownston? When?"

"This morning. I wanted to check in on...my stuff an–"

Her eyes narrowed knowingly. "You mean the wasps, don't you?"

"Well, yeah," I said, getting a bit frustrated, "I couldn't exactly leave them another day. They'd already –"

"Fabia, really? They're wasps!"

"I know, but –"

"The one you brought to the wedding actually killed someone. I don't remember who, but it was someone."

"He didn't mean to. He was just panicking beca–"

"Don't ex–"

"Stop interrupting me!" I shouted before clasping a hand over my mouth. Shock covered her face, mine too probably. I'd never interrupted anyone before.

"Damn, girl. I'm proud of you." She grinned. I slowly lowered my hand. "It's about time you broke away from all the rules while sober. I've been waiting for this day for *ages.*"

I shook my head. "It feels weird."

"But good, right?"

I grinned. Nodded the tiniest bit. Then I sat beside her and whispered, "I cursed today."

She laughed. "Good for you."

"And I kicked Richard."

Her humour faded in an instant. "Arienna, you can't attack him. What did he do?" Her eyes roamed over my body, no doubt looking for bruises.

"Nothing. I hurt my foot more than him. He had to hold me up while I hopped on one leg, clutching at my toes."

She rolled her lips in, fighting back a smile.

Shaking my head, I grinned. "It felt good though. Inside I mean, not in my toes. Those hurt."

"Why did you kick him?"

Sighing, I flopped back on the bed. I wanted to tell her about my attempt to kill him. I wanted to ask her for advice given all the research she'd done for her books. But my desire to keep her happy won out. She'd never had a home before, and I really thought this place could be it...as long as she never found out the truth about my death.

Perhaps, I can convince him to execute me privately, I thought. *Make it look like an accident, something that won't make her want to leave...*

Because she belonged here a heck of a lot more than she ever had in Brownston.

"Because he was going to burn my house down once he found out about the wasps," I said.

"You didn't tell him?"

"I was distracted," I mumbled, the lie sitting tight in my throat. "And it's not like they hurt him." *The traitors.*

She shook her head in disbelief. "So did he kill them?"

"No. He went in and fed them all ambrosia. Then when they passed out, he had his guard take them all away to be released somewhere." It had been really nice, dang it. He'd even let me say goodbye to them, not that any of them had cared. I'd raised them since they were larvae, and they hadn't even had the curtesy to spare me a backwards glance. The next pet I was going to bring home was going to have the mental capacity to love me.

My heart ached, knowing there wouldn't be a next one. The wasps were it, and now they were gone.

"Well, that was nice of him."

"Yeah," I said half-heartedly.

She studied me with all the years of friendship between us. "You okay?"

I nodded. "I'm just thinking about Karl. It's going to be a slaughter." He wouldn't last a second in a fairy ring unless Richard wished him to.

She frowned. "Yeah, that's less nice of him." Laying down beside me, she added, "But I bet it was cool to watch him issue the challenge."

I tried not to smile but failed. "He threw that dagger so close to his feet Karl pissed himself."

Her laughter was loud. "The guy's a prick. I would've killed to see that."

I winced. "But he still shouldn't die. All he did was call me fat."

"What?" She looked at me in bewilderment, her eyes roaming across my slim frame.

"Yeah, three grams too big, according to him."

She snorted. "I'm glad he's dying."

When I didn't respond, she glanced at me. "That was a joke. You're right. He doesn't deserve to die for that. Maybe you could ask him not to kill him?"

"I tried, but he said by insulting me, Karl insulted him and the kingdom, so..." I didn't mention the cruelty in his eyes or the joy. The sneer that had twisted his lips when I'd called him a monster. *There's no one quite like me.*

"Well, I have to get back." Sitting up, she scooted off the bed, then stopped. "Hey, didn't you want to talk to me about something?"

"Oh yeah..." My words caught in my throat. I glanced away. "I just wanted to see if you wanted to explore the city tomorrow?" If I had the time... "What was that library on your To Visit list?"

"Aurelia's Library?"

I nodded. "Yeah, that one. We could go see it; make it a whole day out?"

"Ah, I can't tomorrow. Training, you know?"

Pain laced through me. Wondering if this would be the last time I saw her, I rose to my feet and gave her a hug. But it wasn't the desperate cling to her that I wanted to do. It wasn't the heartbreaking squeeze.

So she pushed me away like always, not knowing the pain inside. Cracking a smile, I said, "Go kick everyone's ass."

Her grin warmed my heart. "I like you cursing."

"Fuck."

Laughing, she headed for the door. Giving me a two fingered wave, she disappeared.

And I vowed, staring at the closed door of my cage, that this would not be the last time I saw her.

I would kill my husband.

I would live to die of old age.

I just had to figure out how.

TWENTY-THREE

To prove himself worthy of the throne, a man must challenge those in line to a fight in a fairy ring.

THE COURT CAN NEVER KNOW

WHAT WE DID.

— RICHARD

I tossed the blade at Jace's feet. When he rose with the knife in his hand and a smirk on his lips, I smiled. "You look a bit pissed there, Jace."

He rotated his wrist, twirling the weapon. "I wonder why that might be?" He chuckled sharply, his laughter a chill across my spine. This was what I'd wanted – the madman – from the moment my own wife had accused me of being a monster.

It was a term that had been spat at me multiple times before – too many times to count – but this time...coming from her...

I shifted onto the balls of my feet, needing this fight.

"Could it be because you flew off without a single guard?" Jace asked, his eyes narrowed in annoyance.

I straightened, not even caring that I was leaving myself open to attack. "Oh, come on," I said dryly. "Irin and Saragese were on me the entire time."

He pointed the knife at me. His smile curved his face in two. "Oh, yeah, they were. It's because you ate my fucking cake."

I licked the icing I'd left on the corner of my lips just to piss him off. My tongue had barely tasted the gosberry and honey blend before I was lunging back, attempting to stay out of his reach. Diving, he rolled into a crouch in front of me. His leg kicked out in an arch, sweeping me off the ground.

My wings snapped out as I fell. They flapped strongly, pushing me up but not fast enough to escape the sharp slice across my thigh. It was a shallow cut. Non-lethal. He was playing with me, considering he could've aimed for my spine.

Scowling, I twisted in the air and dropped back on top of him. My legs wrapped around his neck. His arm came up to stab me, but I knew he wouldn't hit anything major. The bastard never lost control even when pissed.

And considering my challenge was with Karl tonight, I might as well make it fair for him.

I wouldn't want to be accused of being a monster.

Ignoring the agony erupting in my leg, I slammed my elbow onto Jace's head. Over and over and over again in rapid succession.

Cursing, he dropped the knife after the first stabbing, knowing I wasn't tapping out. Lurching backwards, he tried to slam us into the ground, but I flapped my wings hard, keeping us both upright. He stumbled around below me for a few steps before finding his balance. Jumping high, his own wings spreading, he curled up at the waist and kicked me in the skull. *Hard.*

My head snapped sideways. I heard something crack. As blood oozed into my eyes, his other foot came up to break my nose. Throwing my arms in front of my face, I blocked him. Pain shot through my forearms. Then through my calf as the bastard bit me.

An honourable fighter Jace was not.

Then again, neither was I.

Lifting one leg off his shoulders, I slammed it down again onto his balls.

He moaned, and not in a painful way. His strong hands tightened on my thighs before running up them.

"I told you you weren't allowed to do that!" I snapped in disgust.

Another groan escaped his lips. "Do it again, Daddy."

Shuddering, I pulled away from him and landed. "This is why we never spar anymore."

Righting himself, he laughed as his feet touched the ground. "No, it's because you're always such a tease and never finish me off."

My eyes narrowed. I glanced at the dagger between us.

"Go for it," he murmured before puckering his lips and kissing the air.

Shaking my head, I walked to the edge of the cage. "There's something seriously wrong with you."

"You know what's wrong with me."

I stopped, a chill of regret and pain shooting through me. We'd never talked about that night. We never talked about her, yet this was the second time he'd brought her up in as many days. I was torn between being elated for him and hating him. The memories of her ripped me apart, but I was glad he was starting to face what he'd done...what I'd asked him to. Perhaps, he would even start to heal.

Turning to him, I held his gaze. "I'm sorry I asked that

of you."

His smile shone with pain. "No you're not. You did what you did because you loved her."

"So did you," I murmured, acknowledging that truth for the first time.

Pure agony flickered across his face, breaking the smile that had taken up permanent residency since that day. "Yeah."

Walking forward, he picked up the blade. He flicked it into the air and caught it again. On the second toss up, he threw it at my feet in a challenge.

I held his gaze, searching for a trace of the man he'd turned into. But there was nothing but a heartbroken boy looking back at me.

A dangerous heartbroken boy who had every right to hate me.

My nerves pulled tight.

Adrenaline burst through my veins.

Heart hammering, I picked up the knife.

He was on me in an instant, his fists swinging, his feet kicking, his elbows knocking into my ribs and face and gut. I took each one of his blows to heart, hearing her angelic voice in every thump of his fist.

"I have so many dreams for this place."

His elbow snapped my face to the side. A tooth went flying. Blood poured down my chin, staining me with the sins of my past.

"I'll turn the battlements into universities, the arenas into stadiums for dances and plays and games."

Swiping the blade between our bodies, I opened Jace's side. He grunted, twisted, and kicked me straight in the chest. I flew across the room. Landed hard on my wings.

Hissing, I scrambled to my feet – and directly into Jace's fist.

"Our soldiers will come home and our borders will be open. We can't go to war with them if they're our friends, right?"

Her smile haunted me as I stumbled around, shaking my head, trying to focus on the man attacking me. My best friend. My greatest ally.

I raised an arm to block a blow to my side – and took one in the underside of my chin.

"We'll be at peace. Can you imagine that, Richard? Us at peace."

As she twirled in my memories, laughing with pure joy, I hit the ground. The world darkened, narrowing into pinpoints of fading consciousness.

When I awoke, Jace was beside me, his head in his hands, tears sliding down his face. "I loved her."

Blinking sluggishly, I sat up. His face was bruised from the blows I'd managed to land. One eye swollen. His lip cut. But I knew I looked worse. I sure as hel felt worst.

"I know," I said, spitting out blood.

He looked up at me, his eyes raw and full of torment. "Then why do it? Out of everything you could have asked, why that?"

I reached for his shoulder, gripping it hard like I should have done years ago. "Because she loved you."

He flinched, reacting more to those words than he had to the knife in his side. "What?"

"It wasn't just an infatuation Au–" I cleared my throat, her name too hard to say. "My sister loved you, Jace. She talked about asking you to marry her one day."

He jumped to his feet and started to pace. He ran his hands through his air, tugging on the ends. His fingers flexed at his sides, needing something to hit, to strangle. The energy pouring off him was dark and dangerous.

Stilling, I didn't dare move. "She talked about the large

family you would have – once you finally noticed her."

"Notice her?" He spun on me. "I noticed everything about her. You were the one that told me to stay away..."

I held his gaze, seeing my own pain and guilt reflected in them. Out of all the things I'd done in my life, all the monstrous things Arienna had probably heard of, what I'd asked Jace to do that day...what I had done the evening after...that was the worse. "Until I didn't," I said, finishing his thought.

Tears glistened his eyes. They fell down his cheeks and hit the wooden floor with thunderous splats in the silence pulled taut between us.

"Will you do this for me, Jace? For her?"

His muscles completely relaxed. The air rippled with danger. Despite myself, my fingers grazed the hilt of my dagger.

"Why did you tell me?" he asked, his voice low and dangerous.

"Because I want her to enjoy this holiday." The last one she would ever get.

His eyes burned bright with fury. "You could have just asked me to have sex with her. You could have asked me, and I would have said yes." He took a step towards me. My fingers tightened on my blade. Grabbing my tunic, he yanked me towards him. "So why tell me she likes me? Why!"

My heart pounded in my throat, but I kept his gaze without flinching. I would do anything for her. She was my greatest joy in life and deserved all the happiness this fucked up world could give her. "So you would cherish her."

His mouth dropped open as he seemed to struggle to understand the words I'd uttered. Shoving me away from him, he stormed off. "I would have anyways."

"I could have had *years* with her," Jace accused, his eyes wild. Broken just like that day. "And instead, because of you, I only had one night."

"Jace –"

Shaking his head, he stormed off. The door to my private gym slammed shut, leaving me alone for the first time in over two decades. His absence bothered me a lot more than I'd thought it would.

Slowly, I climbed to my feet. There was a healing wand in the cabinet on my right, but I ignored it on my way to the punching bag. Throwing fist after fist into its cloth, I beat my knuckles raw.

"I want you to be king, Dickie."

I slammed my hand into the bag. *Thump.*

"I can't be the ruler our people need me to be."

Thump. Thump.

"But you have to promise me, when we're ready for peace, you'll push for it."

Twisting my hips, I threw all my energy into each blow. Pain erupted everywhere, but I kept going.

I kept going until her sweet voice was drowned out by the high pitch of Arienna's.

"You're a monster."

Thump. Thump. Thump.

"He was my fiance..."

Thump.

"Not a monster like you."

TWENTY-FOUR

Never step into a fairy ring lightly.

THERE CAN ONLY EVER BE

ONE SURVIVOR

— RICHARD

Karl climbed into the bathtub stark naked on shaky legs. I would have preferred to have this conversation anywhere else, but the coward kept pissing himself every time I opened my mouth. The least he could do was go somewhere it could easily be cleaned.

With my back to the door, I caught a glimpse of myself in the mirror. Blood caked half my face. Nasty bruises covered the rest. But the throbbing in my skull had nothing to do with the pain in my jaw and everything to do with this piece of shit in front of me.

Scratch that. A piece of shit was useful. It marked territory. It helped fertilise the ground. It could be used as a weapon, coating arrows and daggers. But this guy? He was absolutely fucking worthless. Killing him would be a kindness, and for a moment, I imagined opening up his neck and spilling his life all over the tub.

But then I remembered Arienna's words. Haunting me still.

Crossing my arms, I waited for him to settle. "There aren't any rules in a fairy ring. You can do whatever you want to survive. Skin me alive, pluck out my eyeballs and juggle them. Kick me in the balls. The rules of honourable combat do not apply, and there won't be any punishments for committing a war crime."

Piss flowed down the drain. Of course it fucking did. The surprise was how he managed to have anything left inside him. What was this? The fourth pee in a couple of hours? Granted, it wasn't a lot each time, but dear gods, how quick was his bladder?

And how in Hel's name had my wife been wanting to *marry* this?

"He's not a monster like you!"

Even with that in consideration, there was no way in Niflhel I was worse than this sorry lump of life.

Except, in her eyes I was.

Shifting uncomfortably, I continued, "Once we enter the ring, the only way for you to exit is by killing me." I waved a hand down my body, ending on the two stab wounds in my thighs. Blood crusted my clothes. "To make it fair, I won't be using a healing wand beforehand. Nor will I use a weapon, whereas you'll have the choice of whatever you want."

"Please..." he begged, his lips trembling.

I scoffed. "You don't think that's fair?"

He shook his head madly. Snot bubbled down his nose and into his mouth. "I'm sorry. I'm so sorry. I didn't mean to insult you."

"But you did mean to insult Arienna."

He sobbed wildly, hiccuping and gasping and putting on all the waterworks. "She...bro-bro-broke my...my h-h-heart."

Never had I wanted to destroy someone's voice box more than I did now and I'd listened to Nicholas sing. The guy couldn't carry a tune to save his life.

"I thought you brownies had a rule about lying?"

"I'm not! I...I d-d-did love her –"

"Pussy?" I cut in dryly. Because there was no way he knew anything else about her. He wouldn't have cheated on her otherwise, wouldn't have thrown away such a gift.

He nodded, and it took every bit of my control not to kill him here and now. The bastard shouldn't have the luxury of breathing the same air as my queen. And once he left these suites, I was having them completely gutted and redecorated. I didn't want his stench anywhere in the castle.

"She's so ti–"

"Another word and I won't give a damn about what she wants. I'll drag your ass to a fairy ring."

He swallowed damn near audibly, his green eyes wide. Reminded of my high scholar, I shook my head in disgust.

"So you have two options. You can either accept my challenge to enter a fairy ring, or..." I paused just to make him squirm. "You can tell me how to woo her."

His mouth fell open as he gasped for air. Arienna's air. My eyes narrowed. "Choose before I choose for you."

When silence was his only answer – though not for lack of trying – I took a step forward.

"I asked her to dance!" he blurted. Shaking violently, he lifted his eyes to mine in a silent plea for mercy.

Didn't he know monsters didn't give mercy?

"What else?"

He gulped, tears and snot streaming down his face.

"Then I took her to dinner. And I – I br-br-brought her–" Another gulp. "Shrooms."

I frowned. "Shrooms?"

Karl nodded like his life depended on it. And I guess, it kind of did.

"That's it? Dancing, dinner, and shrooms?"

His frantic nodding made me want to punch him in the face. Forcing myself to relax, I smiled nicely. "Breathe, Karl."

He sucked in ragged gulps. One after another until he finally had a sense of calm about him.

"Now tell me everything."

He shuddered, holding on to what little strength he had. Or rather, what little survival instinct he had. The words 'Karl' and 'strength' didn't belong in the same sentence.

"She was easy," he said shakily. "It only took dinner and shrooms because Fabia was at the dance. She's a real cockblocker, you know?"

Remind me to get her some shrooms. I smiled. *Make that a knife set.* "Go on."

"Well, she's a bit desperate to please, so you just have to string her along. Insult her while complimenting her..." He trailed off on a hard swallow, no doubt seeing the fury in my eyes.

"What kind of shrooms does she like?" I asked slowly. If I didn't change the subject, forget the fairy ring, I was going to kill him in the tub.

"I don't know. Marson gave them to me to throw away. They were a bit wilted, so he couldn't sell them..."

"You gave. Her. Rubbish?"

His face paled. Sweat broke out on his brow. "N-no, it wasn't like that."

I stared at him, daring him to continue.

"They were g-going t-to g-get...thrown...thrown away any...way a-a-and she −" He yelped as I pulled him up by the neck and slammed him against the tiled wall. A knife was in my hand, pressed against his dick. He whimpered as he closed his eyes. The blade dug into his pathetic flesh.

"Do you accept my challenge to enter the fairy ring?"

When piss dribbled across my hand, I smiled coldly.

"Say no, Karl," I whispered.

Tears flowed down his cheeks. "N-no."

"Good." My knife sliced across his penis. He screamed. Releasing his neck, I slammed my hand over his mouth. "To refuse to accept a challenge means you accept the alternative punishment: a thousand cuts. That was one."

Forcing his mouth open, I took his tongue. "Two."

I hoped he tasted the piss on my hand.

The door opened behind me, and I didn't have to turn to know it was Jace. He never had the courtesy to knock. And despite how we had left things earlier, his sense of duty − his loyalty to his friends, would never let him walk away completely.

"You know," he said, a bite of a smile in his voice, "I don't think this is what Arienna had in mind when she asked you not to kill him."

Freezing with my blade on Karl's ear, I looked into the coward's eyes. "She asked me not to challenge him in the ring. I accepted her request."

The 'man' whimpered.

"She asked you for mercy. To not be a monster, if I heard correctly."

"You didn't."

Chuckling, he stopped behind me. "You think I don't know why you challenged me to a spar earlier? We've been friends for over thirty years. I watched you learn how to walk."

I glanced at him over my shoulder. "I learned how to walk before you did."

"And sitting on my little baby ass, I watched you."

Shaking my head on a sigh, I released my grip on Karl and stepped back. He flopped into the bathtub. The both of us ignored him.

"The alternative is a thousand cuts," I pressed, really liking the idea of continuing.

"But you don't have to give them all at once. And you definitely aren't required to chop something off each time. If he dies, Arienna won't ever see you as anything other than a monster."

I swirled the knife in my hand. "But why should I care what she thinks? She's going to be executed in a few weeks."

His eyes turned serious. "Same reason I cared about Aurelia despite knowing what you had planned for her. We don't get to choose who we care for or how hard."

"What about the Court?"

"We'll tell them the truth: that we lied and she never entered the portal. They'll be forced to drop the charges."

Wiping my blade on a roll of tissue, I then sheathed it. Somehow, I doubted it would be that simple. "Clean him up and throw him out. And get someone to redecorate this whole floor. I don't even want to be able to sense his aura here once he's gone."

Heading for the door, I added, "Have a healer reattach his tongue and penis. Make sure Arienna's there to see it."

Jace chuckled. "I don't think she'll take that the way you want her to."

I turned. "Why not? It's proof of my mercy."

He cocked a brow. I scowled. "How about I patch him up and get him some fresh clothes? Then I'll have him tell Arienna you just let him go."

"Brownies don't lie."

Jace's smile was chilling. "Trust me. This one will."

Sliding my gaze over to the pathetic pulp on the floor, I nodded. "Fine. Do that."

Exiting the suite, I headed for the balcony. Flying up to my rooms, I tugged off my blood-stained tunic and used it to clean my hands. The guards nodded at me. Irin opened my door, and I walked inside, heading straight for the shower.

By the time I finished washing off all the grime, got dried, and dressed, Jace was waiting for me. I stopped in the doorway, staring at him as he sat on the bed, assessing the damage between us. When he smiled, I relaxed.

A knock at the door had Jace rising to answer it. Paul was ushered in with his carts of shrooms, a smile lighting up his face. Fabia came in after him, scowling and covered in sweat.

"You called?" she demanded.

Paul's smile faltered as he glanced at her in horror.

Holding her gaze, I gestured to his carts. "What kind of shrooms does Arienna like?"

"What?"

"I think I was perfectly clear. As a recruit in my guard, you are legally obliged to answer."

She glanced at Jace in irritation, then shook her head. "The glowing purple ones."

My eyes narrowed as I scanned the two carts. There were purple polka dotted ones and glowing green ones, but no glowing purple shrooms. "Did Jace not ask you to bring everything?" I demanded.

"I've never heard of any glowing purple ones, my lord," Paul said, his eyes wide.

"That's because they don't exist," Jace cut in with a chuckle. "Now that you've poked him, stop," he told Fabia.

"Otherwise, you're going to be responsible for his death."

She paled. I smiled.

Good. Now that she understood the seriousness of the situation, I asked again. "Which shrooms?"

Exhaling strongly, she walked up to the carts. "She doesn't really have a favourite. She likes anything and everything if you haven't noticed. Spiders. Rikas. Wasps. Jacolas." She turned to me. "You."

My lips twitched with a smile. I know she'd meant it as an insult given everything else she'd listed was venomous, but I didn't care. She'd said Arienna liked me.

"But she especially likes those with meanings attached to them."

I glanced at Paul for an explanation.

"Some shrooms mean different things," he said quickly. Pulling a solid blue shroom out, he held it towards me. "This is a symbol of prosperity and wealth."

"Do you have one for 'I showed mercy to your pathetic excuse of an ex'?"

"You let him go?" Fabia cut in, surprise lacing her voice.

"She did ask me to," I growled.

"But you challenged him."

"Yes."

"Did you retract it?"

Knowing where she was going, I turned to her with a smile. To retract it was to show weakness, to claim that you were a coward. But it would also let the other person off without any harm to them. "No. He refused, but the thousand cuts I owe him don't have a time limit. I'll give them to him when he's on his death bed."

She studied me, her silver eyes cold in her assessment.

Sighing, she picked up a teal shroom with white polka dots on its rim. "This is Arienna's favourite colour. And she likes animals. Like a *lot*. She's always wanted a mischief of rats."

When I glanced at Jace, he smiled and headed for the door to inform the guards.

"Thank you." Turning to Paul, I said, "Make a hundred boutiques that centres around this colour for the ball next week and send one to her rooms the evening of. I'm assuming I don't have to tell you what will happen if word gets out about this conversation?"

He nodded.

"Good. Then you're dismissed."

As he scurried out the door, I headed for the minibar in my room. Pulling out a bottle of ambrosia and two glasses, I set them on the table and poured. Picking the tumblers up, I handed one to Fabia. She hesitated for a few seconds before taking it.

Settling in my chair, I asked, "Now what kind of food does she like?"

TWENTY-FIVE

A good brownie never checks out books
on murder.

These are some very specific rules...

— Arienna

Dear gods, how was murder this hard? Fabia's books always made it sound so easy. Set fire to someone's house. Throw a toaster in their bathtub. Drop a piano on their head. And then behead them. Easy.

But I lived in the same house as my target. I couldn't get into his suite, let alone his bathroom. And even if I could, what was I going to do? Waltz in there with a toaster under my arm, pretending it was a sex toy?

"Oh, hey, hubbie, want to close your eyes for me while I stick your schlong in a hot warm hole?"

Groaning, I banged my head on my desk. This was never going to work. He was faster than me, stronger than me, and always had a guard on him. As much as I wanted to live, I didn't want to kill Jace or any other innocent bystander just doing their job.

Ugh. If only my freaking wasps had done what they were supposed to do. I lifted my head. Had they not been angry at being left alone without much food? They were murderously aggressively to me 80% of the time – on a *good* day, and yet, he'd waltzed in there with his macho chest and his hot, sexy charm, and they'd just rolled over for him.

The slutty bastards. Good riddance they were gone.

Why? Don't like seeing how they took after mama?

I scowled.

Standing, I headed for the floor-to-ceiling windows overlooking the city, trying to find a bit of peace. The town bustled around me in the soft glow of the morning light. The branches spreading out from the castle were full of shops and attractions I would never get to visit. The nefarious arena where prisoners of war could fight for their freedom. The battlefields were children as young as two started to train. And the beautifully carved library that was situated in the trunk of the tree above the castle. I couldn't see it from here, but I knew of it from Fabia's stories. Its beauty was said to match that of the gods, the building a love message that would make Aphrodite weep.

My eyes widened. *That's it!* The library would be full of "How to Kill People" books. I just needed to grab a few and do my research.

Turning from the window, I scurried to the door of my suite and pulled it open.

"Morning. Hope you two are well. I would like to visit Aurelia's Library, please." I paused, realising that though I recognised the guard on the left from my wedding night, I didn't know either of their names. Holding my hand out to the one I knew, I smiled, "And sorry I didn't introduce myself earlier; I'm Arienna."

The woman stared at me for a second before gripping my hand with a smile. "I'm Marrabel and this is my sister, Saragese. Don't bother offering her your hand. She has a stick up her ass this morning that's affecting her ability to be a decent human being."

Turning to me, a smug smile on her face, Saragese thrust out her hand. "The stick my *little* sister is referring to is 'reason'. I won't tell her how long it's been for King Morningstar."

My eyes widened. *I do not want to know. I do not want to know.*

Ushering me down the hall, Marrabel scoffed, "You're not even in on the bet!"

"No" –she turned to her sister– "but Ajax can offer me a great deal more than you can."

"You mean his dick? Because that's the only thing that can compete with the stick in your ass."

I coughed into my hand. Heat flared across my cheeks.

"Absolutely not. That thing is way, *way* too big to get anywhere near any of this." She moved her hand in a circular motion over her crotch. "He's offered me a full suit of my own design."

"I said I'd pay for one!"

"True, but he didn't eat the last of Mum's pie."

"It was sent to me for *my* birthday."

A goofy, bittersweet smile stretched my lips. This was the sort of relationship I'd always wanted with my sister.

"No, it *arrived* on your birthday, which means she had to send it at least a week ago, which means she sent it after hearing about my promotion."

"Promotion? You got to guard King Morningstar for *one* day. Half a day, even. Irin covered your night shift, and you only got it because Jace had a sick day. And have you been back? No. The pie was clearly for me."

"Did it have your name on it?"

"You don't put icing on pie!"

"And pies are not for birthdays. Everyone know's that. Pie is for 'congratulations on your promotion'."

Unable to help myself, I giggled. Both women turned towards me, their mouths hard, their eyes bright. "So how long was it?" I asked, glancing at Marrabel and winking.

"Oh, you sly little rat."

"Careful," Marrabel teased. "If anyone hears you insult our queen, they'll throw you in the dungeons."

"More like stab me in the gut, slit my throat, and then ship me off to the front lines at Gretadal..."

Shaking her head, Marrabel lifted me in her arms. "I heard he was given permanent latrine duty."

"I heard he was lucky he didn't get his head cut off."

I looked up at her, focusing on the conversation rather than the fact that we were about to launch into the air. "Who?"

"Tinsin. Rumours say our good king overhead him talking about your breasts."

My cheeks enflamed, I glanced down. My discomfort over Tinsin's words turned into fear over falling to my death. I think I'd rather take the public execution. Jerking my gaze back up, I shuddered.

Marrabel's voice turned stern. "You better relax, Your Majesty, because I am *not* fingering you."

Oh my gods. Just drop me now. Pushing my hands against my face, I wished for death. *Ironic.*

As soon she landed on the library's balcony, I was out of her arms and running towards the two large double doors, to solace. No one could talk in a library. No one could talk about fingering or how long it had been since *my king* had had sex...

Looking up from my feet, I searched for reception. My

jaw dropped opened. My brisk walk died a sudden death.

Screw a certain shirtless man with a dreamy chest.

This was beauty.

Designed as an octagon, weathered wooden shelves spanned the full length of the eight sides. They towered six or seven stories high, leading into a series of thick intercrossing beams, which held up a glass dome. And between each wooden shape was a panel depicting a galaxy full of stars.

My breath rushed out of me as I walked further in, staring up at the ceiling. I'd expected this place to be as cold and efficient as the rest of the city. But the shelves had been made with love, the room decorated with splendour. A massive globe, much taller than me, stood proudly in the middle, surrounded by a handful of well-worn sofas and chairs. This was a place of peace. An unguarded sanctuary.

Pulled in by a magnetic force, I walked slowly, my eyes taking everything in. Running my hand along the globe, I was surprised when it moved. Well greased, it shifted without a sound.

I gave it a little push. It spun flawlessly, bits of the world flashing by. The mushroom forests of Yogalha. The diamond caves of Jardo. The lost Temples of Hondu. Ular. Vinsio. Ev'lan'dic. Atheria.

I placed my hand on it at random. It stopped after gradually losing momentum. Aizela. That was where I wanted to go one day, decided as of now. Craning my neck, I looked up at the northern pole. Stepping back, I took it all in. The world was so big. How much of it would I never see?

A sadness came over me. A lost future I would never get.

Walking around, I found Raza, Richard's kingdom. It

was just a speck of colour... A miniscule existence. Ours wasn't even listed.

My gaze turned to the glass dome.

Each one of those galaxies had more worlds in them. Halzaja. Persic. Blódyrió. Konistra. Alazul. Earth. All the places I would never see.

"Can I help you?'

My chest aching with a dull pain, I turned to the woman asking. She was shorter than me, with her hair up in a stern bun.

"Yes. I'm looking for –" I cleared my throat. Taking a deep breath, I smiled innocently. My eyes latched onto the freckle at the corner of her mouth rather than the piercing darkness of her eyes. "A book on murders. Nice murders, if possible. For research."

Blinking rapidly, I added, "Book research, I mean, not real life research, obviously. Ha. Why would I admit to needing it for real life research if that were true? That would be dumb, right? I mean, who would do that? That would be like publishing a 'how I murdered my husband' book after being accused of...murdering...my husband..." Sweat started to break out across my back. I laughed nervously.

She reached for my shoulder, and I flinched, knowing she was going to drag me back down to the dungeons.

"It's okay," she said with a smile. "I'm an author too."

"An author..." I looked at her blankly, then exhaled strongly as I nodded. "Yeah, that's me. Yes, of course, it's for my work in progress."

"What's your book about?"

"Uh..." I shook my head, thinking of Fabia's latest book. "It's about a man who wants to become an assassin, but to do that he has to kill people in various ways as a test."

She nodded. "Sounds interesting. Are you a pantser or

a plotter?"

My mouth worked uselessly as I struggled to recall what those terms meant. "Um...a bit of both?"

Chuckling, she said, "Oh, I know what that's like. I try to plot my books all the time, but the characters end up doing whatever they want."

Gesturing for me to follow her, she headed for the stairs. "You know, I once plotted out a whole book about this woman who had been kidnapped by a vampire. Her sister was supposed to save her at the end with the help from an Elv've'nor agent, who she fell in love with, obviously."

We started to climb.

"Well, sort of save her. They had to put her in a coma to stop a curse from killing her, and in the second book, a telepath had to go into her mind and help her. She then fell in love with him, and the four of them lived happily ever after."

Glancing at me, she snorted. "But do you know what happened?"

I shook my head, glad we were talking about her book rather than 'mine'. "What?"

"The fucking vampire decided he wasn't that stupid and got away at the end of book one. So now the damn thing is a twelve book series. *Twelve.*" She shook her head in exasperation. "And in the second book, my stupid MC kept cutting off his hands. Who even does that? Like dear gods, why? I couldn't leave him alone for *two* paragraphs before off came his hands."

Rolling her eyes, she exited on the fourth floor. Her slow amble took me around the mezzanine.

"So what did you do?" I asked, getting invested in the story.

She grinned devilishly. "I drugged the crap out of him.

Anyway, this is the reference section. I'm sure you'll find what you're looking for."

She waved at a shelf of books, and my eyes followed. *101 Ways to Kill a Queen. The Fastest Assassinations in History. The Cruelest Ways to Die. Getting to the Heart of a Person.*

Looking back at her, I smiled. "I'm sure I will, thank you."

"My pleasure. Let me know if you need anymore help."

As she walked away, I turned my attention back to the books in front of me. Pulling one off the shelf at random, I flipped it open.

Honey, Does This Taste Like Poison to You?

In 1842, a Vylian woman named Yovalin was poisoned by her husband after they'd had a fight about whether the hoovering should come before or after the mopping. She'd claimed it should go after so one didn't have to hoover twice, picking up all the bits that the mop had dislodged. Although her reasoning was flawless, as anyone who had ever mopped would know, her husband declared that to be barbaric and that only 'criminals' would do such a thing.

So that night, he served her, a vegetarian, a stew that contained bits of frog. But what should have been a cruel prank, ended in her death...

Annoyed that there wasn't any mention about what poisonous frog had actually been used, I closed the book and picked another one.

And another.

And another.

And another.

Groaning, I placed the latest book back. There was nothing in any of them that would help me. I had no idea how to wield a weapon nor where to find any poison. I was actually considering going back to the toaster idea.

Sitting down, I dropped my head in my hands.

"Not having any luck?" At Jace's voice, I jumped. If he was here, so was Richard.

Scrambling to my feet, I held the book behind my back. "What are you doing here? Where's Richard? I wouldn't have thought he'd have the time to read."

"He doesn't. Well, not books anyway." Looking over my head, he scanned the shelves.

My blood drained from my face. "It's for research. Book research," I squeaked out. "For my book. That I'm writing. About an assassin."

"Sounds interesting."

"It is."

Reaching past me, he grabbed a book with a chained man on the cover, his arms over his head, a blindfold and gag covering his face. "I'd recommend this one then."

He handed it to me and I took it slowly. My eyes widened. "*Good Enough to Die For?*"

He leaned in with a smirk, "A few of those entries are mine."

My mouth dropped open. The urge to flip through it and see which ones he could possibly mean made my fingers twitch. After pulling a few more off the shelves, balancing them on one hand, he held out his other arm for me to take.

Blinking, I took it.

But my eyes were latched onto the books he was holding. One, two, three...*eleven* books. In one hand. Dear gods, how strong was he?

And was it bad that I found that hot?

My cheeks burned.

"I brought Karl to see you," Jace said, forcing me back to reality as we walked down the stairs.

Shivering, I tried not to picture what that meant. "Will

it be quick?" I murmured, praying Richard would be at least that kind.

"It'll be however long you want it to be."

"However long..." Staring at him, my heart pounding in my chest, I stopped on the stairs. "I want it to be as short as possible. I don't want Richard to drag out his –"

"Oh, shit. No. He's not dying. Sorry, I should've led with that. Richard's letting him go."

"What? What about the challenge? What about the whole 'you insulted my honour and the kingdom' thing?"

Smiling as if he knew something I didn't, he leaned in to murmur, "You asked him to drop it."

"And he did?" I blinked, not understanding. "But why when –" I cut myself off before I could say, 'He's planning on executing me?'

"Do you want us to kill him? Because I could easily cause an accident before we leave the library."

"You can't kill someone in a library!" I hissed.

"On the contrary. Page sixty-nine." He laughed as my cheeks flushed. "And that wasn't a no..."

"No," I blurted. "No. Karl's a dick, but no."

He shrugged. "I've killed people for less."

My brain spasmed. "That's...that's not an excuse!"

"No, it's not a *good* excuse." His lips curled. "Just like it's not a good excuse to leave the castle without Richard's knowledge to...research a book. There are a lot of people that would see your premature death as a good thing."

The air disappeared from my lungs even as confusion flooded me. I wasn't sure if I was being told off or if he was joking. Wasn't sure if he knew what I was planning to do or not. The smile stretching across his lips made my brain hurt trying to figure it out.

"Now come on," he said. "Karl has something he wants to tell you."

I glanced at him. The stairs disappeared beneath my feet. My heart jumped into my throat. My pulse slammed around in my ears.

No, there's no way he knows, I assured myself. *If he did, he wouldn't be walking me down these stairs. He'd be dragging me to the dungeons...*

TWENTY-SIX

Prisoners are stripped of all rights once jailed.

WHAT DOESN'T BREAK YOU...

PETRE WILL.

— RICHARD

Unsurprisingly, I found her in the castle dungeons. Petre loved spending her spare time in the blasted hole torturing prisoners. And since Jace hadn't let me use Karl as an output for my anger, I was almost tempted to join her.

She was in Kiki's cell, the last of the women that had tried to assassinate me. Kneeling over the woman's chest, Petre held a toilet plunger in her hands, the end of which was pushed against her victim's face.

Pinned to her side, Kiki's hands clawed at the ground. Her legs kicked. Her lungs, I were certain, were fighting to breathe.

"Inventive," I said dryly as Jace and I stopped in front of the cell.

Looking over her shoulder, Petre smiled at us, her dark olive skin crinkling at the eyes. As she yanked the plunger up, a loud *welch* made my gut twist. Turning her head to the side, Kiki gasped in air, dark brown marks and bits of tissue stuck to her face.

"You didn't even clean it beforehand – classy."

"I figured if she was going to talk shit, she might as well eat it."

An image of Caroline in Kiki's place made my lips twitch. "And what exactly did she talk shit about?"

"She claimed a certain two girls had been planning to assassinate you." Rising to her feet, she whacked the end of the plunger against the woman's stomach, flicking it clean.

My eyes narrowed. "It is a crime to tamper with a witness' testimony."

"I haven't tampered with anything." Stepping out of the cell, she pulled the dungeon wand out of her tunic. The bars appeared as she waved it. "Kiki has already gone on record stating their purpose that night. I'm just invoking my right to talk to the witness."

"With a plunger?" I asked deadpanned.

She shrugged as she twirled it in her hand. "Given the dimwits I'm forced to work with these days, it's the smartest person I know. At least it doesn't go trancing around thinking it's the fucking Maridal Everdene of our time."

I fought a smile. For everything Petre was, she was a stickler for the laws and she didn't like anyone stretching them further than was honourable. "You mean Caroline?" It wasn't a question.

Her cat-like eyes narrowed. "If she'd just thought about it for a second, she would have realised that pushing the member issue would hurt the Court more than you." Her eyes flicked to Jace. "You would lose him –"

"And you would lose half your members given how many of them have had miscarriages," I finished for her.

Oveyni's laws, as much of a pain in the ass they were, had defined life as starting at the time of conception. And although that law had been scaled back given we were no longer on the verge of extinction, I would use whatever ammunition I had in order to save Jace.

His life was nonnegotiable.

As was Arienna's...

"Quite," she said. "So since you're not here to ask me to drop the charges against him given Caroline will do it for you soon enough, what *do* you want?"

I gestured towards the exit and she followed me down the corridor. The cell Arienna and Fabia had been placed in was empty. She would never revisit this place.

As we exited the dungeons, I said, "The brownie didn't enter the human portal."

Petre looked at me over her shoulder, her eyes shrewd. I kept my face full of boredom, letting her think I didn't care one way or another. Her paranoia would do the work for me.

"You wish to share your crown with her?"

"I wish not to have the blood of an innocent on my hands," I said, keeping my voice flat, "and she could be of use during my trade talks with the brownies."

She smiled. "Not to mention, she has the tits of a whore according to your guards. You had her in your study."

I snorted. "She begged me to, but no. I finished her and threw her out. She's too soft for my liking."

"Ever the gentleman." Her eyes roamed over my face. She could look all she wanted, but she wasn't finding shit. "My Evangeline would eat you alive."

"Your Evangeline had her chance, but she called off our

engagement," I said, purposefully rubbing it in her face that she'd been so close to being the mother of a queen and yet, her own daughter had let her down.

Her scowl made me want to smile.

"Like I said," she sneered, "I'm surrounded by dimwits."

Spreading her wings, she launched into the air. Jace and I followed her through the tunnels up to the first floor of the castle. The baths at the end of the hall played in my mind, the place of my first meeting with my queen – or rather, my first proper meeting with her.

When I'd found her the first night, she'd been so drunk off her ass, she'd thought I was a baby bird that had fallen out of a nest. She'd clicked and cawed at me, flapping her arms as she tried to get me to follow her to safety.

At the time, it had been vastly annoying. The effort it had taken to get her to do anything remotely normal had made me seriously consider dropping her to the forest floor below.

Now, it seemed...cute.

A smile pulled at my lips. I squashed it before Petre could see. I needed to get her to agree to drop the charges before she realised I was invested in this for more than just a political gain.

"I'll bring it to the Court's attention," she said as we passed the guards on the balcony. "Assuming there's no evidence of her entry and you and Jace won't testify to her going in, I could potentially sway them to drop the charges."

"And in exchange?" I asked, knowing it was coming.

She stopped to turn and smile at me. "Nothing. The brownie has nothing to do with our feud."

My blood ran cold. My gut tightened. She never did anything without personal gain.

"Besides," she added as she walked away, "it's about

time we had a queen."

TWENTY-SEVEN

A good brownie never leaves the table
until everyone is done eating.

Eating food or...?

— Arienna

The nerves I'd experienced at my house had nothing on the nerves I was feeling now. There, I'd been able to convince myself that it wasn't really murder I was about to commit. But this? Standing outside Richard's suite with a cake in my hands? And, okay, yeah, this cake wasn't poisoned, but it *was* the cake I was using to get him to lower his guard so that when I *did* offer him the poisoned cake eventually, he'd take it without suspicion.

Smiling nervously as Jace opened the door from the outside, I shifted from foot to foot. I hadn't seen Richard since talking to Karl four days ago. He'd been busy with running the kingdom, and I'd been flipping through book after book trying to come up with a way to kill him. And now I had this idea and Richard was free and Jace was outside rather than right beside him and it was all coming together and I felt sick all the way down to my toes.

All those people that said marriage made a relationship boring had clearly never tried killing their partner. This definitely spiced things up.

I squirmed.

But maybe not in a good way...

Taking a deep breath, I tried not to vomit all over Jace as I cracked a smile.

Which immediately started to slip when he stared at me with a disbelieving grin. Frozen in front of the door, the only thing that moved was the frantic beating of my heart. He knew. Dear gods, he knew. I should've known when he'd offered me that book.

Nonsense. Why would he try to help you kill the man he's guarding? my little voice said, trying to soothe my nerves.

When Jace reached forward with one strong hand, I tried not to flinch. Swiping a finger through the icing, he placed it in his mouth with a little, heart-stopping moan. "I *love* cranberry and cream. You'll have to make me one of these too."

Dumbly, I nodded.

Trembled beneath my skin.

So he doesn't know?

My pulse slowed a bit before beating just as frantically as before.

Dear gods, what if he ate the poisoned cake? I liked Jace. I didn't want him to die. Maybe this was a bad idea. Maybe I should just –

"Go on in," he said with another swipe of his finger. "Richard doesn't like being kept waiting."

With legs that didn't seem like my own, I stumbled inside. The door clicked closed behind me. My heart in my throat, I gulped around it. My nerves frayed.

My hands tightened on the platter.

"I'm in here." Richard's voice called from my right, from inside his bedroom. My pulse spiked. Going in there, where his bed was, was not a good idea.

Rooted to the floor, I called out on a shaky breath. "I think we should eat out here. Wouldn't want to get the bed dirty..."

Images of his bed dirty in a different way, wet and stained, popped into my mind. Biting back a groan, I hurried to the black two-seater sofa. Staying busy, I placed the cake on the dark coffee table and then grabbed some plates and forks from his kitchenette. The open plan of his suite was similar to mine and that familiarity helped me relax a little.

I can do this.

Turning with the plates in my hand, I jumped, having found him right in front of me. The plates flew high, as did the cutlery. His eyes didn't leave mine. Reaching up, he grabbed all four items before even gravity could get a hold of them.

Swallowing hard, my pulse spasming in my throat, I leaned back on the counter.

He was shirtless. Why did he have to be shirtless?

"You brought me a cake?" Richard murmured, leaning forward to put the stuff down.

Screw the bed, he was fucking me right here with his eyes. My hands tightened on the edge of the counter. Dear gods, why did I have to use 'screw' and 'bed' and 'fucking' all in the same sentence? My lips parting, I started to pant.

Pull yourself together, woman!

But it had been four days since I'd felt his touch, and my daily masturbations had done nothing to relieve the pressure building inside me. The pressure that was now building so fast and high that if he just leaned in a little bit more, I would combust.

"Yes, cake. I brought. Eat! We should eat...it." I gulped.

He leaned in.

My heart slammed against my ribcage over and over and over again. So hard I could feel that pulse in my pussy, throbbing with need. Clenching my thighs together, I held on to what little bit of sanity I had left.

Sleeping with him would *not* be a good idea...

Even if the book Jace had recommended was about all the different ways to kill someone in bed...

And Richard, who was also planning on killing me, didn't seem to have the same dilemma of mixing murder with hot, sweaty sex...

"There is something I'd like to eat." His breath hit my neck. "But it's not cake."

Grabbing my hips, he lifted me up onto the counter. I scrambled to jump down, only to realise that the orders going through my head didn't seem to be reaching my limbs. My nerves were fried. My body was his to command.

Breathing heavily, I watched as he spread my legs open and dropped to his knees.

Fuck. Fuck. Fuck. Fuck. Fuck.

I wish I was wearing a dress...

No! Bad, Arienna. Ba– Arching backwards, I forgot why this was a bad idea.

My hands fisted in his hair as he kissed the fabric between my thighs.

My eyes closed.

My mouth opened.

I panted heavy and hard.

Came harder.

His chuckle vibrated against the V of my legs, building me back up again way too quickly. "I seem to have been neglecting my duties as a husband." Opening a drawer, he pulled out a knife. "Allow me to apologise."

I jumped. Fear squeezed my heart, keeping me mute. His arm pressed across my hips, keeping me down.

As thoughts of my blood and guts spilling all across the floor flooded me, I picked up a plate to smash it over his head.

But then he was running the blade up my thigh, slicing the fabric clean through, and his lips were following, and *fuck me*.

The plate clattered back down on the counter.

"That's better," he murmured as he skimmed the tip against my pussy, cutting my panties in half. I clenched, expecting to feel a sting, but there was nothing other than pleasure. *My king* knew how to wield a knife, and why in Hel's name did I find that sexy?

I should be terrified...

He placed the knife down beside me, the clatter of the metal calling my attention. My eyes latched onto it. My fingers slowly reached for it.

Sliding his hands under my ass, he gripped my cheeks and hauled me to him. As I fell backwards from the momentum and the pleasure, I couldn't stop a cry from escaping. Bowing under his wet caress, I caved for just a moment. Just for this moment.

After all, why should I suffer through abstinence in my last days? I was punishing him, not me. And clearly, he didn't have an issue with fucking me while having plans to kill me, so why should I?

Equality and all that...

Moaning, I dug my hands in his hair and ground my hips against his mouth. His fingers slipped inside me, curling as his tongue licked and claimed and worshipped.

Panting, I moved with him. His tongue lapped against me. Long slow licks that set my soul on fire. His fingers pumped inside me, pushing against my squeezing wet muscles until I could no longer breathe. Just gasp for air. Gasp and moan and cry out in pleasure as he built up the pressure inside me.

So close.

I was so flippin' close...

"My king!" I panted, writhing beneath him, chasing that beautiful release.

His tongue stroked me.

His fingers claimed me.

His lips nibbled across mine.

Just a few more seconds and I would –

Abruptly, he pulled away.

His fingers left me.

His mouth lifted.

When I tried to reach for him, he grabbed my hand and kissed the rapid pulse at the base of my wrist. Licking me off his lips, he murmured, "That's punishment one."

I blinked at him. Slowly. In confusion.

Punishment?

For what?

My eyes widened. Did he know? But how? This cake wasn't even poisoned!

The knife!

My eyes flew to it beside me. My fingers itched with the urge to grab it, but in a one-on-one fight, I knew I wouldn't win. I needed to let him think I was weak and helpless before going for it.

Scolding myself for not grabbing it earlier, I trembled in anticipation.

He leaned in, his breath whispering across my lips.

"The second punishment I owe you, I'll give you right before you leave."

Pressing his mouth against mine, he kissed me fully. His tongue tasted of me, so I tried to turn away, but he grabbed my chin, holding me still.

He claimed my face's lips as well as he'd claimed my pussy lips, and soon I was panting beneath him again. I reached forward to undo his belt, but he stopped me with a grip like iron.

"Not tonight. Tonight is your punishment."

I whimpered in frustration.

"Did you think I'd forgotten my promise at your house?"

My brows furrowed. *What promise? What –?*

A gasp escaped me as my eyes flew to his. A smirk curled his lips. A dark, sexy smirk that made me want to service him. To beg him to finish what he'd started. But he wouldn't, I knew.

Because this was punishment one...

"Every second you don't answer is another punishment I will give you."

And two would come soon...

Panting, I whimpered.

Grabbing my hips, he lifted me off the counter. I sagged against him, my legs not wanting to hold me. What they wanted was to be wrapped around his waist...

I clutched at his chest.

He moved back. *The bastard.*

"Go on. Take the plates over while I grab the ice-cream." He ran his lips across my neck. "And if you even think about touching yourself, I'll chain you to my bed and leave you there."

Grabbing the plates pushed into my hands, I stumbled into the sitting room. The cutlery rattled as I put it down with shaky arms. My breaths came out in uneven gasps. My brain stayed fried.

Dear gods, I'm screwed...

No, you're not, remember? That's the flippin' issue...

I pressed my thighs together. Flicking my gaze to the kitchenette, seeing him not facing me, I slid a hand down my stomach.

"I don't make light on my promises, Arienna."

Snatching my hand away, I sat down on the sofa and swallowed. Needing to keep my hands busy, I grabbed the cake, then realised I hadn't brought a knife.

"Can you grab..."

I trailed off as a knife was handed to me. It was sharp enough to stab him with, but I wouldn't be fast enough. I knew that. I needed to be smart.

And pray tell, how was letting him touch you 'smart'?

Forcing a smile, I cut him a slice and then me. "Is that enough?" I asked as he settled in the chair across from me.

Squirming beneath his gaze, I tried not to touch myself. Tried to ignore the little voice in my head mocking me. Though really, it was *my* voice. Wasn't it supposed to be on my side? If it was living in my head rent free, the least it could do was be supportive...

"It's perfect."

And the way he'd said that, holding my eyes and not even looking at the cake...

Shivering, I grabbed my plate and started to stuff my face.

"Want some ice-cream?" he asked. A spoonful of it was offered to me. I held out my plate as he deposited it beside my portion.

"Thanks."

"The pleasure is all mine."

Lowering my eyes, hoping the ice-cream would cool

me down, I ate a huge chunk of it. Salted caramel. The worst flavour in the world.

Trying not to spit it back out, I swallowed dutifully.

The heat in my cheeks did not go down.

"So how was your day?" I asked, unable to stand the silence. Normally, I was fine with the quiet. Fabia didn't like talking nearly as much as I did. But with Richard, the silence seemed deafening. Charged. Heated.

I ate another big bite of my ice-cream. The following brain freeze filled me with regret.

"It was fine." He paused. "Yours?"

"It would be better if you'd finished −" I stopped, my mouth falling open in horror. It seemed it wasn't just my body that was the traitor. My flippin' mouth was too. Images of me down on my knees, my mouth full in the way it wanted to be, flooded my thoughts.

And my flippin' thoughts!

Dear gods, this is why I needed Fabia. If only she still hated Richard. If only she wasn't being indoctrinated into this cult, then I could ask her for advice.

She'd be a much better murderer than I.

She already had arson on her track record. Murder was merely a step away.

Choking down my cake, I hoped he didn't realise what I'd been about to say.

But his eyes said he did as they lightened with laughter.

And freaking gods, he was beautiful.

Finishing my cake, I jumped to my feet. "Well, this was nice. We should do it again tomorrow." *With poison.*

"Sit back down. It's rude to leave before everyone is... finished."

My traitorous body lowered me onto the sofa.

My heart beat strongly in my vagina.

Archery.

I needed to pick up archery.

Shoot him from afar.

Because this close stuff wasn't working.

Holding my gaze, he lifted his fork to his lips.

Memorised, I watched as his mouth closed over it.

Panting, I reached for the knife and cut myself another slice of the cake. I didn't feel like eating anymore, but I couldn't just sit here.

As I raised my fork to my mouth, he asked, "Do you have a safe word?"

I choked, very gracefully spitting cake all over my plate. "What?"

He handed me a serviette. With shaky fingers, I took it.

"I'll take that as a no," he murmured with a bit of humour colouring his words.

"Wh-why do you need to know?"

His smile told me everything.

Oh fuck me, I'm in trouble.

"I uh – I..." I shoved some more cake into my mouth, only then remembering I'd just spat it all out. I was eating second-hand cake. Trying not to gag, I swallowed.

Swallowed like a good little girl.

My breath catching, I placed my plate on the coffee table. It clattered with the same nervous energy that was rattling my body.

"Mine's 'peace treaty'," he said softly. His lips closed around another bite. I wanted them to close around me.

"You have..." I swallowed. "A safe word?"

"Of course. It's not exactly a one-way street, now is it?"

I opened my mouth, then closed it again. I'd had no idea, but it made sense. "Oh."

"We won't do anything you're not comfortable with."

"Like leaving me as horny as Zeus?" I muttered.

Flippin' mouth!

He smiled. "That's called edging. And trust me, you'll thank me for it."

Under the heat of his gaze, I believed him.

Eating the last of his cake, he placed his fork on the plate and set it on the table. "There. I'm all finished. You can go now."

Disappointment filled me.

But I grasped onto the very, very, *very* thin slither of sanity I had left and climbed to my feet.

Just as I reached for the door, a hand shot past my face and slammed onto the wood. Strong fingers turned me around. His body caged me in. Remembering the night in his office, I started to tremble. Electricity shot through me.

My thighs became wet.

Looking into my eyes, he murmured, "I almost forgot to give you your second punishment." He reached into his trouser pocket and pulled out a remote control vibrator.

My eyes widened.

My breath became laboured.

Holding my gaze, he slipped the toy inside me.

My muscles clenched around it. His fingers pressed against my clit, making me spasm.

Leaning in, he kissed my neck. Licked his way up to my ear.

"I'll see you tomorrow, my queen."

Pulling me aside, he opened the door and pushed me out.

As I stumbled into the hall, my face enflamed, I placed my hands in front of me. My jumpsuit was cut, as was my underwear.

And the bastard had just pressed the button.

TWENTY-EIGHT

A good brownie never refuses an invite
without a good reason.

Unfortunately, contemplating suicide

is not a good reason.

— Arienna

I was never coming out of my room again. Not even to
kill him. I was okay with death now. After last night, after
Jace had looked at me knowingly when I had stopped in
the middle of the hall to 'tie my shoes' – slip ons, by the
way – I was okay with dying.

Groaning, I held the pillow over my head and screamed
into it. Perhaps, I was going about this all wrong. Instead
of trying to kill him, I should be killing me. Give myself a
nice, comfortable death because the gods knew, going to
his room tonight was going to end in disaster.

A knock on the door instantly froze my thoughts.

Was it him?

I was on my feet and out of the bedroom in a second.
The last thing I needed was to have him enter my rooms.

"Your Majesty, we have a messenger here to see you."

Pretending it wasn't disappointment rushing through me, I tugged on a dress and said, "Okay. You can let them in."

The door opened and a red-haired man strolled in with a bouquet of my favourite coloured shrooms in one hand. In his other, was a flat box balanced on his palm. Black with a lilac bow wrapped around it, it screamed class and luxury.

My lips parting, I watched, memorised, as he placed both items on the table.

"King Morningstar will be here at six." With a slight bow at the waist, he exited.

My stomach twisting with nerves, I reached a hand towards the flowers and plucked out the card.

FOR YOU, MY QUEEN

Handwritten.

He'd taken a moment out of his day to write to me.

A smile twitched at my lips.

A giddiness filled my chest.

Shaking my head, I put the card back. Who was to say it was even his handwriting? I had never seen it before. He'd probably had the shroomist do it.

Pulling the bow off the box, I lifted the lid and froze.

Another handwritten card stared back at me, and it was, without a doubt, *his*.

THESE ARE FOR YOU

CHOOSE TO WEAR THEM OR NOT,

BUT THE TOY IS NON-NEGOTIABLE.

Swallowing, I placed the card on the table and lifted out the dark purple dress. It unfolded all the way to the floor. Two thick black belts wrapped around its middle, and sewn into its black corset was a galaxy of diamonds.

I sucked in a ragged breath as I held it up to my chest. Nicholas had definitely not picked this one out.

Looking back in the box, I pulled out the shoes – black strappy heels with diamond studs. My size.

But it was the jewellery that my eyes were snagged on. A leather choker necklace with the symbol of the Raza kingdom in the middle: a raven with a snake in its talons. Matching earrings with dark purple gemstones making up the snake's body, as well as three black bangles and a ring.

These weren't the sort of gifts you gave someone you planned on executing.

They were what you gave –

My breath caught.

– your wife.

Fingering the amethyst in the choker, I imagined what a future here could be like. Toe-curling, hot, and sexy for certain. But maybe also kind. And soft. And...loving.

With time perhaps.

Time I didn't have.

Because my hot bastard of a husband was okay with the Court killing me.

Sighing, I put everything back inside the box. I couldn't wear any of this. The card caught my eye again, making me shiver. *Especially not the toy.*

I refused to be some sex object he got to play with before my death date. I was a person with my own dreams and desires and all. The fingering I'd only allowed because of my fear of flying. The oral I'd accepted just to get close to him...and, okay, because it felt amazing.

But this? Playing wife to a husband that didn't really want me?

Pain sliced through my chest.

That I could not bare.

Glancing at the clock, seeing I had only an hour to get ready thanks to my day-long moping session, I headed for the bathroom. After a quick shower, I started to style my hair. Brushed my teeth. Applied a bit of makeup.

Naked, I walked through the sitting room. My eyes lingered on the gifts. The card.

Hurrying into my bedroom, I grabbed a random dress Ajax's daughter had picked out for me: a lilac floor-length beauty with a low back and slits running up to the thighs. After pulling it over my head, I slipped on a pair of black stilettos, then made my way into the sitting room.

Over to the box.

My fingers trailed once more over the choker.

I could wear it for me...

Not him.

With a shaky breath, I lifted the piece around my neck. Threaded on the earrings. Looking down, I realised that the dress he had sent would be a much better match than what I had on...

For me, not him.

Changed completely, dressed in everything he wanted, my mind latched onto the toy I'd left on the bedside table.

Non-negotiable.

Before I could decide what to do about it – whether he'd see me not wearing it as more of a challenge – the door of my suite opened without notice.

As my eyes landed on *my king*'s face, time stood still. He looked regal in his suit – a black jacquard tailcoat with amethysts on the lapels, black trousers held up with a set of crisscrossing silver studded belts, and a black button-up shirt underneath a purple waistcoat with buttons made up of the Raza symbol.

My mouth watered.

His hand moved at his side, his fingers and thumb

rubbing together.

His eyes narrowed. "You're not wearing it."

I took a nervous step back.

Liquid heat pooled inside me as he advanced.

"I said it was non-negotiable."

I moved around the breakfast bar, putting it between us. "I didn't think it was a good idea. This get up looks expensive, like there will be other people around, and..." I stopped as he rounded the bar. He wasn't supposed to do that.

"Oh, there will definitely be other people around." The gap between us vanished. My heart slammed against my chest, feeling cornered, caged, boxed in. "Everyone of importance will be there. Now where is it?"

My eyes flicked to my bedroom. "I- I threw it away."

"Did you now?" He growled low and primal, and fuck me, who needed a toy? His hand ran up the side of my waist and over to cup my breast. Squirming beneath his touch, I tried not to throw myself at him completely.

"Lying is cause for another punishment," he murmured, his other hand trailing up my thigh. "As is defying a non-negotiable order."

Trembling, I started to pant. "I'm not...lying."

His hands stopped in their caresses as he stared me in the eyes. "You're not?"

My lips parted to say no, but the hot look in his violet pools was a bigger warning than any threat.

Leaning in until his scent enveloped me and his body pressed against mine, he growled, "I asked you a question, my queen."

My hips bucked on their own accord. Memories of last night, of sitting on his counter with my legs spread and my hands in his hair bombarded me. Running his hand down my thigh, he made it to the top of the slit. My pulse spasmed. My pussy grew wet.

"Every second you don't answer..."

"No!" I blurted, my eyes wide in uncertainty. "Uh, I mean, yes?" Crap. How had he phrased the question?

"So where is it?"

I squirmed as his fingers feathered across my sensitive skin. He was so close to touching me, to releasing a bit of that pressure.

"My bedside table," I gasped.

"And did you like wearing it?" The tips of his fingers played with the seam of my underwear.

A hot flush cresting my cheeks, I nodded.

"So do you want it in you now?"

And the way he'd said 'it' brought all kinds of images crashing down on me. His fingers. His cock. The toy. I didn't care; I just wanted something of his. Something –

Moaning, I closed my eyes and rocked my hips as a finger slipped under the fabric and stroked me. "Yes!"

"Good girl."

Cupping my breast, he leaned down and kissed my neck. Two fingers parted my wet lips. Ran the full length of them over and over again before sinking inside and claiming what was his.

Mine, I corrected. *For me, not him...*

As he raised his head, I leaned forward and kissed him. Gasping against his mouth, I rode his fingers. His tongue stroked past my lips. His hand squeezed my breast before trailing up to the top of my dress and pulling it down. The corset trapped it from sliding all the way, but it bared my breasts for him to view. To touch. To worship.

And gods, did he.

First with his hand.

Then with his mouth.

Licking my breast, he placed his thumb on my clit. As I

arched into him, against his hand, his mouth, he sucked my nipple in between his teeth. The sharp scrape of pain had me bucking and crying out in pleasure.

One of my hands wrapped around his hair, holding him close. My other joined him inside my dress, but he quickly pulled it back out.

"If I watch you touch yourself, I'm going to come all in my trousers."

With his words hot in my ears, I came all over his hand.

His lips sucked on my nipple harder.

His fingers pumped faster.

As he dragged out my orgasm, building me straight into another one, he released my breast and kissed me on the lips.

His tongue laid claim.

His hand cupped me.

And then he stepped back, licking his fingers clean.

Sagging against the counter, I watched him. My lips parted. Desire snaked through me. Dropping to my knees, I reached for him, but he took a step back.

"We're out of time. The ball is starting soon."

With my brain a fuzzy field of pleasure, it took me a few seconds to comprehend what he'd said. "A ball?"

Sucking in a sharp breath, I rose to my feet. Everyone would be there. Maybe even the Court. I needed to look presentable and innocent to them, not like some sex slave unfit to rule on her own.

Images of me collared and tied to him filled my mind.

I ignored them.

My pussy had a hard time doing the same.

"Yes," he said, walking towards my bedroom.

Shaking my head, I struggled to regain my composure. Hurrying to the bathroom, tugging up the top of my dress,

I checked my reflection to make sure I looked presentable.

He'd left a large, prominent hickey on my neck.

Great.

The blush across my cheeks went from a pale pink to an undeniable red as he appeared behind me with the toy in his hand.

Pressing a large hand between my shoulder blades, he pushed me down. My hands rested on the sink as he bent me over and kicked my legs apart.

Breathing hard, I held his gaze in the mirror as he hiked up my dress and inserted the toy inside me. Lifting his hand, the same one he'd moved earlier, he repeated the rubbing of his fingers.

Strong vibrations through my pussy had me sagging against the sink, gripping the edge as tightly as I could. My breaths left me. Ragged and raw.

Dropping to his knees behind me, my king pulled my panties down to my ankles and –

Laughed.

A deep bellied laugh that had me jumping in surprise.

"What in Hel's name is this?" he asked, running his fingers across the middle of my right cheek.

My eyes widened. Embarrassment filled me. But when I tried to straighten and pull my dress down, one strong hand held me pinned to the sink. He towered over me. His eyes met mine in the mirror – light with humour.

My breath caught.

Gods, he was beautiful.

Rolling his lips around for a bit, he grinned, clearly struggling for words. My throat tightened.

"Do you really have a tattoo…" His laugh hit me all the way to my core, squeezing my heart tight. "Of a bucket full of cum on your ass?" he asked, his lips twitching.

I groaned.

"With a cat sitting inside the bucket, licking its lips, and saying, 'This pussy loves milk'?"

"No?" I tried, my voice a mere squeak.

Reaching around my body, he grabbed my chin and forced me to turn my head. As his other hand cupped my tattoo, he kissed me slow and deep. His laughter rumbled against my back and across my lips, burrowing deep into my soul.

Crackling a smile, I laughed with him.

Lowering his head, he kissed my neck.

Then my shoulder.

Then my back.

Moving his way down my spine, he spread my cheeks, cupping and squeezing them in his hands. His tongue slid across my tattoo. "Tell me what else your pussy likes."

I spasmed, my thighs tensing, my core clenching. "Your tongue," I breathed, all laughter leaving me. Closing my eyes, I moaned against his caress.

His tongue slid down my ass to my wet lips. Kissing them, he slipped his tongue inside.

Gasping against the sink, I laid my body against it. The cold stone rubbed against my nipples. Between it and him, my body was overwhelmed with sensations. Hot and cold. Soft and hard. Moving and still.

Trembling, I spread my legs further apart, giving him more access. To me.

For me.

Closing my eyes, I reached behind me and pushed my cheeks against his face. His tongue licked from my pussy to my ass. Massaging the hole, he increased the vibrations in the toy.

Pressure built inside me.

I squirmed against his face.

Pooled in my core.

I screamed his name.

Jerking and spasming and moaning, I came hard.

Stars lined my vision.

Clouds brewed between us.

And electricity shot through me, leaving me weak and trembling above him.

Licking me clean, he lifted one of my legs up to slip it out of my underwear. Then the other. Leaving me bare.

The vibrations slowed.

His head lifted.

Rising, he kissed my shoulder and lowered the bottom of my dress.

"We really do need to go," he murmured, pulling me upright.

The strength of his grip was the only thing keeping me moving as we strode down the hall.

My thoughts scattered.

But in the haze, one sentence shone like a beacon:

Dear fucking gods, I have to have sex with him before I kill him.

TWENTY-NINE

The Court is a queen's greatest ally.

ONLY WHEN THEY DON'T REALISE IT.

— RICHARD

I should've fucked her in the bathroom. Maybe then my brain would focus on something other than the way she would feel squeezing over me. Riding me. Sucking me. Taking my cum inside every little hole she had.

I wanted her down on her knees or against the wall or sitting on my lap. Hel, who was I kidding? I didn't want 'or'. I wanted 'and'.

Over.

And over.

And over again.

I could still taste her on my lips. Could still feel her pressing her ass against my face. Could still hear her little moans of pleasure as I licked her to completion. She had taken over every one of my senses.

Wrapping my arm around her waist, I pulled her to me. She stumbled against my side, her breath leaving her in a little pant. But despite my urge to turn to her, to take her lips with mine, I kept my attention on King Dravr.

"The borders are non-negotiable. The Court will not give you any land they deem as ours. Now, I understand your frustration –"

"Frustration? We will lose a tenth of our kingdom overnight!" His grey eyes cut like steel, but they bounced harmlessly off the armour I'd been forced to wear since I was a child.

My fingers rubbed against Arienna's side, activating the toy on its lightest setting. She jerked against me, and I stroked my hand down to her hip, then back up again.

She had a fucking tattoo.

Of a cum bucket.

With a cat inside.

"You will lose all of that in months if you do not take this deal," I said, reminding King Dravr that he had been on the verge of losing this war when I'd called for a truce.

His lips tightened. His eyes narrowed. I held his gaze without flinching.

Thoughts of filling her with that much cum consumed me.

"But as I said," I continued from before, "I understand your frustration, which is why I'm offering open borders between us. Your people will not be forced to move. I will appoint them a council that respects your culture, and they will work closely with your lords to make sure life for them is as they wish it." Lowering my voice, I added, "But the border line is non-negotiable."

The toy is non-negotiable.

His scowl deepened momentarily before relaxing. "And you'll give me full access to your markets?"

My fingers slid down to Arienna's thigh, to the top of the slit in her dress, and rested on bare skin. "If your merchants have the licenses outlined in the agreement, then yes. That will more than make up for the losses from taxing those villages."

I could see the thoughts racing across his chiselled face. He was decades older than I, his black hair streaked with grey, and there was a tiredness in his eyes. He'd been born into war, as had I, but unlike me, he had already crested his prime. This treaty would allow him to live his last few years in peace.

He would take the deal.

Pursing his lips, he said, "I will sign tonight."

I smiled, my fingers trailing across Arienna's thigh. "I am glad to hear that."

As King Dravr walked away, I leaned down to whisper in my wife's ear. "Is there something wrong, my queen? You're looking a bit flush."

Her gasp made my cock jump.

"You know why," Arienna breathed as she leaned into me. Her hips gyrated ever so slightly against my thigh, and I couldn't help myself. I grinned.

My hand slid across her leg. My fingers grazed the inside of it. "Shall I tell everyone you've caught a bug and take you to bed?"

She jerked against me, breathing hard. I increased the pace of the toy. "You know," I murmured against her ear, "you have this annoying habit of making me repeat myself."

Shivering, she looked up at me. "N-no. I want to stay here."

"Are you sure?" My fingers crept upwards to her bare heat.

She nodded jerkily.

"In that case," I said, removing my hand to grab hers, "may I ask you to dance?"

She stumbled behind me as I pulled her towards the centre of the hall. Confusion looked cute on her, especially when mixed with sexual disappointment.

Catching the gaze of the lead musician, a woman with golden hair, I nodded. Instantly, they began to play. The metallic tunes picked up rhythm as the drums thundered throughout the room.

The crowd parted into two sides as people rushed to declare their loyalty. King Dravr stood on one side, and I on the other. Our people clamoured behind us, their arms swinging in rhythm to the song.

"What's happening?" Arienna asked, a tinge of fear in her voice.

"Just stay beside me."

Fabia appeared in the crowd on my left, shoving people aside as she made her way closer. A grin curved her lips. Dressed in the dark leather uniform of the recruits in my guard, she looked ready to dance.

The drums increased in tempo.

My hand tightened on Arienna's. As Jace and Fabia appeared beside us, the golden-haired woman started to sing, her voice gritty and raw. As one, the two sides ran towards each other.

Arienna screamed as she teetered in her high pumps. Fabia cried out as if she was going to war. Jace laughed like a madman as he kept pace beside me.

I collided with King Dravr, knocking him aside. He stumbled into the man who'd just been about to ram into Arienna. Pivoting around, I turned to face her and took the brunt of the next man on my back.

She looked up at me as if I was crazy.

The world stopped moving for just a moment.

Despite the crowd jostling around me, it was just us two.

For this breath in time.

Our eyes peering into each other, seeing nothing else.

Then her gaze shifted to the left, where Fabia was being slammed back with the others.

Laughter erupted from them, and a large grin slowly spread across my wife's face. Launching herself into the mob, she screamed with delight.

My heart stopped. She was so little, surrounded by warriors twice her size.

Lunging forward, I tried to grab her arm and pull her back to my side, but she was jumping and moving and jiving to the beat. And then she was being lifted above their heads and passed around on hands stretched high above.

Jace shoved me to get me moving. "Relax," he shouted over the music. "Saragese and Irin are on sniper duty. They've got her covered."

I lifted my eyes to the beams above us but saw only darkness. Forcing myself to relax, I started to move in rhythm to the beat, but my gaze never left my wife.

When she was deposited back beside me, bubbling with energy, I picked her up in my arms and kissed her. My hand slipped through the slit in her dress. She tensed as a gasp breathed across my lips.

At the feel of the toy, I rubbed my fingers together, setting it off.

Her legs wrapped around my waist. Spreading my wings, I took to the air.

Dozens of others did the same behind me, dancing above just as fiercely as they had on the ground. Flying her to the edge, I wished the music wasn't so loud so I could hear her moans. The way she was bucking against my hand, I knew she was making them.

Landing at the head of the banquet table, I put her down. I was just about to kiss her again when Jace landed beside me.

"Incoming," he said a second before Caroline and Petre appeared behind us.

Removing my hand, I placed it on Arienna's hip as I turned us around. "Petre, Caroline, to what do I owe this displeasure?"

"We're here to meet our future queen. You've hidden her away for far too long." Petre's silver and green eyes latched onto Arienna like a spider did a fly. She reached up and touched her hair – long black locks set in a tight bun with sharp needles poking out of it. A subtle threat. One I did not take kindly.

My fingers burned with the need to release the knives strapped to my forearms. But I forced myself not to move. We were in a crowded ballroom with the Vylian king and queen in attendance. Any sign of discord in our ranks would give them the idea that they could push for more than the terms outlined in our agreement – something Petre wanted just as little as I did.

Arienna was safe here.

My hand twitched.

Nudging me, Jace pierced me with his gaze.

I forced myself to relax, to focus on Arienna's presence beside me. "She is not queen yet; her attendance is not mandatory," I said, rubbing my fingers together, increasing the pace of the toy.

"Nor is her absence." Smiling, she turned to Arienna. "Are you aware, Your Majesty, that once crowned, your power will trump his? You'll have the entire army at your command. Don't you think you should be well educated before taking on such responsibility?"

And there it fucking was: why she hadn't put up much of a protest when I'd told her that Arienna hadn't actually committed the crime I'd accused her of, why they hadn't tried to kill her yet just to spite me. They were working a new angle: seeing whether or not she would have the guts to kill me and take my place.

The dumbasses.

My wife didn't have a murderous bone in her body. She even loved wasps, the evil fuckers, and they hadn't made her feel anywhere near as good as I did.

My hand tightened on her hip. I hoped not anyway.

How would that even work? Would their stingers –

Before the image could properly form, I yanked my head out of that very deranged gutter. Clearly, I was sex deprived. Which brought me back to my earlier thought: I should've fucked her in the bathroom.

Or my study.

Or my chambers.

Fuck, hindsight was a bitch.

"I do," Arienna replied, making my blood run cold. The last thing I wanted was for her to be alone with them.

"She'll be trailing me now that our honeymoon period is officially over," I cut in before Petre could say whatever it was she wanted.

Caroline's sneer was blatantly hostile. "She must also learn the role of the Court – something you cannot teach her."

"And once she learns everything else from me, I will send her over." By the time that happened, we'd be a democracy and there wouldn't be any court.

Caroline growled, "Do you think we're stupid?"

"Frankly? Yes."

She took a step forward before Petre grabbed her arm. Jace was already in front of us, his hand on his blade.

"Let's go, Caroline. He can't hide her forever."

As they flew back into the crowd, Arienna pulled away from me. A frown marred her lips. "Am I really going to start trailing you on your duties?" she asked.

Sitting down, I pulled her onto my lap. "Only if you want to."

"But why?"

I glanced down at her, my brows furrowed. "I thought you wanted to learn about your role?"

"I do. I just thought you didn't want me involved."

"I don't," I said, sliding my hand down her soft thigh. The Court was a dangerous place where anger reigned and grudges were held forever.

I didn't want to watch her lose her innocence. To come to hate the world as I did. As all fairies did.

I wanted to keep her as she was.

Her heart on her sleeve.

A massive fucking heart too.

Marvellous and perfect.

Turning her chin, I took her lips and started touching her underneath the table.

THIRTY

A good brownie doesn't give their friend
a poison-making gift set.

I didn't know that's what it was, but

it's nice to know, I wasn't the first...

— Arienna

Grabbing Richard's hand, I tried to get him to move his fingers, but he was stubborn in his decision to stop. He had built me up so close, so flippin' close – *again* – and now he was turning off the toy – a-fucking-gain. He'd been doing it all throughout the meal. On. Off. On. Off.

Exhaling in frustration, I dug my fingers into his, trying to force them to rub each other, but he was a lot stronger than me. He removed my hand easily.

My eyes narrowed. I was going to remove his cock, stuff it, and then turn it into a dildo. See him try to deny me then.

He chuckled as he finished off the last of his dessert. "Patience, my queen."

And I wanted to stab that dessert and throw it in the

bin because it should've been me. His mouth should've been on *me*. I should be the blasted dessert.

"Fine," I growled. "I'll do it myself." I reached between my legs, but he grabbed my hand and pinned it to his thigh.

Leaning towards me, he whispered in my ear, "No one gets to touch you but me. And if you do, I will tie you to my bed tonight and leave you until morning." He nipped my ear. "A couple more hours and we can go. The signing ceremony will start soon."

Scowling, I exhaled strongly and envisioned exactly how I was going to kill him. Wasn't there an animal that died if it didn't get laid in time? A rodent of some sort? A rat or squirrel or – ferret. Yeah, that's what it was.

I was going to pay a witch to change my king into a fucking ferret, build him up every day but never let him release, and then watch the fucker die.

And then maybe, *maybe* he could understand how I was feeling right now.

"Just leave it on for, like, a minute more," I pleaded.

Shaking his head with a smirk, he rose to his feet. *The bastard.*

Narrowing my eyes, I imagined him as a ferret.

And then realised there was a massive flaw in my plan.

If he was a ferret, how the heck would I build him up?

I would also have to be a ferret, and I had absolutely no idea how I would then tease him. Ferrets teeth were sharp, weren't they? So fellatio was out. And I wouldn't have any clothes to strip off. Or any boobs to flash him.

Ugh, this is why I needed Fabia. She would have an answer to this.

Looking around for her while Richard walked over to King Dravr, I spotted her standing at the end of one of the tables with a group of leather-clad guards. Pushing to my feet, I hurried over to her. Halfway there, the vibrations started again, causing me to almost stumble.

I reached out a hand, grabbing hold of the edge of a table. An unattended glass of ambrosia beckoned to me, and I picked it up before continuing on to Fabia.

She broke away from Marrabel and the others as soon as I approached. When she reached me, I asked, "How would you arouse a ferret?"

"Wait until it's in heat and then scratch it on its back."

"Oh. Would that be the same, you think, for someone that had been turned into a ferret?"

She cocked her head to the side. "Depends on the spell, I guess."

My breath caught as the toy turned on and off, on and off, pulsing inside me with an intensity I could barely stand through.

"If they keep all of their memories and know who they were before being turned, then you could probably get them going with regular porn."

My legs turned into jelly. I needed to sit down. I hadn't come off the previous edge that long ago. I was too close, had been all night.

I raised my glass to my lips and took a shaky sip.

"Regular being whatever they used to watch, obviously, not just what's seen as 'the norm'. Like monster porn or dinosaur. Why?"

"Oh, no reason..." I trailed off to swallow a moan. The pressure built inside me. I needed to get back to my seat.

But I'd only taken a step before Fabia asked, "What's going on?"

My eyes widened.

Gods, please tell me she can't hear it vibrating.

Chugging my drink, I took another step, desperate to escape. My thighs quivered as the frequency increased.

The bastard was going to make me come while talking to my best friend. I was never going to forgive him for this. "Nothing," I rasped, taking another step.

Grabbing hold of my arm, she rooted me to her. And gods, did I not want her – or anyone – touching me right now. Well, anyone other than him. My king. The bastard with the controller.

"Are you sure? Because something smells really fishy."

Snorting my drink back into my glass, I coughed and whacked my chest. *Dear gods, just take me now.* "What?" I croaked, pulling out of her grasp.

"Cut the crap, Arienna. Marrabel told me about your visit to the library the other day."

"The library..." I blinked, trying to wrap my head around how that tied in with the vibrator going off inside me. Avoiding her gaze, my fingers tightened on my glass as I struggled not to give in to the urge to touch myself. He'd kept me on edge all night, varying the speeds so I couldn't get used to it, slowing it down when I needed it to go faster. My thighs were soaking wet. Next time I was going to have to wear underwear. And a liner.

"Yes, the library," she snapped. "Where you told Jace that you were checking out certain books in order to do 'research'."

My eyes flew to hers. If my cheeks got any hotter, I was going to die of internal heating. "He recommended the book. I'm not into necrophilia, I swear."

"What?"

"The book called *Good Enough to Die For*. It's not for research on things I want to try in bed. It's –" I stopped in sudden realisation. Drat. *That's* what she had been hinting about this whole blasted time.

As the vibrator's speed went mental, I wrapped my arms around myself and bit back a groan. I really needed him to stop now. I clearly wasn't able to concentrate on this conversation otherwise.

"When were you planning on telling me you were trying to kill him?"

"What? No, I'm not." I smiled, the picture of innocence, needing her to go away.

She stared at me deadpanned. "You don't have an interest in gore. You get squeamish when I just suggest watching anything scary. So why else would you have checked out a dozen books on ways to kill people?"

"You don't know. Maybe I want to kill someone else?"

Her silence made me squirm. Or maybe that was the vibrator pushing me to the edge of orgasm.

Dear fucking gods, this was not the time to be having this conversation.

"I think Richard's calling for me, so if you'll excuse –"

She grabbed my arm again, making me want to die. "Tell me what you're planning so I can fix this."

"Let me go." I clenched the muscles in my pussy, trying to mute the sensations, but it didn't work. The room suddenly felt too hot, my body like a current of electricity.

Shoving her off me, I looked towards Richard. He had always known when I was close; he had always stopped right before, but if he didn't right now, I was going to –

My eyes latched onto his.

He smirked and raised his hand to his mouth. As his fingers rubbed against his lips, my breath caught, my legs quivered, and I came. *Hard.*

Thunk.

The following noise made me freeze. Nothing but my pussy moved – that pulsed and pulsed and pulsed as it rode the waves of ecstasy.

"What was that?" Fabia demanded.

I refused to look her in the eye, knowing damn well

what that was. If he'd just left my underwear on, this never would have happened. The toy would still be inside me instead of between my feet, visible to all as my dress didn't quite reach the floor.

My face most certainly a deep crimson, I whispered, "Please don't look down."

The bitch looked down. "Oh dear gods. Is that –"

Placing a hand over her mouth, she laughed. "That's disgusting. I was touching you while…?"

Groaning, I covered my face in my hands. "Please never speak to me again."

Her laughter made me wish I had a bottle of pills on hand. Or a knife. Either one would work.

"You have to pick it up," she whispered.

My eyes widened. "What?"

"You can't just leave it there. That's probably against, like, a dozen health and safety violations. There's food in here."

"But not on the floor."

"Arienna –"

"Can't I just kick it under the table?" My eyes flicked to the nearest one. People stood around it. A *lot* of people. All eating.

"No."

"But I don't have anywhere to put it. There're no pockets in this thing."

She laughed, her eyes way too suggestive for my liking.

"Wait," I said, my attention fastened on her trousers. "You have pockets. You could –"

"Oh, hel no."

"But you're my best friend. Best friends have to –"

"Not doing it."

"Please? I'll pick it up and put it in. You'll just need to hold it open."

"Fuck that."

"Come on," I said desperately. Any moment now and someone would see it. It was bright pink between my black shoes, and so very clearly a sex toy. "I'll tell you why I checked out the books."

Looking at me, Fabia's laughter faded. "You owe me big time."

"The biggest."

I started to lean down when she grabbed my arm. Quickly releasing it with a shake of her head, she said, "Wait. I'll go get some serviettes."

"Okay, but hurry."

As she left, my attention went back to Richard. He sat in his seat at the head of the hall, talking to the Vylian king. But his eyes were on me. Hot and smouldering.

Feeling bold, I raised a hand to my lips and sucked in two fingers.

The challenge in his eyes left me shaken.

"Oh, ew, stop," Fabia protested as she stood beside me.

Jerking my fingers out of my mouth, I snatched the serviettes from her and bent over to grab the toy. As I crouched there on the floor, I really wished Niflhel would open up below me and swallow me whole. When it didn't, I slowly rose.

"Make sure it's wrapped well."

"I'm going to need more serviettes," I mumbled beneath my breath.

"What?"

Squirming with embarrassment, I repeated myself a bit louder.

Pretending to gag, she walked back to the table.

Oh my gods, I was going to have to ghost my best friend.

Move country.

Go into hiding.

Never come out again.

Or die.

That would work.

And it didn't even seem that bad anymore.

When she came back, I swapped the wet serviettes over for dry ones, wrapped it well, and then handed it to her. Shuddering, she opened a pocket in her suit bottoms and I shoved it in.

"You owe me your-first-born-child level of owing." Grabbing my arm, she pulled me far away from everyone else. "Now tell me about the books," she said softly. "First, why? I thought you liked him." Dropping my arm, she shook her hand as if it was dirty.

"I do."

"But?"

I hesitated, not wanting to tell her. She had really settled in here: joining the guard, making new friends, finally finding a home that accepted her for her. I didn't want to ruin that.

"Arienna. I have your fucking toy in my pocket. You better start talking."

Looking down at my feet, I mumbled, "He's planning on killing me."

"What?"

Sighing, I pulled her further away from the party and lowered my voice. "According to Ajax, my execution is still going through. Richard didn't cancel it because he doesn't want to share the throne."

"And you verified this?"

My heart breaking, I nodded. "He pretty much said so himself."

Her face paled. Then it hardened.

"For fuck's sake, girl," she growled, shaking her head.

"Why in Hel's name are you letting him shove toys up your vagina then?"

I winced, doubting she would take, 'he's really fucking hot' as a good defence. It sounded like a bad defence to me, and I was the one enjoying it. "It was inserted before he confirmed it?" I tried.

She looked at me like she wanted to throttle me. "But you checked out the books four days ago," she said slowly.

"Yeah, well," I said defensively, "why should I have to suffer? He's the only guy I can sleep with now that we're married. I didn't want to die with Karl's dick being the last I've ever had." I grabbed her shoulders. "Fabia, he lasted *four* seconds and had my mum's and my sister's vagina on it."

She shook her head, but a tiny smile graced her lips. "So what's your plan?"

Glancing around us, I leaned in closer. "I'm going to poison him. It's actually really clever. I baked him a regular cake and gave it to him yesterday to get him to lower his guard so by the time I give him the poisoned cake, he'll eat it without question."

"You do know he has a taster, right?"

"Yes," I said as if I hadn't just found that out yesterday. "I'm not stupid. I have a plan for that. I'll mix the poison on only one slice, the side facing me as Jace will most likely try from the side that's facing him. This will also let me eat it with Richard so he doesn't suspect it's poisoned."

"And what poison are you using? Because it'll need to be tasteless and odourless."

"I know..."

"So what is it?"

I glanced away.

"Arienna –"

"I don't know yet."

"Wait, you're saying you don't even have it yet?"

Exhaling in frustration, I said, "Well, it's not like I can just waltz into a shop and ask for poison." I glanced at her. "Right?"

She gave me a deadpanned stare. "So let me get this straight. Your whole plan to stop yourself from dying is to poison him with a poison you don't even have nor have any idea of how to get?"

"You're making it sound dumb," I grumbled.

Her eyes were full of judgement. "Arienna, you are just feeding him cake with this plan. Regular ass cake. How is that not dumb?"

"That's not fair. You're leaving out the poison."

"No, *you're* leaving out the poison."

Before I could counter that, she added, "Why didn't you tell me earlier?"

"Because I didn't want to ruin this for you." Wrapping my arms around my waist, I hugged myself. "You're the happiest I've ever seen you, and I saw you the day you punched my sister in the face."

"Your sister is a dick."

"She's..." I said, trying to defend her but coming up empty. "Whatever, that doesn't matter. You're happy here. I didn't want to ruin that."

"And how did you think I would take it after watching you die in the square?"

I glanced away, my face heating. This had sounded so much better in my head. "I was going to ask Richard to kill me in a way that looked like an accident," I mumbled.

She stared at me, gobsmacked. "An accident?"

"I figured that's the least he could do..."

"How was he possibly going to pass off pulling your intestines out of your ass as an accident? Oh, hey, Fabia, look at that, I forgot to use lube?"

Shaking her head, she took a step away from me and then came storming back. "You are – you are – Ugh." She clenched her fists as she looked up, then back down at me. "I'll get you the poison."

"What? How?"

She breathed out slowly, regaining control. "You know my chemistry set you got me?"

I nodded.

"Yeah...well, I haven't actually been using it to create new drinks."

"Fabia!"

"What? It's for research for my books. I have to get the smells right. And the taste and the symptoms."

"Fabia!" My jaw hit the floor. She was going to be the death of me.

"What? I only eat a little. And look at me, not dead. It's fine."

I shook my head at her. Wasn't I supposed to be the dumb one, the one that needed looking after? The heck that was true now. "When you came down with a sudden bug on my birthday –" I said sternly.

"Yeah...that was antrix."

I had no idea what that was, but it sounded bad. I placed my hands on my hips.

She rolled her eyes. "Hey, you had wasps. You don't get to get on to me about my dangerous hobbies. And it's way less dangerous than yours."

"You're eating poison! On purpose."

"And you lived with murderous wasps."

"No, because Hyatt was the only one that murdered someone and he left right after."

She raised a brow as she crossed her arms. "You really want to argue technicalities because the wasps were not the first dangerous stunt you've pulled."

I opened my mouth and then closed it again. To be fair, she had me there.

"Fine," I huffed in defeat. "Make the poison, but then I'm destroying that chemistry set."

She shrugged as if that was acceptable. "So when are we doing this?"

The way she'd said it so flippantly, so assuredly made my blood run cold.

I didn't know if I wanted to do this anymore now that there was an actual possibility of success. Tonight had been amazing. The room was decorated with the same bouquet he'd sent me – my favourite colour too. The dress was a perfect fit. The jewellery was something you gave a wife you loved – though fair, there was nothing to say he couldn't take it back off my dead body.

But he'd been attentive and sexy and protective this whole night. He'd even taken me dancing... And okay, I wasn't even sure if I'd call that dancing so much as just people hitting each other and pretending it was fine, but, like, he'd done it with me.

Did I really want to kill that?

When it had just been me attempting it, I had known deep down, that it wouldn't really work. That I would mess it up somehow and he would live. But it gave me the pretence of having at least some standards about who I slept with. This way, I wasn't really having sex with my executioner; I was seducing my executioner to kill him, and that sounded infinitely better. Classier. Way less slutty.

And okay, I didn't want to die, but despite everything, I really liked him. Like really, really liked him.

"I think we should do it tonight," Fabia said, cutting into my internal ramblings.

My chin jerked up as I stared at her. "Tonight?"

My heart pounded in my chest.

Tonight was too soon.

I needed to think. I needed to –

"Yeah, tonight." She nodded firmly. "When everyone's here and slightly buzzed rather than guarding his room. I'll slip in there now to help you hide his body later."

"But what about making the poison?" I asked a bit desperately.

She waved a hand. "Oh, I already have loads to choose from."

"But...I haven't baked him a cake yet."

"So just grab one from here. Trust me, if he's already putting toys inside you, he is not going to care if the cake you bring is one you made or not. He's just going to want to eat it off you."

Grabbing my hands, she gave them both a squeeze. "It'll be okay," she said. "I've already thought of a way to make it look like an accident. Once he's dead, we'll pour a bottle of ambrosia down his throat, then throw him out the window. They'll just think he fell, too drunk to fly. It'll be fine."

I looked at her in horror.

"Trust me." She released my hands and nodded. "I'll see you there. Give me an hour or so before you come up."

Before I could think of what to say, Fabia disappeared into the crowd.

And only then did the words come to me.

One word, actually.

"*Fuck.*"

THIRTY-ONE

Truces are for the weak.

THERE IS NOTHING HARDER THAN

GETTING SWORN ENEMIES TO STOP

KILLING EACH OTHER

—RICHARD

For the first time in many generations, there was peace between us and the Vylians.

A fragile peace.

But one nonetheless.

As King Dravr straightened after having signed his name beside mine, I leaned down to pick up the piece of paper. Holding it above my head, I showed it to all.

"We are now no longer enemies," I boomed, my voice carrying across the hall. "We are no longer at war. Our friends and family held captive as prisoners of war will now be returned to us – tonight."

Gesturing to Marrabel, I signalled for her to retrieve the prisoners – both mine and Kind Dravr's. They'd been stationed outside after having been bathed, finely dressed, groomed, and their wounds healed.

Complete and utter silence reigned as they walked in. For a second.

Two.

And then noise erupted – chaotic sounds of happiness and movement as people swarmed to greet their loved ones.

I turned to look at King Dravr. Disbelief hid behind his mien of strength – a feeling I shared wholeheartedly. This had been months in the making, and still it did not feel real.

Nothing about tonight felt real.

It had been amazing.

Too perfect.

Like a trap.

Searching the crowd, my eyes went back to the spot where Arienna had been standing. She was still there – alone now, and my stomach twisted with unease.

Spreading my wings, I flew to her. Jace landed behind me, silent as always. "Are you ready to go?" I asked.

She shook her head, the world in her eyes as she looked at me. "N-no. You've just done something amazing. We should stay and celebrate a bit longer."

I scowled. Dammit. I knew I shouldn't have let her orgasm. I should've left her on the edge instead of giving in to her pleas. Holding her gaze, I lifted my fingers and rubbed them together.

She shivered, but she didn't clench.

My eyes narrowed. A sadistic grin curved my lips. "Did my little queen take it out?"

Her lips parted. Her cheeks flushed. "N-no?"

I took a step forward.

She took a step back.

Breaths left her lips in a frantic beat of arousal.

"Wha– what are you doing?" Her eyes flicked around the hall. No longer on me, and that deserved another punishment. One I would be all too happy to carry out. "We're in a crowded room. There are people –"

"There are always people around me," I informed her as her back hit the wall. Her corset was pushing her breasts up in a most erotic way. Rising and falling, her tits begged me to touch them. To taste them. To mark them as mine as I had her neck.

Towering over her, I raised my hand, brushing the back of my knuckles against her plumped up mounds. She should always wear corsets. Or nothing at all...

Looking into her eyes, I smiled. "I do believe you lied to me. That's such a bad habit."

"I..." She trembled, her gaze softening with arousal. "I didn't?"

She was such a bad liar, my wife. Always making her statements sound like questions.

Lowering my hand to the slit in her dress – every dress should have slits – I burrowed it under the fabric at the front of her thighs. When I touched her wet heat, her head lolled back against the wall, bearing her neck to me. And who could resist accepting such a gift?

Leaning down, I licked the base of her throat. Suckled and kissed as the crowd shifted behind me, their presence increasing my arousal. She was such a naughty temptress, my wife.

Sucking her skin into my mouth, I marked her, claimed her so everyone would know she was mine.

So the Court would know.

So fucking Tinsin would know.

I growled at the memory of his words. *You should have seen her tits, Cal. They are the perfect size to slip your dick in between them.*

I should've made them the last words he'd ever spoken.

But instead, I had let him off lightly.

Fucking mercy.

I kissed my way up my wife's neck to her ear.

And she was the reason for it. Another thing deserving of punishment, no?

A smirk playing on my lips, I sucked her lobe into my mouth just as I feathered my fingers across her pussy. Slipping a digit between the slick heat of her labia, I pushed inside her hole. "I don't feel a toy there." I grabbed her ear with my teeth. "Where is it?" I growled, loving how she shivered in response.

She really was going to be the death of me.

One of these days, someone was going to kill me while I was distracted. Already, the crowd had disappeared into silence, leaving just her and me.

"It..." A beautiful crimson painted her cheeks. Her eyes lowered to the floor. Her breaths came out ragged and raw. She mumbled something so softly I couldn't quite make it out.

But then the words registered.

And the widest fucking grin spread across my cheeks as I released her ear to look at her.

"It fell out?" I repeated, wanting to make sure I had heard correctly.

The smallest nod moved her head.

"It. Fell. Out?"

Looking up, her eyes pleading with me to be quieter, she whispered, "Yes."

"And where is it now?"

I hadn't thought it was possible, but her face turned even more red.

A foreign warmth built inside my chest and spread to every part of me. It wrapped me in its arms, making me slightly uncomfortable in its entirety.

"Fabia...has it," she squeaked.

"Fabia..." My eyes crinkled as I stood upright, no longer trying to tease her body into coming back to my chambers right now. "Why does she have it?"

"Because she has pockets," she mumbled, her words falling into each other to create a jumbled mess.

Laughing, I pulled her into my arms. I needed to hold her, touch her, kiss her. Just be here for a moment.

Until my duties called me back as they aways did.

Tilting her head up, I kissed her. Breathed in every breath she released. Tasted every particle making up her sighs and moans. Mine. It was all mine.

"My lord," Jace said, ripping me away from her.

Stopping abruptly, I turned to face him.

But I could feel her body behind me. Hear her ragged breathing that she was desperately trying to control.

My eyes shifted from Jace to my brother. A tightness enveloped me, putting me back on edge. "You're here," I said, scanning the crowd around us. He hated crowds. Ever since Dorothy had done what she had, he avoided them like the plague.

So if he was here, that only meant one thing: bad fucking news. I'd known tonight was too good to be true.

"What is it?" I demanded, my thoughts full of what it could be. The civil war finally starting. An ambush set up by King Dravr's men. The Alzans or the Okahi having finally pushed into our territory. The damn Court having decided that a 'member' included family members and they'd now be charging Jace with treason. Because of something I'd ordered him to do.

Fuck.

Blinking, Nicholas looked at me in confusion. And then his grin spread wide across one half of his face. The other was pulled tight, melted into expressionless uselessness. "Relax, you paranoid bastard. I'm here because it's an important night and Fabia convinced me I shouldn't miss it." He held out a hand. "So congratulations. You did what no one thought you could."

"Except for us," Jace cut in, pointing at both him and Nicholas. "We believed in you."

Nicholas tilted his head to the side in a gesture that said, 'not really'.

My stomach tightened; I wasn't quite ready to relax. "What are the reports on the Alzans and the Okahi?" I demanded.

Grasping my shoulder, he shook it. "Gods, man, relax. This is a night of celebration." He tilted his head at Arienna. "Just go back to fingering –"

She gasped and I shoved him away.

But a smile graced my lips.

Coming up beside us, Jace wrapped a heavy arm around each of our shoulders. "We should have a drink for Aurelia. She would've loved to have seen this."

My smile fell.

Nicholas tensed.

"You have to promise me, when we're ready for peace, you'll push for it."

Holding my brother's gaze, I nodded jerkily. When he did the same, Jace released us and walked back to the long tables.

"Who's Aurelia?" Arienna asked, her voice soft as if she feared encroaching on something she shouldn't.

"Our sister," I said, not looking at her.

"The one you killed in a fairy ring?"

My jaw tightened. "No. The one who died from cancer."

Nicholas turned away, and I didn't blame him. The lie we had spread about her death haunted all of us. But the

Court could never find out what we had done. If they did, my crown would be taken from me, and every law and treaty I'd brought into existence or helped draft would be overturned. Oyveni's Law of Ascension was clear: a man could not become king unless he proved himself by killing his opponents in the fairy ring. All of his opponents.

But I hadn't been able to bring myself to kill Aurelia that way, to leave her soul trapped in the magic of the ring, forever hungry, left to feed on the drops of blood spilled by new challengers.

Our bitch of an older sister had deserved that and more.

But not Aurelia.

Not kind, sweet Aurelia who had sacrificed herself in order to save our kingdom.

When Jace returned, he came with four glasses. He gave one to me, one to Nicholas, and then one to my wife.

My breath caught. She didn't know Aurelia. She didn't know what our sister had done, what we had done... I didn't want Arienna's toast to be meaningless. I wanted it to matter because it mattered to me, mattered to all three of us.

But when Arienna looked at me, her pale pink eyes full of concern and empathy, I knew Aurelia would have wanted this.

She would have loved her – my queen.

Nodding at her, I turned to Jace. "To the woman we all loved."

A shudder ran through him as he lifted his glass. "To the queen she would have been."

The only queen I would have gladly stepped down for. I'd begged her to take the throne so I wouldn't have to, but she'd refused.

"We are at war on all fronts," she said sadly. *"I am not*

the ruler they need right now. You are."

My fingers tightened on my glass. A soft touch on my other hand caused me to look down. My wife's fingers threaded through mine and squeezed. A squeeze I felt all the way in my heart.

"To the pain in the ass she was," Nicholas said with a soft chuckle.

Despite the agony in my chest, I smiled. She had been such a pain and not just because of the end.

My smile slipping, I raised my glass, as did Nicholas and Jace. We'd just started to lift them to our lips when Arienna cut in with a soft, "To the wonderful bookworm who would have loved that library." Tears shone in her eyes.

Burned in mine.

Tossing my head back, I swallowed the entirety of my glass.

To Aurelia.

Everything I do is for you.

THIRTY-TWO

A good brownie doesn't deliberately destroy someone's belongings.

Then don't wear something with an excessive amount of frickin' buttons.

— Arienna

Double freaking drat.

What was I going to do now?

I definitely couldn't kill him after I'd toasted his dead sister. I'd broken a lot of rules recently, but I wasn't a monster.

And you know, the whole, I might very well be falling in love with him thing.

I winced, hearing Fabia screaming in my brain, telling me how dumb I was.

And perhaps I was dumb and naive and whatever else she wanted to call me. But I was also right in this. I knew it in my heart. I could not kill him.

I did not want to kill him. My previous attempts not withstanding, of course. I mean, it wasn't like I'd actually succeeded. And as Fabia had pointed out, I hadn't really done anything other than feed him cake.

Except...I'd somehow managed to convince my best friend to hide in his bedroom with a bottle of poison. A friend who was expecting me to lead Richard up there so we could kill him. Together.

Fuck.

When his hand wrapped around my waist, I jumped. "A bit sensitive there, my queen?" he murmured, pulling me into his arms.

His cock pressed against me, growing harder by the second. His hand explored the back of my body, making me as sensitive as he'd claimed I was. But it was his eyes I was drawn too. Haunted and guarded, they lacked the heat from before Nicholas' arrival.

Raising a hand, I cupped his face. He leaned into my touch. Turning his lips, he kissed my palm.

My breath caught as I stared at him, his cloaked pain, his unsaid words. If a picture was worth a thousand, then this silence was worth them all.

"Nicholas," he said, looking at me, seeing only me, "tell King Dravr I've retired for the night."

Before I could protest, he dragged me through a door I hadn't even seen. It closed behind us flawlessly, its edges undetectable in the sudden dark. No trails of light marked where the hall was. No noise. No laughter or clinks of glasses.

Just silence and darkness.

And him.

And me.

I shivered, goosebumps rising across my skin, trailing behind the path his fingers were making. Up my arm. Across my shoulders. My collarbone. Spanning my neck.

Grabbing my throat, he hauled me to him. His lips touched my face, moving down and across my cheek, seeking my mouth.

I shoved down all the thoughts rushing through me – the panic about Fabia, the guilt about setting him up to die, the realisation that I didn't want what I'd thought I'd wanted, the fear of dying...the hope that I wouldn't, that he would step in and save me.

The darkness consumed all of it, stripping me bare, leaving me just as a woman in love with a man who was hurting.

Parting my lips, I kissed him back. Roamed my hands over his body. His clothes.

He was wearing too many clothes.

Frantically, I tugged at them, shoving his jacket off his shoulders, undoing the button on his waistcoat.

And another one.

And another.

Oh my gods, how many were there?

My hands roamed across his chest, trying to find them all as my breaths came out needy and desperate.

I wanted him inside me now.

I wanted to see him.

His piercing.

His cock as it slid into me.

But it was pitch black.

Soundless except for our breaths and the pounding of our hearts.

Having nothing but touch to hold on to, I touched. Grabbing the sides of his waistcoat, I ripped them away.

Pop. Pop. Pop.

Thank the bloody gods.

But when my hands landed back on his chest – his supposedly naked chest, I groaned.

Another flippin' shirt blocked my path.

With a dozen flippin' buttons.

Chuckling against my mouth, he grabbed my hands. "Such an impatient little slut, my wife."

A bolt of electricity shot through me.

"You're so fucking wet for me, you can't wait, can you?"

His words made me flush. A good, delicious flush I felt all the way down to my toes.

Panting against his lips, I moaned, "Make me your cum bucket."

He froze.

Lifted his head.

I leaned forward to kiss him, to find him in the darkness, but he evaded my mouth like a flippin' ninja.

Just as frustration started to build inside me, it was shoved to the side by horror.

What if my breath stank? What if he was no longer kissing me because it smelled like ass?

Oh my gods, my breath smelled like ass.

Which was ironic because his lips were the ones that had been on my ass.

Subtly, I tried to exhale strong enough for me to smell it, but all I could smell was him.

"Say that again," he said, humour colouring his words and making me blush for an all together different reason than before.

Oh my gods.

That's what it was.

I'd done it wrong.

And now I'd taken us out of the mood.

And he wouldn't fuck me and –

"Arienna," he pulled my name out, making it sexy, making me shudder in anticipation. Leaning down to my ear, he nipped it in between his teeth. His breath fanned across my neck; his words rumbled against my skin. "Did you just ask me to turn you into my cum bucket?"

My pussy quivered.

My body relaxed.

I most definitely had not said that wrong because those words were flippin' sexy coming from him.

"Yes?"

His laugh shocked me. Stung just a bit.

But then his lips were on me again.

And his hands were undoing the lace of my corset.

Shoving it down.

Pushing up my breasts.

Lowering his head, he burrowed his tongue in between them. "Your wish is my command."

He kissed his way across one mound to its nipple. Licking around it, he kneaded his fingers into my flesh, massaging me, building me up until I was gasping and moaning and waiting for him to put his freaking mouth on my flippin' sensitive bud.

"Richard," I moaned.

"Yes, my queen?"

"Play with my nipples."

His chuckle left me quaking. "I am *playing* with it."

Exhaling in frustration, I snapped. "No, not like that. Like –"

My head fell back.

My back arched.

As his lips closed around my nipple, I dug my fingers into his thick curly hair and moaned.

Dear flippin' gods. His mouth should be immortalised. There should be a business for that. Making moulds out of mouths and then casting them with a spell so they could move with such heat and grace.

It would bring an end to necrophilia, that was for sure. The slogan could be: Don't let their kicking off stop you from getting off.

Oh, no, wait, that sounded more like an advertisement *for* necrophilia.

I jerked beneath his sucking, nibbling lips. My thoughts scattered. If he would just stop for a second, I could think of a better slogan.

But when I opened my mouth, all that escaped was a moan.

Releasing my breast, he moved his attention to the other one. His hand trailed down my stomach. Through the slit in my dress.

Arching back as his fingers touched me, I writhed against the wall. Or door. Or whatever it was pressing against my back.

The image of a towering beast popped into my head for a second.

I shuddered, imagining a thick cock that had spikes and barbs and knotting sacks.

I really needed to keep out of Fabia's search history...

"Who knew my queen was such a naughty little slut?"

His words snapped me back to him. My hips bucked from his caress.

"Did you like being played with in front of everybody? Looking in their eyes and wondering if they knew you had a toy going off inside you? Did you touch yourself when I wasn't looking?" He pressed a finger against my labia, slipped it right between them.

I shuddered, the pressure inside me building towards an eruption. "Yes." My breath hitched. "I liked it."

"And did you touch yourself?"

I shook my head. Realising he couldn't see me in the dark, I said, "No."

"Good girl. Because it's mine, isn't it?"

I nodded. Leaned my head back against the wall. His

finger slid up and down the length of my pussy. Gods, I was close. I just needed him inside me. Needed him to touch me like I'd wanted to touch myself all evening. "Yes."

"Say it. Say, 'My pussy is yours, my king'."

A beautiful heat raced through me. His lips sucked on my breast. His finger stroked. Clutching his hair, I said, "My pussy...is yours..." Moaning, I squirmed against the door as his finger rammed inside me.

"*My king,*" he growled.

Whimpering, I bucked my hips. "My king."

He shoved another finger inside. Lowered his other hand to rub my clit. "Good girl," he said, his mouth full of my breast.

Riding his hand, I tugged on his hair, pulling him up, pulling his lips to mine.

He kissed me to the same pacing of his fingers. Long slow licks matched his thrusts. As my body came alive in the darkness, under his touch, growing too sensitive, I grabbed his hands to stop them. I squeezed my pussy around his fingers, trying to fight the waves of pleasure begging to be released.

"Stop," I panted. "I want you inside me when I come."

His fingers stilled.

Drawing them out, my fingers still clutched around his wrist, he lifted them to my breast. A wet slickness spread across my skin.

Shivering, I waited for what I knew was going to come next.

Bending his head, he licked my chest clean. "Guide me in then," he said as his tongue lapped at me, tasting me on me because he knew he couldn't taste me down there without making me come.

Reaching for his trousers, I yanked frantically on the

crisscrossing belts. I was too close. His kisses were slow and leisurely, but I was already on the edge. My hands trembled. My pussy clenched.

The flippin' belts weren't coming undone.

My cry of frustration was covered up by his rumble of laughter. His hands pushing mine out of the way, he undid his buckles. A soft cry of relief escaped me. He licked his way up my breasts to my neck. Biting my ear, he said, "Pick a number higher than three."

"Sixteen," I gasped, not really paying attention to his words anymore. I just wanted his cock out of his pants. Wanted it inside me.

Shoving down his trousers and boxers, I reached for him. A shudder of pleasure swept through me as I gripped his hard, thick cock in my hand.

I pumped up and down its length. Once, twice as he grabbed my waist and lifted me.

I wrapped my legs around his hips.

Guided his cock to my pussy's entrance.

Moaning, I flicked my finger across his piercing as he finally pushed inside me.

His groans matched mine.

His thrusts.

His pulse.

His need to come.

With my hand over his chest, his quick beating heart, I rode him hard.

My breaths came out harder.

My thighs quivered.

My stomach clenched.

As every nerve ending was flooded with heat, I begged, "Harder. Please."

And fuck me, he actually did it.

Not faster.

Not more frantic.

But *harder.*

With each strong thrust, he filled me.

With each pull back, he left me empty.

Only to slam in with a strength that left me shaken.

Bruised.

On the beautiful flippin' edge of ecstasy.

Again.

And again.

And a-fucking-gain.

Grabbing the back of his neck, I arched to meet his thrusts. His fingers dug into my waist. His cock pounded into me, the metal of his piercing a heavy weight inside me.

Reaching between us, I rubbed my clit.

Closed my eyes and screamed.

As I clenched around him, gasping and moaning and begging, he slowed his thrusts. His mouth was suddenly on mine, swallowing each and every noise I made. His hands cupped my face as he kissed me deeply.

Pulling out most of the way, leaving just the tip, he murmured, "That's one."

With a slow, hard thrust he filled me again.

In...

My pulse skipped around in my chest.

...and out.

My pussy clenched around him.

In...

Digging my fingers in his hair, I arched against him as I pushed his mouth down to my breasts.

...and out.

Slowly, ever so slowly, he built me back up again.

And it didn't matter this time when I begged him to go faster. When I cried for him to rail me harder.

Death Do Us Part

He took it slow.
In...
...and out...
...and in again...

THIRTY-THREE

A good brownie never breaks a promise.

*Unless there's sixteen of the
fuckers. Then they should get
the option of tapping out.*

– Arienna

If you asked me a few hours ago, if I wanted to come sixteen times, I would've said yes. Like hel fucking yes. Like sign me up right this second yes. Like I'll sell you my first born child yes.

But now?

After the eleventh orgasm?

After my legs had gone past the point of trembling and fully stood in the area called 'can't bloody well feel them'?

After my heart felt like it had run a marathon and was now about to pole vault into a heart attack if he simply looked at me like he wanted to start again?

After I'd come so many times I was starting to feel dehydrated?

Yeah...no. I was done. Completely and utterly done,

and if he touched me in a sexual way ever again, I was going to cry.

His elbow nudged mine as he shifted on the floor beside me.

Eyes widening, I shoved him away and rolled down the tunnel. "No!" I shouted. "No, no, no, no, no. You have to stop. Go watch porn or something. I'll pay for a hooker. Or three. I don't even care."

I wrapped my arms around myself, then dropped them to my sides again, not even liking me touching myself.

Ugh.

Everything was so flippin' sensitive.

"Just please don't touch me anymore." Tears leaked out of my eyes in pathetic drips of desperation. They would've been flowing rivers had I had any liquid left inside me.

And the vagina wasn't even connected to tear ducts, I was pretty certain.

That was just how done my body was with the whole thing.

His chuckle made me shiver, made me recall how he'd laughed with his fingers inside me when I'd asked to become his cum bucket.

Ugh.

Even his freaking laugh was just too much.

When the air shifted in front of me, signalling his close proximity, I whimpered. "Please, no."

"You picked sixteen," he murmured, his two calloused hands roaming across my naked body. "I still have five left to give you."

"I didn't know that's what the number meant!" I tried to swat his hands away, but he grabbed them at the wrists and pinned them above my head. Holding them with one hand, he lifted one leg over my body and crawled on top of me.

Cupping my breast in his free hand, he kissed my face. I turned my head, dodging his lips, but he just lowered his mouth to my neck.

My body – my traitorous, dumbass body slowly started to heat again.

Whimpering, I squirmed beneath him.

"And don't think you can try to fake the rest of them like you did with the last two," he growled with my nipple in between his teeth. "Each one you fake, I'm going to add two to your final number."

"You're a monster!"

His teeth released me in an instant. He shifted on top of me, the heat of his face settling above mine. "Say your safe word then." His words were soft and challenging.

In the darkness, I couldn't breathe.

Trembling, I struggled to keep my ass on the ground. I could feel the hard end of his cock, the cold piercing on my stomach. And I *wanted* it, dammit. Because my body, as he was constantly showing me, wasn't mine anymore. It was his.

His to command.

His to pleasure.

His to take.

Ugh.

The flippin' traitorous bastard.

"But..." I swallowed. "But I never picked one out."

"So use mine this time. Say it and I'll stop."

His hand slid down my stomach to his cock. Gripping himself, his knuckles rapped against my flesh with every upward pump.

Another whimper escaped me.

But 'peace treaty' never did.

Chuckling, he kissed my throat. Made his way back down my body, licking and sucking and worshipping.

I could hear his hand moving against his shaft and I wished it was mine. He pumped himself hard. Trailed the end of his cock down my skin before sliding it in between my thighs.

Pushing against my entrance, he slammed into me. My back arched. A cry escaped.

As the wet slurping of our bodies echoed in the tunnel, he rubbed my clit and kissed my lips.

He wrapped one of my legs around his hip, but I didn't have the energy to keep it there. When it slid off him, he slid out of me, turned me over, and forced me to kneel low.

His cock trailed a wet line across my ass.

His hand slapped my left cheek, causing me to jump despite my exhaustion.

Grabbing my ass, he pulled me onto his shaft. His hands jerked me up and down, forcing me to ride him at a pace I couldn't keep.

The pressure built inside me.

The hard thickness of him filled me.

The grunts and moans of his pleasure, the hard slap of our bodies, consumed my senses until I was lost in an ecstasy I both hated and loved at the same time.

Exhausted but horny – what a horrible feeling.

His thumb pressed against my back hole. Already wet, it slid in without resistance.

"I'm going to fuck this later tonight. After you've had your sixteen, I'm getting mine."

He slapped my ass again. Fucked me faster. Harder.

Reaching down, he grabbed my throat and bent me backwards.

His cock was like a machine inside me. Pumping with a stamina that shouldn't be possible. How was he still going? Scratch that, how was he still *hard*?

Despite myself, I started to pant.

Started touching myself.

Squeezing my breasts, then trailing down to my clit.

As he pounded into me, his hand tightened around my throat, cutting off my airway. A fuzzy dizziness crept into my mind, my body, making me feel alive and sluggish at the same time.

I gasped for air he wouldn't let me have.

I rubbed myself for an orgasm my body wouldn't give me.

Reaching my hand up, I grabbed his wrist, trying to pull him away.

His lips touched my ear. "Come for me first. Then I'll let you breathe."

My pussy clenched.

My lungs ached.

As my body became heavier, fuzzier, I surrendered to the sensations.

To him.

Squeezing his cock, I came on a shuddering wave of ecstasy.

His hand relaxed.

I sucked in air.

The dizziness subsided, but my body still buzzed, still hummed from the feelings he'd given me.

His hand tightening on my throat again, he shoved his thumb all the way up my ass and slammed me all the way down on his shaft.

A groan escaped him as he came inside me for the first time tonight.

One to twelve.

"*Fuck me,*" I breathed.

He chuckled. "I am."

THIRTY-FOUR

A good brownie always covers for their friend.

Even at the destruction of

her own vagina.

— Arienna

By the time he carried me out of the tunnel, I was half asleep in his arms. My dress had been placed back on me at some point, but I doubted I looked presentable. He sure as hel didn't with his waistcoat and shirt missing buttons and his jacket being covered in wet cum from having been used to clean us up.

My head resting against his chest, I yawned lazily.

His chuckle vibrated against my cheek. "Satisfied, my queen?"

"Exhausted," I mumbled. Satisfied had left the station twelve orgasms ago.

Flinching away from the bright light as he stepped out into a hall, I tucked my head tighter against his chest. I'd just started drifting off again when a thought popped into my head.

A person, really.

Jerking my head up, I froze. "Where are we going?" I asked, suddenly remembering that my best friend was waiting in my king's chambers with a bottle of poison – an act that could see her executed for treason. "And where's Jace?"

My blood ran cold as I waited for a chuckle that wasn't my king's. I had no idea if Jace had been in the tunnel with us. It had been so dark and he was so quiet. Oh my gods, he'd been there. The whole bloody time. Just waiting for us to finish.

Me to finish.

Sixteen.

Fucking.

Times.

Shrinking into Richard's arms, I wanted to disappear and never be seen again.

His hands squeezed my side and thigh. "Jace is most likely waiting outside my chambers, which is where we're heading," he said as he stepped out onto a balcony.

My arms would've tightened around his neck if they weren't so floppy and useless at the moment.

I looked around us, my head still heavy from all we'd done. Or rather, he'd done. I'd kind of just laid there for two-thirds of it. The last three orgasms, I don't think I'd moved at all.

The world was dark around us. It was still night, which meant not as much time as I'd thought had passed had actually passed. I'd been expecting the sun to be peaking through the branches of the city by the time we walked out of the tunnel.

Shifting me in his arms, he spread his wings.

And for the first time, the thought of flying made me

smile.

Fabia didn't have wings.

She couldn't have made it up to his floor without help.

Which meant she couldn't be there waiting because asking someone to take her up to her rooms to pick up a bottle of poison and then higher up to Richard's chambers would have been a dead giveaway to her plan. She would have been charged with treason just for asking.

Relieved, I started to relax again.

As the sounds of the party rumbled through the night, I closed my eyes and breathed deep.

I would tell Fabia about my change of heart tomorrow. I would get her to understand that even if it ended in my death, I couldn't kill him. I loved him.

Regardless of whether he felt the same, I. Loved. Him.

My lifemate.

The other half of my soul.

The one the gods had fated me to be with.

A smile broke out on my lips. As I listened to his heart beating beneath my cheek, I breathed slow and deep.

In...

...and out.

In...

The jostling of his arms woke me. As he shifted me to make it through the door of his chambers, I peered up at him with sleep-filled eyes.

"Morning, beautiful," Jace called from close behind us.

I turned my head to look at him. A smile graced my lips.

His knowing grin though caused a twinge of unease to shoot through me.

"He did that number thing, didn't he?" Jace's laughter jerked me fully awake as embarrassment coloured my cheeks.

"How high did you go?"

Scrambling, I tried to get down so I could run away. Richard's arms tightened around me, holding me there, holding me in range of Jace's teasing.

"Triple digits?" he asked.

When I whimpered, Richard kicked the door shut in his face. But I'd felt his hands move on my body as they'd flashed numbers at his friend.

His cockiness made me smile.

"I'm never going to talk to him ever again," I moaned as Richard carried me into his bedroom.

"Trust me, there is nothing we could do that would shock Jace."

I peeked up at him. "Nothing?"

He nodded.

"What about monster porn?" I pressed. "Tentacles and tails and stuff? And monster dicks. With barbs."

Stopping at the foot of his bed, he looked down at me. "Is that the sort of stuff you're into?"

"Oh gods no. I'm asking for a friend."

"A friend... Fabia, you mean?"

"No," I said, dragging the word out to give me time to think. "You don't know her."

"Mmhmm."

"So would that bother him?"

"No."

"What about bondage? Or wand play?"

"You've never had wand play or done bondage before, have you?"

"No, but I don't see what that has to do with anything."

His grin was full on delicious. Had my pussy not been

completely wrecked and desensitised, it would've wetted with desire instead of throwing close the labia gates and drying up the moat.

I was not having sex again tonight.

Maybe not even the whole month.

"You'll see," he said, his words like a promise. Walking around to the right side of the bed, he pulled the blanket back and then laid me down. Stripping the dress off me, he tossed it on the floor.

I sighed in contentment as he kissed my forehead and tucked me in. I closed my eyes, breathing deep, relaxing. But when he didn't crawl into bed beside me, I asked, "Where are you going?"

Looking up, I found him in front of the doorway.

"I have a few things I need to get done tonight."

"Like what?"

He hesitated, and it was like a blow to my heart. He still didn't want me here. In his business. Sharing his crown.

"Never mind," I mumbled, giving him an out. Myself one too. "I probably won't understand it, anyways."

"Yeah, it's a bit complicated."

Closing my eyes, I fought the tears.

"But maybe in the morning after you've had some rest we can go over a few things?"

My eyes snapped open. I stared at him, wondering if he'd meant it. Hoping like hel that he did.

"I would like that. I'm actually pretty clever. I know that doesn't always come across, but I pick things up pretty quick."

"I don't doubt it." He grinned. "My little cum bucket."

Groaning, I closed my eyes. "Don't say it like that." All cute and funny and cringey. "Make it sound sexy again."

Lowering his voice, he growled, "I don't doubt it, my

little slutty cum bucket."

I half-giggled, half-moaned. I could listen to the deep rumble of that voice all day.

"Good night," he said. "I'll see you in the morning."

As he flicked off the bedroom light, a smile spread across my cheeks. He wanted to see me in the morning. I was sleeping in his bed. Actually sleeping – thank the gods. Fuck, I was never complaining about Karl's four seconds ever again.

A hand flew over my mouth as I giggled.

But it wasn't mine.

Eyes widening, I rolled to the other side of the bed, away from the hand reaching up from beneath. My body hit the edge and continued over. My arms flailing, I tried to grab hold of the mattress. But all I'd grabbed was blanket. Smacking onto the floor, I yelped. Then sucked in a breath as I realised there was something beside me.

Slowly, I turned my head to look under the bed.

Fabia's wide eyes stared back at me.

My jaw dropped.

Before I could ask her how in Hel's name she'd made it into his room, Richard burst through the doorway.

"What happened?"

He was down by my side in an instant, crouching by my head. If he looked around for an intruder, Fabia was screwed.

I sat upright and winced. Grabbing my head, I tried to rub the pain away. He pulled my fingers away to look at my scalp.

"Is it bad?" I asked, hoping it was a gusher so he'd be forced to take me to a healer and Fabia could then sneak out.

"No. No blood, though there is a lump."

I hissed as he touched it. "Sorry," I said, my mind

racing for something to say that would make him leave so I could sneak Fabia out of here. "I had a nightmare and must have rolled off the bed."

He frowned, no doubt doing the maths of when I'd fallen asleep and when my first REM cycle would've been.

"I have always been able to jump straight into REM sleep," I gushed. "I dream straight away."

"Uh huh," he said, helping me to my feet. "What was it about?"

"REM cycle? It's when –"

"No, your dream."

"Ah." I glanced away as I shuffled the blanket around my shoulders, making sure it reached the floor, covering the gap below the bed.

"It. Was...about...wa...sps."

"Wasps?"

"Uh huh." My fingers twisted in the blanket. *I'm so frickin' stupid. Wasps? My babies? Scary? Come on.* But I was committed now. There was no going back. I just had to sell it. "Don't you know they're venomous?" I asked. "That's pretty scary."

At least, that's what everyone had been freaking telling me, as if I didn't know.

His eyes narrowed. He wasn't buying it.

Reaching, I said, "Hey, it's a dream. It doesn't have to make sense." I smiled innocently, my heart thundering in my skull.

He inclined his head in agreement, but he didn't look like he believed me.

Ugh. Fabia, you totally owe my vagina for this, I whined.

Reaching forward, I ran my hand over his chest. "You know what I just realised?" I winked.

He looked down at my head, watching as it trailed past

his stomach.

"I really need a shower." I batted my eyelashes despite wanting to do nothing but crawl into bed and fall asleep. "Do you want to join me? I think I might have trouble washing everywhere. Dead limbs and all that." Another wink.

He grabbed my hand. "What's going on?"

"Okay, fine, you caught me." Pulling my hand away, I glanced down, pretending to be embarrassed. It was easy enough. All I had to do was think about Jace. "I rolled over to sniff your side of the bed. Then I started to play with one of your pillows when..." I trailed off, hoping that would be enough.

"Play with one my pillows?"

"Yeah. You know." My cheeks heated for real, knowing I would have to actually say the words. "Rubbing myself... on it... Masturbating."

He crossed his arms. "Sixteen orgasms wasn't enough for you?"

I tilted my head to the side, cursing Fabia left and right for having to go through this. Shrugging, I said, "But that was before my nap. I'm all –" I swallowed, choking the words out. "Ready to go again now. And you were busy. And I couldn't really...be bothered to go another sixteen rounds. I just wanted a quickie, you know? And this has nothing to do with your...performance, I promise, but like...sometimes a woman just wants to...you know, cut through all the...faff...and just...get. To. The. End..."

"The end?"

"Uh huh."

"By faff do you mean foreplay?"

I winced. My body was going to hate me for this later, I just knew it. "Yeah," I said slowly. "But only sometimes. Most of the times, foreplay is great. Required even. But...

Yeah."

When he didn't say anything for a few minutes, I glanced up.

His eyes were narrowed in on me. Hot. Dangerous.

I gulped.

"Show me," he murmured.

"What?"

"Show. Me. I want to know how to get my queen off quickly when she, how did you say it? Wants to cut through all the faff."

My jaw bounced off my boobs and hit the wooden floor. "You want me to..." At the thought of him watching me pleasure myself, my body started to respond.

"Yes. I want you to show me how you touch yourself so I can learn."

Oh my gods, that was the hottest thing I'd ever heard, and my body, my very exhausted body, really wanted to do this.

Holding his gaze, I started to lower myself onto the bed.

Then I remembered Fabia.

"The shower!" I blurted as I straightened. "I'll show you in the shower. It can get a bit messy, you know, and uh, I want a clean bed to fall into."

Grabbing his hand, I dragged him towards the ensuite.

His feet padded behind me.

His eyes lingered on my ass.

I could feel them stroking me.

"I'm going to fuck this tonight."

Although he'd stopped after I had hit number sixteen, realising that I was seriously out for the count, I knew that if I stepped into the shower with him now, he was going to make do on his promise.

The things I did for my friend.

Fabia would frickin' owe me for this.

"So I'll show you how I get out – off," I said loudly, hoping Fabia got the message. "And then we're going to bed, where you'll join me. Right?"

"Whatever you want, my queen," he said, his voice husky and deep.

I bit back a groan at the clear promise in his tone.

My vagina and ass were going to hate me forever.

THIRTY-FIVE

Consummation is not required for the legality of a marriage.

BUT IT'S A FUCKING MAJOR PLUS.

— RICHARD

My eyes were riveted on her hands as she sat across me in the shower. The water cascaded over me, bouncing off my head and shoulders, steaming up the room. Little beads trickled down her skin, beading on all the parts I wanted to taste. She was stretched out in front of me, on her back, with her fingers spreading apart her pussy lips.

My cock twitched with arousal despite having already come four times in the last hour.

But as she'd said, that was before.

This was now.

As her fingers rubbed on her clit, not even going in yet, I cupped my balls, kneading them, pretending it was her touching them.

My cock grew rock hard under the heat of her stare,

under the touch of her hand on her own body. I wanted her sitting on my cock. Riding me with her tits jiggling in my face. I wanted her standing with her back to me, arching as I fondled her breasts. Lying down missionary style with my cock in her tight little ass. Her pussy spread open for my view. Just as it was now.

Grabbing my cock, I squeezed it hard, imagining my fist was her ass.

Closing my eyes half-way, I growled in pleasure.

Her fingers slipped inside herself.

"Spread your legs more," I ordered, my view currently obstructed by her hand.

Dutifully, she did so.

My breathing increasing, I played with my balls as I stroked my cock.

She raised her other hand to grab her breasts.

A growl escaped me as she kneaded herself, as she pinched her nipples like I wanted to. Sitting all the way over here was torture. I wanted to touch her, taste her, claim her like I'd had before.

But I also wanted her squirming. Wanted her to beg me to touch her after realising her touch wasn't as good as mine.

As my faff-filled touch.

My eyes narrowed. I bit back a scoff.

Bucking my hips, jerking into my hand, I lifted my gaze to hers.

Women liked that, didn't they?

It made them hot.

It would make her beg.

Her breathing turned into little pants.

A triumphant smirk curled my lips, knowing she would break soon.

Her pants turned into quick moans of pleasure.

Her hand on her breasts squeezed harder.

Her hand on her pussy rubbed harder, her fingers now back out of her.

My smile slowly faded.

Fuck, she was actually getting close.

As she arched back against the wall of the shower, her eyes closed, her mouth open, I pumped myself harder.

Fuck me, she was hot.

Releasing my cock, leaving it throbbing, I leaned forward and grabbed her leg. With a sharp tug, I pulled her towards me. She slid down the wall until she was fully on her back.

Panting, she looked me in the eyes as I knelt between her legs.

Lifting her ass and back off the floor, I guided my cock to the entrance of her pussy and shoved in.

She wrapped her legs around me. Her arms reached over her head, pushing her breasts up, making them perky.

Leaning forward, I grabbed one in my hand.

My wings spread out behind me.

My balls pulled tight.

Gasping and moaning, she squeezed me on every thrust. So tight. So fucking perfect.

Rolling her nipple in my fingers, I pinched it hard, building myself right up to the edge.

Right before I was about to come, I pulled out. Pressed the head of my cock against her ass.

With a sharp push, I crested the hole. Just the tip – the very sensitive tip, which she squeezed with her tight little ass.

Throwing my head back, I growled and emptied a full load inside her. Lubricating her. Getting her ready for me.

Releasing her breast, I grabbed both her hips. Ever so

slowly I pulled her down onto my cock before I could go soft.

I watched as her initial wince relaxed into arousal. Waited for her breaths to pick up again.

Moving gently, I stroked myself inside her. Half strokes to build the both of us back up again.

Her ass was so tight around me.

Her pussy was in clear view below me.

Along with her breasts and face.

"Gods, you're beautiful," I groaned as I spread her pussy apart, opening it up for a full view.

I rubbed her clit as she had done – in steady circles rather than in a fast hard speed.

Her hips bucked.

Her eyes closed.

As she reached for me, I leaned down and kissed her breasts. She held my head to her, arching on a moan of pleasure.

Fully hard once more, I started to pick up the pace. She met me thrust for thrust. Matched me breath for breath.

Sucking and licking her tits, I then trailed my lips up to her mouth.

I slipped two fingers inside her at the same time as my tongue.

She moaned into my mouth, a hot sexy moan that had my balls clenching on the edge of release.

"Gods, I love the noises you make."

Grabbing her throat, I lifted my head to look her in the eyes. "Do you know how hard you're squeezing me right now?"

My hand tightened around her neck.

"Do you know how good you feel?"

Clenching my fingers, I cut off her airway.

Her eyes widened. She fucked me faster.

I smiled. "Does my dirty little slut like it when I choke her?"

She nodded above my hand. Her ass slammed down on me. Over and over and over again. So fucking tight.

As her eyes started to flutter close, I released the pressure on her neck. She sucked in a ragged breath. Her gaze refocused on mind.

"That's it. Good girl. Look at me when I cum in you."

My hand squeezed her again as she was squeezing me, but her eyes never left mine.

Thrusting faster, harder, deeper, I bowed forward on my release. My hands clenched around her hip and throat. My lips found hers in a desperate kiss.

As her tongue stroked across mine, soft and lazy and sluggish, I removed my hand from her neck, and breathed into her mouth.

She sucked in the air I gave her.

Her breasts pushed against my chest.

Sliding out of her ass, keeping my lips locked on hers, I lowered her back to the floor.

"Are you okay?" I asked, sitting back, shifting so I was no longer kneeling on the hard surface.

Raising a hand to her throat, she nodded. But it wasn't entirely steady.

Opening my arms, I said, "Come here. Let me clean you."

She crawled into my embrace under the spray of the water, her back to me. Reaching between her legs, I cupped water in my hand and washed her. My lips grazed her neck. "Safe words are used freely. Anytime you want me to stop, you say it, regardless of whether you think it'll ruin the moment for me," I explained as I rubbed my cum off her thighs. "Do you understand?"

She nodded.

Tilting her chin, I forced her to face me. "Don't do that brownie shit where you never speak up or complain about your partner's sexual performance. You tell me, okay? Anytime you don't feel comfortable, regardless of how far along we are, you tell me."

She looked into my eyes, searching for what, I didn't know. Slowly, she nodded. "I understand."

"Good." Reaching behind me, I grabbed the shampoo and squirted a glob onto the top of her head. Moving the angle of the spray away from us, I started to wash her hair. "I like to do scenes," I said. "I'll want to push you to the limit, and I'll want to keep pushing until you trust me to do everything."

Wrapping one arm around her as I continued to scrub her scalp, I held her tight.

"Trust is the biggest thrill for me."

There was a moment of silence, and then the softest, "I trust you."

My heart squeezed. I ignored it. I refused to take advantage of her naivety.

"You don't know me," I countered. Not like I wanted her to. "And considering you haven't tried bondage or wand play yet, I'm not even going to suggest the other stuff right now. We can build up to it."

Standing up to grab the shower head, I started to wash the shampoo away. "If you want to, that is."

She nodded. "I do."

Despite my brain telling me she didn't know enough to know what she wanted yet, I smiled.

I continued to wash her in silence, just basking in her presence, in the feel of her wet body beneath my hands.

When she was all cleaned, I pulled her into my arms and kissed her under the hot spray of the shower. She sighed against my lips. Content. Happy, I hoped.

Because tomorrow, day one in Niflhel would start for her. The Court would tear her to pieces, trying to break her into their puppet. I would mitigate as much as I could, but our world was not a kind one and I could not be everywhere at once.

I hated the idea of her losing everything that currently made her her.

But the dice had already been cast. Now I had to sit back and let them roll.

Turning off the water, I grabbed a towel and started to dry her from her hair down.

She smiled at me the entire time, an emotion in her eyes I wasn't yet ready to label.

"Go on to bed," I said as I hung up the towel and grabbed one for myself. "I'll be there in a second."

Picking up my toothbrush, I watched her tight little ass walk away from me.

Towards my bed.

Where she would be when I crawled into it.

That foreign warmth settled in my chest again, as did the fear that this couldn't last.

Nothing good ever did.

THIRTY-SIX

A good brownie...

I'm not a good brownie.

— Arienna

My vagina was still uncertain, but my ass frickin' loved me. *Who knew that anal could feel so good?*

As I hurried into the bedroom, I stopped beside the bed. Dropping to my knees, I checked underneath it.

No Fabia.

And no bottle of poison.

Thank the gods.

Sighing with relief, I lifted my head and crawled onto the mattress. But just as I was about to draw the covers up and fall asleep, my eyes snagged on the closet door.

It was open just a crack when earlier, it had been completely closed.

A horrible feeling settling in my stomach, I walked towards it. My hand reached out. Twisted the knob.

Swinging the door open, I found Fabia crouched inside, poorly hidden among the black suits. Gods, Ajax wasn't joking when he'd said Richard's entire fashion sense centred around black armour with pockets.

Shaking that thought aside, I focused back on Fabia. "What are you still doing here?" I whispered harshly.

"Me? What took you so long to get here? I said one hour."

"And I was hoping you'd be gone by the time we came in." Glancing over my shoulder, making sure Richard wasn't about to come in, I lowered my voice some more. "I don't want to kill him."

"What? Arienna, this was your idea." She sucked in a sharp breath, struggling to control her volume. "You practically begged me to give you some poison."

"I did not," I protested. "You volunteered. Very quickly, might I add."

"Because you were already trying to kill him."

"But not *really*," I said, ignoring how lame that excuse sounded even to me. "I kind of just fed him cake."

Fabia rolled her eyes. "With the plan to butter him up to poison him. Or more likely, knowing you, waiting until he accidentally died of obesity. But whatever. It doesn't matter." She crossed her arms. "Because he's still planning on killing you, so I'm sorry if you got attached, but if it's between him or you, I'm choosing you every time."

"Fabia, you'll get charged with treason!"

"Not if it works."

"But it won't! I didn't even bring any cake with me."

She looked away.

But she didn't look worried.

My gut flipped around, then shot up into my throat, shouldering my heart hard in the process. "What did you put it in?" I asked, my voice trembling, my hands shaking.

"Fabia, where is it?"

"This is for your own good."

Reaching in, I grabbed her shoulders. "Tell me where it is!" I hissed, anger and desperation pouring out of me.

But they bounced off the wall of her stubbornness. Realising she'd never tell me, torn between outing her and saving Richard, tears burned my eyes. Shoving her back in the closet, I raced into the kitchenette and started opening up cupboards.

I pulled out everything that was already open and threw it in the rubbish bin. Anything she could have contaminated.

"What are you doing?" Richard asked as he strolled out of the bathroom, his towel around his waist.

"I saw roaches." Trembling, I threw out a whole box of unopened cereal. "They've probably laid their eggs in everything. We have to get rid of it all just to be sure." Opening the mini-fridge, I pulled out the cake I'd made. Guilt crushed my shoulders. This was all my fault. I never should have told Fabia.

"Arienna," Richard began, but he didn't finish his sentence. Reaching out a hand for the breakfast bar, he sat down on one of the stools.

"I'm not crazy," I said, pulling everything out and chucking it. The bin got full all too quickly. "I really saw a roach."

I refused to look at him, refused to let him see the tears rolling down my face because he would know then. He'd know I knew.

"Trust is the biggest thrill for me."

And of course it would be. Who did he trust in this life? Jace and Nicholas. That was it. Everyone else was out to kill him, and I couldn't be one of those people. I coul–

A hard thump stopped me cold.

My blood drained from my face, my whole body, it seemed, as I turned towards him.

Or rather, where he'd been sitting.

The breakfast bar was empty.

His stool was lying flat on the floor.

Next to his body.

Dropping the milk I was holding in my hands, spraying it all across the floor, I scrambled over to his side. "No. No, no, no, no, no."

Grabbing his shoulders, I shook him.

He didn't react.

Pressing my head against his naked chest, I listened for a heartbeat.

The softest thump.

Anything at all.

There was nothing.

Just silence.

I had killed my king.

No!

An unholy noise ripped through the air.

Monstrous and cruel, it bounced around the room, tainting everything with its darkness. Snuffing out all the light and happiness, it overwhelmed me, suffocated me.

And then I realised it was coming *from* me.

My lungs. My heart.

Broken.

Shattered.

Guilt-wracked.

Empty.

Trembling, I clamped my jaw shut.

I refused to accept this.

I wouldn't.

When I shook him harder though, he didn't wake up.

Desperate, I slapped his face. *Hard.*

Pain shot up my arm.

But still he did not move.

"No!"

Tears ran down my face. Pinching his nose shut, I took a deep breath and placed my lips over his. Exhaling, I filled his lungs. Breathing deep, I did it again.

"Jace, stop her!" Fabia yelled. "There can still be traces of poison on his mouth!"

Strong arms wrapped around me. I was lifted into the air.

"Get off me!" I hissed, pulled at his fingers. Wrapping mine around his thumb, I yanked it the wrong way, just needing him to release me.

Crack!

I looked at the backwards finger in horror. My stomach revolted as I released his thumb. I hadn't wanted to hurt him. Just like I hadn't wanted to hurt Richard, and yet, I'd done both.

"Stop, Arienna. Just calm –"

"I need to bring him back!" Slamming my head against his chest, I hit him over and over again.

"Bring him back?" Fabia shouted. "You can't bring him back!"

My nails scraped into his skin. "Yes, I can. I read about it before. I just need to pinch his nose and –"

"Pinch? That's for someone who can't breathe!"

"And he can't!"

"No, I mean – Oh, for fuck's sake, Arienna." My best friend appeared in front of me. My *ex* best friend. Her eyes were full of pain but not regret. How could she have done this? How could she have done this to me?

"I used anguku poison," she said sternly. "It's quick and painless, but nonreversible. You can't bring him back."

Trembling in Jace's arms, I cried, "But necromancers

do it all the time."

"Necromancers put a bit of their own soul into the corpse. It's not the same thing."

"So what are you saying?" I asked frantically. "I just need to put his cum back inside him?"

"What? No. Their own –" She shook her head. "How are you even equating a soul to cum?"

"Cum makes babies! Babies have souls." I didn't have time to explain this. Necromancy needed the body to still be warm to work. I had no idea how long that gave me, and I'd never attempted necromancy before. I would need time to get it right.

I *had* to get it right.

When my feet touched the ground and Jace's arms released me, I collapsed to the floor. Crawling on my hands and knees, I made it to Richard's side. I placed my hands on his chest, feeling for warmth.

"What are you doing?" Fabia hissed. "Why did you let her go?"

The jacket! I need the jacket.

"I figured she might as well try."

"You know it won't work."

Ignoring them, I raced into the bathroom and picked the jacket up off the floor. Shuffling it in my hands, I tried to find the wet smears, praying that they weren't crusty yet. I'd never timed how long it took for semen to dry before. What if it had been left too long? Did the soul disappear when the cum was no longer viable? *How do I not know how long cum can last outside the body?*

My shoulders bowed forward in relief as I finally found the clumps I was looking for. Except they were already crusty...

It didn't matter. I had to try.

"Arienna, stop. You just have to accept he's gone!"

Kneeling beside him, I prayed that this would work. I didn't want to think about a future without him. He was my lifemate. I loved him. "So what do I do?" I whispered hoarsely. "Do I just put it in his mouth?"

"I'm no necromancer," Jace drawled, "but that sounds about right."

Trembling, I placed the jacket in Richard's mouth and dragged it across his tongue. "Come on," I prayed. "Come on, come on, come on. Hel, if you give him back to me, I promise I will sing your praises as long as I live."

"I think you need to give him some more," Jace said.

Pulling the jacket out, I realised the splodge was gone. Shifting it around, I scraped another clump onto his tongue.

Tears rained down my cheeks.

The world blurred.

He blurred.

This had to work.

Why wasn't it working?

"You mother fucker," Fabia said slowly as I tried a third time, my hands shaking. "He's not dying, is he? That's why you're just standing there. Why we're not dead yet."

My head jerked up.

My heart grabbed hold of her words.

"He's not?" I breathed, praying it was true.

Jace smiled, but it was heartless and cold. "No."

I blinked. I didn't understand. "Then why isn't he moving?"

"Because it knocked him out. She must have used a hel of a dosage, way more than the necessary amount."

I pulled the jacket out of his mouth and leaned down to check his pulse, my head on his chest. Nothing.

And then, there.

A slow thump.

A sign of life.

Holding him tight, I cried. "I don't understand. Why let me try my hand at necromancy then?"

"Well, I wasn't going to until you mentioned putting cum in his mouth." He shrugged. "The fucker ate my cake; I wasn't going to pass this opportunity up."

"Opportunity...?" He was insane. This was insane.

"How did you know we'd poison him?" Fabia asked, her voice a lot stronger than mine.

"What else were you going to do? Get close enough to stab him?" He shook his head, then pierced me with a stare. "I knew you were planning on killing him from the moment I learned about the wasps. So I made sure any plans you 'thought up' were ones I approved of."

The disappointment in his eyes cut me down like wheat at harvest time. Caving in on myself, I wrapped my arms around my waist and tried to breathe.

He turned to Fabia. "And I swapped out all of your poison with another – one he's immune to. Did you really think I wouldn't recognise them when I had them boxed up and brought back?"

"But why not just leave them there?" I asked, wiping at my tears. "Why go through all this?" Why hurt us like this?

His words, although soft, made me flinch. "Because I really hoped you wouldn't."

"I didn't want this," I whispered, my voice ragged and raw.

"But it happened."

"Because he was going to kill her!" Fabia shouted as tears rained down my cheeks and drowned any defence I had.

"No, he wasn't."

She snorted in disbelief. "We know the decision is not

his to make. It's the Court's and they –"

"Were convinced by Richard to drop all charges."

I sucked in a ragged breath. My hands covered my mouth. It was for nothing. All of this, this *heartache*, had been for nothing.

Knowing this would be the last time I would see any resemblance to peace on him when I was in his presence, I ran my eyes over his face. Searing it into memory. This moment, despite all the pain, would be infinity better than what I would face when he woke.

When he learned what I had done.

When he looked at me as if I was the enemy.

When he treated me with the coldness I deserved.

"So what happens now?" Fabia asked, but I didn't care. Execute me or not, I was already dead.

My life was over.

I'd killed it...

Jace's voice sounded so far away. "When he wakes up, he'll decide if he wants to charge you with treason."

THIRTY-SEVEN

Treason is punishable by public
execution.

And the king is the executioner.

– Richard

She'd killed me. My own wife...

For over twenty years, I've been avoiding assassination attempts left and right. By professionals, hired hitwomen who had been honing their skills for years.

And yet, it had taken an incompetent brownie less than a week to kill me.

The irony of my situation wasn't lost on me.

But it was too crushed by my fury to make me smile.

"Where is she?" I demanded as I pulled on a pair of trousers.

"I don't think it's a good idea –" Jace began.

"She's my wife," I growled. "I'll see her whenever the fuck I want."

And I wanted to see her now. I wanted to look her in

the eyes when I charged her with treason.

"Tomorrow, I'll take you to her. But not now. Not when you've just come to and you're not thinking straight."

"For fuck's sake, Jace, you're my guard, not hers." I shoved my arms through my tunic. Strapped on my knives.

"And I am guarding you."

"Like you did when you didn't warn me she was trying to kill me?"

"Yes, actually. There's more to life than being a king. Aurelia would've –"

"Stop bringing her up!" I roared. Slamming my fist into the wall, I pulled back and did it again. Again and again until my hand was bleeding and the pain in my knuckles matched that in my chest. "She *poisoned* me."

"So what?" Jace said so flippantly it cut through the furious haze, just for a moment.

"What do you mean 'so what'?"

He walked towards me, his eyes downcast. His body language soft and nonthreatening, trying to coax me into relaxing like I was some wounded animal backed into a corner.

"I mean," he said slowly, "that everyone you know has tried to kill you at least once. Including Nicholas and I, and you got past that."

I shook my head. "That was different."

"No it wasn't, and you know it."

My jaw tightened. I refused to look at him.

"And if Aurelia hadn't stepped in, we would have." His voice cracked ever so slightly. "When you told us that you planned on killing her, we thought the idea of power had finally gone to your head. That you were doing it just to take the throne. That she would die in a fairy ring, forever trapped and never knowing peace... You didn't even fight us when we came for you."

Tears burned my eyes in memory of that day. Nicholas had wanted me to die quickly, but Jace had wanted to drag it out. The pain in his eyes...

"You didn't blame us after either," he said softly. "Fuck, you gave me the job of protecting you."

"I didn't want to kill her." My voice came out strained. I closed my eyes, clamping down on the agony burning my throat.

"None of us did. But you also knew it was the only way to save her soul. To give her a chance at reincarnation. We should've believed in you, just like Arienna should have. But we didn't. Our crimes are the same."

I shook my head, refusing to listen. "So you think I should just forgive her?" I spat. "I *trusted* her."

And she'd broken it.

Stabbed me in the fucking heart.

"She tried to bring you back, you know."

I recalled her throwing all the food in the bin. Frantic. Wild. Pain in her eyes. Tears rolling down her face.

I shook my head.

"She tried to kill me."

"Technically, Fabia was the one that managed it. Did you know, she has a blueprint of the tunnels?" A touch of pride filled his voice.

My eyes narrowed. "Charge her with treason too then and burn the –"

"I've already destroyed her copy."

The anger in my chest didn't loosen. It wasn't enough. Punishing them from afar wasn't enough.

As I strode for the door, Jace stepped in front of me. A knife embedded into the floor between my feet. "Pick it up," he said.

"Jace –"

"I issued a challenge. Pick it up."

"My anger isn't with you."

"It's not with her either. It's with you, and I'm going to let you beat it out of your system."

I scoffed. "How is it with me? I'm not the one that poisoned me."

"No, but you are the one that set her up to die to begin with."

Guilt rammed into my anger, and the two battled it out inside me. A need to move coursed through me. A need to fight through the pain making it hard to breathe.

Slowly, I bent down and picked up the knife.

Jace smiled. "When you were passed out, by the way," he said, rolling his shoulders, "I convinced Arienna to feed you your own cum. A necromancer's trick, I told her."

My eyes narrowed. I tossed the blade in the air and caught it again.

"She loved you enough to try anything."

Growling, I charged.

The knife sliced through the air. He jumped back. Smacked my arm across my body. Grabbing my wrist, he twisted it backwards. My shoulder popped. The blade dropped. Kicking it away, he spun us around and threw me against the wall.

I crumbled to the ground, dust raining down on top of me.

"I thought you said you were going to let me beat it out of my system," I said accusingly as I rose to my feet. Using the wall, I popped my shoulder back into place.

Grinning, he shrugged. "Yeah, but this is more fun. Also, I absolutely hate what you've done with the place. I have been wanting to redecorate for ages."

Shaking my head, I went in cautiously this time.

With each swing of my fist, I thought about what

Arienna had done to me.

With each blow I took, I thought about what I had done to her.

I'd been so worried about the Court destroying what made her her, but in the end, I had done it.

I had made her feel like she'd had to make the choice between me and her.

I was to blame as much as she was.

More so.

As we fell to the ground with Jace on top of me, I threw a fist into his face. His elbow knocked me in the jaw, snapping my head sideways, filling me with a pain I deserved.

Fuck.

Jace had said she'd left here crying.

That she'd refused to leave me until he'd told her that it would be better for me, easier for me if she wasn't here when I woke.

Raising my arm, I slammed my elbow into the base of Jace's neck. Shoving him off me, leaving him wheezing in pain, I rose to my feet and headed for the door. "Thanks for the talk, but I'm going to see my fucking wife now."

THIRTY-EIGHT

A good brownie always says sorry.

sometimes 'sorry' isn't enough.

— Arienna

At the opening of my door, I shot out of bed, my heart in my throat. Hope and fear mixed together. He had come himself – everyone else knocked.

Stumbling over my feet, I skidded into the sitting room. My eyes latched onto his face. My blood ran cold. And despite murder having gotten me into this mess in the first place, I wanted to try again.

Someone had hurt him.

Someone had bruised his cheeks and cut open his lips.

Someone was going to die.

"Who did this to you?" I asked, my chest heaving, my fists clenching.

Given I was already going to Niflhel for hurting the man I loved, I might as well throw in a few more murders.

Couldn't exactly go to hel twice.

"Was it someone from the Court?" I demanded.

He smiled. "No."

"Who then?"

Walking to me he picked me up in his arms and carried me back into the bedroom. My legs wrapped around his waist. My hands cupped his face as I stared into his eyes.

Pained.

Guarded.

Broken.

I'd done this to him.

"I'm so sorry," I whispered. "I never meant to actually go through with it."

He didn't say anything, just laid me down on the bed, on top of the covers. As he stepped back to strip off his clothes, I watched him in confusion and bewilderment. I didn't know where we stood. Surely, that simple apology couldn't have been everything he needed to hear, all I'd needed to say to make it right between us.

My eyes roamed over his heavily bruised face.

My heart squeezing, I understood.

"You suffered a concussion."

He laughed hollowly as he pulled down his trousers. "Probably."

I scooted off the bed, needing to get the healing wand out of the bathroom, but he stepped in front of me, one arm braced across the door.

"Get back in bed."

My mouth opened and closed as my brows furrowed, trying to understand. "But I tried to kill you."

"And it's made me fucking tired. Turns out, immune or not, my body doesn't like being poisoned."

"So why are you here?"

He stepped forward and lifted me in his arms. "Because

you're here." He'd said it as if that explained everything.

But it didn't.

Why wasn't he upset?

Why wasn't he full of the nerves hounding every piece of my body?

"But I *tried to kill you*," I said again.

He lowered me down on the bed. "And as Jace pointed out, I tried to kill you first."

My breath caught. Trembling, I looked him in the eye. "Jace also said you called off my execution."

"I did."

"Why didn't you tell me?" That would have changed everything, stopped everything...

I shook my head; I couldn't blame him for my actions.

"Because I didn't know you knew it was ever in play. Now go to bed." Irritation lined his voice as he shoved me under the covers and crawled in beside me.

Sitting up, I pushed them back off. "Why aren't you angry?"

"I'm trying not to be," he replied through clenched teeth.

"But why? You have every right to be. I. Just. Tried. To. Kill. You." I shoved his shoulder, wanting him to be angry with me, wanting something other than this cold, distant dismissiveness that I didn't know how to cross.

Didn't know how to fix.

Tears burning my eyes, I shoved him again.

"For fuck's sake, woman, just go to sleep."

"No. Not until you tell me why you're not angry."

"I'm not."

"But you want to be."

"No, I don't."

"Yes, you do."

"Fine!" He jerked up out of bed, throwing the covers

onto the floor. "You want me angry? You want me to tell you I was so fucking pissed with you, Jace had to talk me out of charging you and Fabia with treason?"

Tears fell down my cheeks, but I refused to flinch away from him. I deserved it. All this pain and anger. I'd hurt him. "Yes," I said.

Clenching his jaw, he shook his head, reigned in his control, shut me out. "Just go to sleep."

"No." I shoved him when he tried to lay back down.

Grabbing my hand, he yanked me on my back and then rolled on top of me. "Don't make me do this."

"Do what?" I growled. "You're not doing anything!" I shook my head. "I tried to *kill* you." My voice broke. My whole body trembled with the pain of my own actions. I couldn't stand him pretending like nothing had happened, like everything was fine between us.

It wasn't.

It was broken.

And damaged.

And unfixable.

But he was here.

And I didn't know what that meant.

I didn't know...how to begin to fix this.

I needed him to tell me.

Wanted him to care enough to *want* to tell me.

He was here wasn't he?

"Why are you here then?"

"I told you." His jaw tightened again. Fury flared in his eyes. And pain, so much pain.

"Because I'm here? The woman who tried to kill you? That doesn't make fucking sense!"

His lips crashed onto mine, robbing me of my next words. His tongue stole into my mouth, rough and angry and moving with all the trapped emotions he wouldn't say.

Perhaps couldn't say.

Lifting my head off the mattress, I pushed against his mouth. My hands roamed over his body, holding him to me, holding me to him, closing the gap between us in the only way I knew how.

A shallow way when I wanted depth.

"I'm sorry," I whispered against his lips, tears falling down my cheeks. "I'm so sorry."

"Shut up," he growled. "Stop fucking saying that."

I flinched beneath his words, his harsh tone. My heart hammering in my chest, my pulse in my ears, I feared that this was goodbye sex.

Tearing my lips away from his, I reached up and slapped his face. *Hard.*

He stilled. A darkness poured off him, enveloping me and making me tremble.

But I refused to cower. I refused to let him push me away when he clearly wanted to be here.

I didn't know what I was doing, didn't know how to apologise with something other than sorry, but I would try anything – everything to show him I meant it.

"Then punish me," I said, my voice wavering, my eyes challenging in their desperation.

"What?"

"Push me to my limit," I said, praying he understood what I was asking because I had no idea how you were supposed to go about this.

"Arienna." My king said my name like a curse. Like a warning. Like he knew what I wanted but refused.

But I didn't care. He couldn't hurt me more than I was already hurting.

"Do it." I slapped him again. "Punish me."

Growling, he moved off the bed, off me. Running his

hands through his hair, he turned away. I sat up, staring at him, my everything in my throat.

"My king," I breathed.

He spun around, his eyes hot, his face twisting with too many emotions to name. "If we do this, you have to promise me you won't lie. If I ask you how you are, you'll fucking tell me the truth. None of that brownie shit."

I shook my head. Then nodded. Realising I was already messing it up, confusing him, I said, "Promise. None of that brownie stuff. Complete honesty."

He sucked in a breath.

We stared at each other, letting the silence speak for us.

Growling, he stepped forward. "Green means you're good to continue. Yellow means you're okay but getting uncomfortable. Red means I tone it back down, and 'peace treaty' means I fucking stop, do you understand?"

I nodded, needing him, needing this – whatever *this* entailed. "Yes."

"Arienna," he warned.

"I promise."

"Then get out of bed and on your knees."

I was on the floor in an instant, kneeling in front of him, staring up into his eyes.

"Hand me my belts." I leaned down, my hand groping the floor as I searched for his discarded clothes. I didn't want to move my eyes from his.

"Now," he snapped.

Glancing away from him, I looked down. Snatching up the two belts, I handed them to him.

He grabbed them, along with my hands. Looping one belt through itself, he tightened it around one of my wrists and then the other. Locking it tight, he dragged me across the room. My knees scraped against the hard wood floor.

Hauling me up underneath an open beam, he tore off my slip and twisted it into a rope. He tied one end around the belt binding me. Spinning me around, putting my back to him, he tied the other end over the beam. I raised up onto my toes, my arms stretched tight above my head.

I could feel him behind me, the tension in his body as he stepped in close against me.

"Do you know what you're being punished for?" he demanded.

I tried to turn my head to look at him, but a hard grip on my chin forced me to stare ahead at the wall.

"For trying to kill you?" I said, my body shaking in anticipation.

The second belt slapped my ass. I jumped, a yelp leaving my lips as my skin stung.

"Colour," he growled.

I wanted to just blurt out green, but I forced myself to stop and think. To give him the truth. "Green," I breathed.

His hand slapped me this time, not as hard.

"Do you know what you're being punished for?" he asked again.

I struggled to think, not understanding why my answer hadn't been correct. Wasn't that the issue between us? The massive flippin' gap between us? "N-no," I stuttered, hating to have to admit it. That I didn't know him enough, us enough.

It had only been a week, I reasoned.

That should have been enough.

He was my lifemate.

The literal other half of my soul.

"You're being punished," he said, grabbing my ass, rubbing the sting out of my skin, "for breaking my trust."

My heart in my eyes, I turned my head to look at him, but I'd barely moved before the belt slammed down on my ass.

I cried out, the pain shooting up my back and down my leg.

"Colour."

"Green."

"Don't fucking lie to me." His hand cupped me again, his fingers kneading away the bite of the belt.

"*Green.*"

The physical pain I could take. The emotional pain, the knowledge that he was hurting this badly because of me? Knowing that if I stopped, this pain would run through him? That I couldn't deal with.

"Don't fucking do this for me," he growled. "I need to be able to trust you."

His hand slammed on my ass. I pushed into his palm.

"Green," I breathed, and I meant it. I knew he wouldn't hurt me. And with every slap, I could feel the tension pouring out of him.

Grabbing my hips, he spun me around. My slip twisted above me. The beam creaked.

Dropping to his knees, he scooped my legs over his shoulders and kissed me. I bucked against his mouth. My hands fisting, I grabbed the silk holding me up. I wanted to touch him. I wanted to hold his hair in my hands, pin him to me, and swear I'd never give him reason not to trust me again.

His tongue licked between my labia. I arched on a moan as he ate me out like I was his last meal on death row. His fingers digging hard into my ass, he bit my pussy. Sharp pain mixed with pleasure.

Turning his head, he sunk his teeth into my thigh. I cried out, knowing he was bruising me, marking me, maybe even breaking the skin.

His tongue swept over the pain, trailed to my opening

in soft licks that left me weak.

"*My king*," I breathed, close to the edge of orgasm.

His hand spanked my ass as his tongue dipped all the way inside. He thrust in and out of me as he rained slap after slap down on my aching skin.

Twisting against my bindings, my hands opening and closing as I desperately wished to hold him, I lifted my hips, pressing my clit against his face.

But as soon as I started to rub myself against him, he pulled back. Breathing heavily, he dropped my legs off his shoulders and stood. Grabbing my jaw tight in his hand, he squeezed it. "Bad girls don't get to come," he sneered.

Leaning down, he kissed me hard. His teeth scraped against my bottom lip. When he sucked my tongue into his mouth, I jerked back from the pain. It was surprisingly sharp. Grabbing my chin, he pulled me back to him, and did it again. I flinched, the pain bringing tears to my ears.

But it was the knowledge that he'd done it deliberately, that he was hurting me for the purpose of hurting me that made my heart skip a beat. Made my skull pound with fear.

When he sucked it a fourth time, really freaking hard, I ripped my face out of his grip on a cry, my bruised heart in my throat.

"Red," I panted meekly, hating that I'd had to. Hated that I didn't trust him enough to stop on his own.

He pulled back to look me in the eyes. I glanced away, ashamed that I'd stopped him from doing what he needed to.

Rubbing his cheek against mine, he nudged my head back up. Peppered little kisses across my skin. Soft and loving and tender.

Forgive me, they seemed to say.

The tension that had been radiating off him since he'd

entered my rooms slowly started to dissipate.

"I'm sorry I didn't check in with you," he said as he ran his tongue down my neck. "But you need to tell me too. You never mentioned a yellow."

I trembled beneath his caresses, puzzled by the sudden softness he was expressing, tensing in fear of the pain to come.

"Tell me what turned it into a red," he said, his hands trailing up my body to feather across my breasts.

A tear slipped down my check. I trembled harder. The binds suddenly felt too tight. Too restricting. Making me too vulnerable to a man that wanted to hurt me, to really punish me for almost killing him.

I tugged against the beam as another tear slid out, my breaths coming faster, my pulse just as quick.

Cursing, he lifted me up and wrapped my legs around his waist. "Hold on to me," he said. "Give your arms a break." He ran his cheek across mine again, like a cat searching for comfort. "Hey, look at me."

I squeezed my eyes shut, not wanting to see the rage and fury in them. The monster that wanted to hurt me.

Stroking my back, he dug his fingers into my shoulder blades, massaging the muscles there, forcing me to relax physically if not mentally.

Slowly, I peeked into his eyes and sucked in a ragged breath when I saw tenderness radiating back at me.

"You're not mad?" I asked, confused and hurt and still on the edge of being afraid. If he wasn't mad, why had he hurt me?

"I am but not because you called red. I'm mad at myself for not checking in, and I'm upset you didn't call yellow first." He kissed me, a quick peck on the lips. "This is about trust, Arienna. Building trust, and we can't do that without communication." He ran a hand through my hair, cupping the side of my face. "Do you understand?"

"You hurt me," I murmured. "On purpose."

"Yes."

"Why?"

Glancing away, he exhaled roughly. "To punish you." His eyes met mine again. "When I woke up and Jace told me what you did...I wanted to hurt you like you did me. An eye for an eye."

"I'd deserve it," I said softly.

"No, you don't," he said firmly. "But my frustration is still there. It doesn't go away just because I've decided to forgive you."

"Why are you forgiving me?" I asked, so afraid of the answer being that he needed me for his kingdom. For something, anything other than just me.

He kissed me softly, his lips moving against mine. When his tongue brushed against me, I struggled not to recoil. But he didn't force his way in, just rubbed my lip in between his until I was panting for him.

Slowly, ever so slowly, he slid his tongue inside my mouth. As he stroked it against mine, I could feel the silent apology in his touch. In his kiss.

My hands twisted in the bindings, wanting to touch him, needing to touch him.

Running his hands down my back, he kneaded the tender skin of my ass.

When he lifted his head, I chased after him, wanting more of the gentle sweetness.

"For the same reason, you decided not to kill me, I imagine," he murmured, making my heart jolt and then quicken.

Sucking in a sharp breath, I looked him in the eyes and saw all my love looking back at me.

Guarded though.

Uncertain.

Leaning forward, I tried to kiss him, but he moved his head back. "Do you want to stop with the scene?" he asked.

I paused, not sure which one I wanted more – the gentleness or the punishment. The former was amazing, but it felt off...distant. Like he was restraining himself to give me what I wanted. But the latter...the latter felt like him.

Him giving us a second chance.

Him working through the emotions he was dealing with.

It felt like a building of trust.

Of a future.

Taking a deep breath, I lifted my chin. "Green," I said strongly before sticking out my tongue.

A slow grin curved his lips.

Cupping my face with both hands, he took my tongue in his mouth and sucked just hard enough to cause a bit of pain. But it wasn't as sharp as it had been before.

Shuddering beneath him, I nodded when he pulled back to look at me.

After a second of silence, he removed my legs from around his waist and stepped back. "Tell me what you're being punished for," he demanded, an edge to his voice that made me shiver.

"For breaking your trust."

"And will you break it again?" Bending down, my king picked up the belt he'd dropped.

"No."

The sharp bite of the belt against my thigh had me jerking against the binds.

"Are you sure?"

"Yes."

He hit me again, this time on the other side. "Are you lying?"

"No."

Holding my gaze, he wrapped the belt around his fist, the buckle on his knuckles.

My pulse spiked. Swallowing, I started to tremble.

When he raised his hand, I flinched, but I didn't cower, wanting to take the pain. Needing to take it. Because as much as he claimed I didn't deserve a beating, I felt as if I did. I had hurt him. Almost killed him.

I had to pay for that.

But his hand came down softly on my cheek. The cold touch of metal scraped against my skin, but not enough to bite. He trailed it down my neck. It was only when he got to my breasts, that he dug the prong in deep enough to scratch.

When I jerked from the sting, he grabbed my breast painfully. "Don't move," he growled as he carved a red line into my skin.

Grabbing hold of the silk holding me up, I clenched my jaw and tried to stay still.

He drew a curve at the top of the line, and my breath caught when I realised he was scratching an R into my skin.

An M followed it.

Richard Morningstar.

My body was his.

"Tell me who owns these tits."

I swallowed, working my tongue around my mouth. "You."

Dragging his belt-wrapped fist down my body, he stopped at the top of my pussy. The bite of the prong cut into me again. I fisted my hands, trying not to move.

"Tell me who owns this pussy."

"You."

Turning his hand over, he trailed his fingers between my labia. The leather belt moved roughly against my skin, chaffing my thighs.

Looking me in the eye, he moved his hand harder. Faster. Punishing me.

"Colour?" he demanded.

"Green," I gasped, finding pleasure in the pain, the way he was watching me, studying me to make sure I was okay.

My hips began to move with him.

My lips parted.

My eyes became half-lidded.

Removing his hand, he left me panting. "Bad girls don't get to come, do they?" he asked.

I shook my head.

"And have you been a bad girl?" He uncoiled the belt. As it dropped to the floor, I nodded.

Raising it, he whipped it across my breasts.

I screamed and jerked against my binds. The beam creaked above me. My eyes watered. My chest rose and fell rapidly and even that hurt.

"Colour?"

"Yellow."

He smiled. Leaning in, he kissed me as if he loved me. His tongue stroked inside my mouth, making me pant. His lips rubbed against mine, making me wet. Desperate.

"You've done so well, my queen," he said as he pulled away. "Are you ready to stop being a bad girl?"

I nodded, my eyes fastened on his.

"Then pick a number."

My breath escaped on a whimper. Our time in the tunnel felt like such a long time ago. Before he'd been poisoned. Before what we'd started to have had been ripped apart. Before the pain in his eyes was put there because of me.

"Seventeen," I breathed.

He studied me for a moment as if he wasn't sure if he should continue.

"Seventeen," I said again, needing this new beginning for us.

His jaw ticked. Nodding sharply, he raised the belt. My eyes widened as he smacked it across my chest. I jerked out of instinct, but it hadn't hurt anywhere near as bad as the previous one. "Count them," he said.

My voice shaking, I said, "One."

He raised the belt again.

Hissing in a breath, I said, "Two."

The third one made me cry out. The fourth one made me scream. But he never put too many in a row that made it hurt too much. He helped me – helped us, get to sixteen, and all I'd had to do was trust him.

Trust him so hard I could barely breathe.

My pussy clenched.

My body vibrated with expectancy and hope.

"Colour?" he demanded, flexing the belt at his side.

"Green."

Flicking his wrist, he cut the belt through the air as he raised it.

I tensed.

Held his gaze.

Slapping it across my flesh, he hit hard enough to cut through skin.

Screaming, tears pooling in my eyes, I sagged against my binds. My orgasm ripped through me so hard and fast, I felt as if I was going to pass out.

Richard's hands were on me in an instant. Lifting my ass, he slammed his cock into me. My muscles clenched around him, pulsing through my orgasm, squeezing him tight over and over and over. He pulled out, slammed back in. Grabbing my throat, he kissed me hard.

He squeezed me until I couldn't breathe.

Fucked me until I couldn't think.

His teeth bit into my shoulder.

His hands massaged my breasts.

And then his arms were wrapping around me, holding me down onto his cock, as his head fell back and he groaned.

THIRTY-NINE

A royal's duty is to the welfare of their subjects.

A HUSBAND'S DUTY IS TO HIS WIFE.

— RICHARD

She sat tight on my cock, her pussy still pulsing around me. Growling against her ear, I tensed inside her, causing her to moan. Her little whimpers were what I currently lived for. The feel of her body was mine to control, to use, to protect.

The trust she'd given me tonight eased the tension in my shoulders, lessened the gap between us.

Releasing one arm from around her, I reached up to undo the belt around her hands. As soon as she could, she wrapped her arms around me and nuzzled her face into the crook of my neck.

"You were such a good girl," I said as I carried her into the bathroom. "But you didn't have to take all that."

Lifting her head, she kissed my cheek. "I wanted to."

My arms tightened around her. My cock jumped inside her. Setting her down in the shower, I aimed the spray at the floor, away from her so it wouldn't sting across her skin. I grabbed the washcloth, wetted it in the warm water, and then brushed it gently across the bruises I'd left on her neck.

Lowering the cloth to her breasts, I stopped just before touching them. They were red and raw and bleeding. Bruises were starting to form, hard lumps rising beneath the skin.

"Do you want the wand?" I asked softly, my stomach twisting with the knowledge that I had done this to her. My chest tightened with the knowledge that she had let me. That she'd trusted me enough to stop. My little queen was going to be the death of me.

Lifting a hand to trace the initials I'd carved into her, she shook her head. "I'm thinking of getting this as a tattoo." Her hand lowered to the other RM. "This one too."

Groaning, I pulled her onto my lap. She hissed as the spray hit her sensitive skin, but she didn't move away. Grabbing my cock, I pushed it inside her. We needed to rest, to clean up and go to bed, but my body needed hers again.

My fingers digging into her hips, I lifted her up and down on top of me. She clenched with a moan, her lips finding mine for a hungry kiss before I pulled away to look at me entering her. At her pussy gripping my cock as she took me all in. At the RM, my mark, scratched at the base of her.

Growling, I moved her faster, harder. Pounding deep inside her, I held her down for a second before lifting her slowly off me, then shoving her down again.

She arched on a cry, her little pants making me feral.

Leaning forward, I took her breast in my mouth, the

one marked as mine. My tongue ran across the initials, licking off the blood, soothing the pain I'd given her.

"Gods, you're so good to me," I moaned, her nipple in my teeth, my tongue flipping across it. "You feel so good, so perfect."

I slammed her down on my cock.

Lifted her off slowly.

"You did so well during the session."

Her fingers in my hair, she twisted her torso and lifted her other breast to me. I took it greedily, sucking and licking as I had the other one.

She cried out, an edge of pain to her voice.

Lifting my head, I looked at the state of her chest. Ragged and raw. Seventeen whips she'd taken. "You're so fucking good to me," I growled as I kissed the cut the last smack had given her.

I slammed her down on my cock.

Lifted her off slowly.

Reaching between us, I rubbed her clit until she was bucking and crying for mercy. Taking her lips in mine, I stroked my tongue inside her mouth. Teasing. Building. Claiming.

"Did my perfect fucking queen like being whipped?" I asked, looking her in the eye.

Half-lidded, she stared back at me, her lips parting on her little pants and whimpers. "Yes."

I slammed her down on my cock.

Lifted her off slowly.

"And does my perfect fucking queen like it when I come inside her?"

"Yes." She clenched around me, started to squirm. Her hands slapped at my chest as she struggled on the edge of release. My balls grew tight.

"Gods, you're so fucking hot."

Grabbing the back of her neck, I kissed her on the mouth. Her breaths mixed with mine. Her groans and moans were mine to take. Her trust, her control, all mine.

As my chest expanded with all she was giving me, I rubbed her clit harder, just like she'd shown me earlier.

She bucked on a cry, and holding her down, I shot my seed deep inside her.

My arms wrapped around her.

The spray beat down on both of us.

Our breaths mingled in hard pants, hers flowing into my lungs, mine flowing into hers.

"I love you," she whispered. "I never meant to hurt you."

Stilling, I struggled to hold her gaze. Cupping her face, giving myself an excuse to look away, I kissed her slowly. "Just promise you won't ever again."

She nodded, tears streaming down her face.

I kissed away each one. Held her tight as the words she'd said bounced around my skull, marking me. Her betrayal still cut through my chest, but it didn't sting as much anymore.

She trusted me.

And for now, that was enough.

Keeping my dick inside her, I picked up the washcloth and gently began cleaning the abrasions and cuts on her breasts. She jerked away on a hiss when I touched the bruise on her left one. Ever so gently, I cupped it, then patted it with the cloth.

The tension in her back eased as I made my way down her body. I wiped away the blood crusted around my initials. Spreading her legs, I tended to the rashes on her thighs. Massaged the bruising on her ass.

Finished, I put the cloth down and prepared to stand up with her still wrapped around me, but she picked up the towel and touched it to my face.

I froze.

Looking her in the eye, I allowed her to tend to the wounds Jace had given me.

My chest expanded.

Her three little words bounced around my skull.

"Who did this to you?" she asked, an edge to her voice that made me smile.

"Why? Are you going to poison him?"

She glared at me, her eyes hard, but there was guilt behind her fierceness. "Just give me a name and I'll sic Fabia on him."

Laughing, I shook my head.

Despite the sadness in her eyes, she smiled. "She's a bit scary, isn't she?"

"A little," I admitted. "Bit impressive too."

Swallowing, she glanced away. Taking a deep breath, she looked back at me. "What's going to happen to her?"

"Nothing. If the Court learns she tried to kill me, they'll force me to execute her. If I refuse to do my duty as king, they can strip my crown from me."

"They can do that?"

"Yes. But if they try without good, proven cause, then it's my right to kill them for a false accusation. It keeps us in balance with each other."

"Sounds horrible."

I shrugged.

"So you can't punish her at all then?"

I shook my head.

"That's not fair."

My eyes sharpened on her, my gut tightening with unease. I didn't want this night to be the one where she changed. "Do you want her punished?" I asked slowly. "She's your best friend."

"She tried to kill you. She deserves something." She paused, fury in her eyes. "What if you had Echo do it? Make her run extra laps or something?"

"Make her fight in the pit unarmed?" I pushed.

She winced. "That sounds bad."

"It is."

"I don't want her to die."

"She won't."

"Or get hurt too much."

"That, I can't promise."

She frowned. "Maybe just the laps then?"

My gut unclenching, I cupped her face and kissed her. "I'll tell Echo to give her extra laps then."

"Like a hundred?"

I smiled. "A hundred and one."

Wrapping her legs around me, I rose to my feet, turned off the shower, and stepped out. She leaned her head against my chest as I patted her back with a towel, not wanting to rub the bruises on her ass and thighs. Slinging the bath sheet around us, I carried her to the bedroom and laid her down on the bed.

I wanted to take her to mine where she belonged, but the entire suite had been upheaved during my talk with Jace. I'd take her there in a couple days when the mess was cleared and the room decorated with her belongings.

Kissing her gently, I finally slid out of her. After patting dry the front of her body, I used a corner of the towel to clean up the cum, as well as my penis, taking special care around my piercing. Infections were a bitch. Laying down on my stomach, I placed an arm across her chest. She snuggled against me and closed her eyes.

I watched her fall asleep, my chest tight, my throat locked.

Nothing good ever lasted in this place.

But she would.
I'd make damn fucking sure of it.

EPILOGUE

Every citizen has the right to challenge
another to a fight in a fairy ring.

GIVE HIM HEL, FABIA

- RICHARD

"Are you sure it's okay for me to be here?" Arienna
whispered as she squirmed next to me, seated on the
queen's throne. Her chair was taller than mine. More
prominent. But the way she kept twisting her fingers in
her dress and fidgeting on the wooden seat made her look
inexperienced and small. Something to dismiss. "I haven't
been crowned yet."

"Relax," I said. "No one is going to challenge your right
to be here, and if they do, I'll kill them."

She stilled, looking at me with uncertainty. Before she
could ask if I was joking or not, something she asked
often, I signalled to Jace for us to begin.

The doors opened. A man strolled in, roughly twenty
years old, a cane clinking against the floor in sync with

his left foot. I recognised him and I knew what he was going to ask. Glancing at Arienna, I hoped she was ready for this. She'd grown up somewhere without war, had never seen the consequences of it. Hearing about it was never the same.

"Nando." I nodded in respect.

"My lord." He winced, his eyes darting to Arienna in embarrassment. "Your Majesty." He bowed. "Sorry I didn't address you first. I wasn't born when the last queen..." He swallowed.

"It's alright, Nando." I glanced at Arienna. "Isn't it, my queen?"

She nodded, her eyes fastened onto the cane. I knew what she was thinking: why bother with it when he had wings? A question that would be answered when Nando turned around to leave.

"What can we do for you, Nando?" she asked.

I stilled, a nervous energy flowing through me. Every quarter Nando came to me, and every quarter I had to turn him away.

He glanced at me, disappointment already in his eyes, before looking straight ahead and lifting his chin. "I would like to request accessibility ramps be built between the levels of the city. I have the thousand signatures required to bring this to the Court's attention."

"Nando..." I said slowly, not wanting to introduce Arienna to this side of my world anymore than I wanted to tell him no. But a king's duty was to his people, not to a single individual. "I will bring this matter to the Court, but although we are at peace with the Vylians, the expenses needed to keep our southern borders safe still don't allow for excessive spending on this scale."

"I understand."

Arienna looked at me, a desire to help clear in her eyes.

I shook my head. We couldn't help them all.

"Thank you for your time, Your Majesty." He bowed to her. "My lord." After another bow to me, he turned to leave.

I tensed, my eyes on my wife.

Her blood drained from her face. A gasp escaped her lips. Raising her hand, she folded in on herself.

Nando faltered, his hand tightening on his cane.

"Wait," Arienna called as she rose. I stood behind her, ready to grab her should she take a step forward. I didn't want her to get in the habit of approaching these people – people who often were assassins in disguise.

"How long does it take you to traverse from Rokula District to Prasin District?"

I looked at her, bittersweet pride filling my chest. This life was going to break her if she stayed in it too long. Fortunately, she wouldn't have to.

"Three hours, Your Majesty."

Arienna turned to me. "And you?"

"Fifteen minutes."

"That doesn't seem fair."

"It's not," I said, "but we don't have the funds to build a ramp between every branch of our city. Let alone in all the other cities too."

"So what about a type of bus service? We could use the birds."

"There's nowhere for them to land."

"Then what about creating a taxi service?"

"There is one," I said softly, "but nobody ever uses it."

"Why not?"

Nando looked down at the ground. "It's a pity service."

"What?"

"You're dismissed, Nando."

Lifting his chin, he nodded. "Your Majesty. My lord."

Bowing, he left.

Arienna turned to me as soon as the door closed. "I don't understand."

Before I could explain how seeking help was seen as a weakness here, the next person strolled in.

"Sup," he said and I hated him instantly.

I hated him even more when my wife grinned widely and took a step forward.

What was with her shitty taste in men?

Before me, obviously.

Grabbing her, I rooted her to my side. My blood chilled as my eyes narrowed on the man. A brownie. One of the criminals I'd been asked to bring back.

"Lief," she said happily.

"Ari, babe!"

My fingers tightened on her arm. I didn't like that she knew him, and I sure as hel didn't like that he felt like he knew her enough to use a nickname.

"You will address her as 'Your Majesty'," I growled. "Anything else and I will cut out your fucking tongue."

"Richard," she hissed, turning to me in surprise and disapproval.

But my eyes didn't leave him. My free hand twitched with the need to draw a knife as I remembered what his crime was. He was a rapist, and all I could think about was his hands on my wife. His cock. Her being too polite to tell him to stop.

A growl escaped me.

Lief took a step back. "Okay, okay, chill," he said, holding up his hands. "I'll call her Your Majesty."

"What do you want?" I snapped, wanting him out of here. Needing him out of here before I fucking killed him. "Actually, you know what? I don't fucking care. Say one word and I'll kill you."

"Richard!" Turning to me, she placed a hand over my heart. "What's wrong?"

She cupped my face, drawing my eyes to her. Concern and confusion looked back at me from two pink pools. But there wasn't any fear, shame, or a desire to be out of this asshat's presence.

"Talk to me," she murmured.

And it was then that I knew: Lief hadn't touched her.

A small portion of my tension eased.

"How do you know him?" I asked softly. "And don't say his fucking name."

My little queen frowned. "He lived on my street. Well, he did before his house burned down."

"What happened to it?"

She ducked her head.

"Arienna," I said, stressing her name, warning her not to test me on this.

She blew out a breath. Lowered her voice. "Fabia burned it down."

"Fabia..."

The fucking bastard.

My eyes shifted over her to him.

The fucker was smiling.

Spreading my wings, I released my wife and flew down the stairs. I was on him in a second. A knife was in my hand. Then it was in his stomach. My arm was around the back of his neck and I was pulling his ear close to my mouth. "Just relax," I growled. "It won't be as bad then." Yanking the knife up, I hit his ribcage. Pulled back to aim again when a scream shattered my resolve.

Shoving him away, I turned as the door opened behind me.

Arienna was sprawled out on the floor at the base of the stairs, cradling her arm and crying.

"Get him out of here," Jace ordered whoever else had come in with him. "And grab a cleaning wand."

Lunging into the air, two flaps of my wings had me landing beside my queen.

"Where does it hurt?" I demanded as Lief's screams faded behind me. If he'd hurt her, I was going to skin him alive.

"Ow, ow, ow," she cried, her face mostly hidden by her hair.

I stilled, a smile pulling at my lips, the tension easing from my shoulders. She was faking it. I could hear it in her too-high voice that didn't quiver with nearly enough pain.

She held her arm to her chest as she slowly sat up. She glanced at me through her hair. "It's fine," she assured me. "Feeling much better now."

I reached for her, my eyes never leaving her face. "Just a moment ago, you were crying in pain."

"I wasn't *crying*," she said as I took her arm to study it, just to check and make sure. "I was just informing you that I'd fallen." Her arm shook in my hands. Her face was pale. Her eyes flicked around me, then widened and I knew she was seeing the blood and bits that inconsiderate asshole had left behind.

"Clean it up," I said over my shoulder, not looking anywhere but at her. "Now."

"We're already on it," Jace replied.

Cupping her face, I moved my head so I was back in her line of sight. "Look at me."

"Why did you do that?" she asked. "I thought you were going to kill him."

"Is that why you 'rushed down the stairs and fell'?"

Her eyes snapped to mine. "His scream... How do you live with them?"

My jaw ticked as the door closed behind us, shutting us in together, the mess now most certainly gone.

"It's part of being king." Raising her arm to my lips, I kissed my way from her wrist to her elbow. "But don't scare me like that again."

Her lips worked, but no sound came out. Cursing myself for stabbing the prick in front of her, I pulled her into my arms. "I'm sorry you had to see that," I said.

She blinked. Shook her head. "I don't get why you did it."

Before I could find the words to explain without hurting her, changing her, a knock sounded on the door.

"What?" I snapped as I turned, not bothering to mask my irritation. Fabia strode in, fury in her every step.

My jaw tightened, knowing exactly what she was here for. Every citizen had the right to challenge another to a match in the fairy ring.

"No," I said before she could even open her mouth. My eyes narrowed, locked on my wife's best friend's face. "You will not speak about this now."

I lowered my voice, making sure the point went home. As hotheaded as she was, Fabia was still a recruit in my guard. To disobey a direct order from me would get her discharged.

Her fists clenching, she clearly struggled to keep whatever she wanted to say down. Her eyes flicked to Arienna. Her breath exhaled sharply. Nodding, she turned on her heels and left the room.

My shoulders tense, I headed for the doors.

"What was that?" Arienna asked as she scurried after me.

"Nothing." The lie slid off so easily, but it sat heavy in my chest. I didn't want to hide anything from her, but she'd greeted Lief with a smile of purity. She didn't know the monster he truly was.

"Richard –"

Stopping suddenly, I pivoted around and grabbed her by the waist. She yelped as I lifted her off the ground. Kissing her hard, I silenced her questions. "Don't ask me," I said against her lips. "I don't want to lie to you."

"Then don't."

Exhaling roughly, I trailed my free hand to her ass and squeezed. "It's not my secret to tell."

Her eyes searched mine. A frown pulled at her lips that I wanted more than anything to soothe away. But telling her wouldn't do that.

Nor would hiding this from her.

"Is Fabia in danger?"

"No."

"Is she hurt."

I hesitated. "Not physically."

"Then what's wrong?"

"I can't say."

"Does it have something to do with what you did to Lief?"

"Arienna, please."

Her lips pursed and she looked away, but she nodded.

After a quick kiss, I lowered her back to the ground. "I need to talk to her in private," I said as I exited the throne room. "Stay here with Jace."

She made a noise of protest, but nothing substantial passed her lips.

"Look after her," I ordered him as I passed.

He didn't bother with an answer, and I didn't pause to listen.

Catching up with Fabia down the hall, I grabbed her arm and pulled her into a room. The door shut behind us, leaving us in the dark. After flipping on the light, I turned to her.

"I know what he's accused of," I said, looking her in the eye.

"Then why won't –"

"Because Arienna doesn't know, does she?"

She looked away, her jaw tight. "I never felt the need to tell her."

"And I get why, but if you challenge him, she will find out."

Her emotions warred across her face – her need for revenge, her need to protect her friend.

"I'll have Echo enrol him in my guard," I said.

Her eyes snapped to me. Her lips parted, but then they stilled. As she searched my face understanding slowly took root. "Accidents happen..." she murmured.

I nodded. "Especially in the pit. Choose your moment. And Fabia." I waited for her to focus on me and not on whatever thoughts were coursing through her mind.

"What?"

"Make sure the fucker suffers."

AUTHOR'S NOTE

Hello everyone!

Thank you so much for reading *Death Do Us Part*. I hope you've fallen in love with these characters just as much as I have.

For although I'd planned for this to be a standalone, it's now turned into a six book series (minimum). The next book, *For Better or For Worse,* will follow Richard and Arienna again as she learns to become a fairy queen. So if you'd like to be the first to hear any news about it, sign up to my newsletter (links on the next page).

Many cheers and happy reading,

PS: A special shout-out to the Koala Hospital in Port Macquarie, Australia. It's an absolutely fantastic non-profit that focuses on the conservation of, surprise, koalas. If anyone else can spare any change, please do! https://shop.koalahospital.org.au/

5 REASONS TO SIGN UP TO MY NEWSLETTER

1 Have the chance to end up as a character in one of my books!
2 Have the chance to join either my beta/ARC reader team.
3 Download sneak preview chapters.
4 Get all the latest information about upcoming releases.
5 Get free book banners and other cool promo.

Sign me up now!
https://mirandagrant.ck.page/0e074e4e9c (direct)
mirandagrant.co.uk (sign-up form)

3 REASONS TO LEAVE A REVIEW

1 They give me the strength and confidence to keep writing. The more reviews, the faster I write.
2 Chance to see your reviews inside one of my books.
3 I will love you forever.

Burn Baby Burn

EVERYTHING IS ABOUT TO BURN

We all know the story. Cinderella's father remarries. She gets a shitty new family. He dies in a tragic accident and she is forced into a life of servitude.

But what happens when Ella's father is brutally murdered and she's sold to the Romans? What happens when she meets a dark fae who tempts her to embrace the embers in her heart? When he shows her the fire she was born with and coaxes those powers to light? What happens when he tells her that she doesn't need a prince.

She needs a crown.

The Little Morgen

She kills without mercy

On her thirteenth birthday, Thalliya watched her entire
family get slaughtered. The humans cut off their fins and
hung their heads from their Viking ships. Left cradling
what few pieces remained of her twin, Thalliya screamed
to the gods for vengeance.

Answered by the Goddess of Love and War, Thalliya
now guards the seas without mercy.

He fights without fear

Ragnar is hired to take care of the mermaid terrorising the
western seas. With seventeen kills under his belt, he
thinks little of venturing into the Mouth of Hel. It'll be a
quick job with a quick pay…

But when his ship is wrecked and the majority of his
crew is drowned, Ragnar realises that it's not a mermaid
he's hunting. It's a morgen, a dark mermaid, that's hunting
him.

And there's only one way to kill one of those.

You have to get her to fall in love.

Bjerner and the Beast

He's Sworn to Protect the Emperor at All Costs

When he was a child, Bjerner sacrificed his eyes to the
Goddess of Death. Raised as a warrior, he's now a trusted
member of the Varangian guard. As he struggles to keep
the emperor alive, Bjerner is forced to take a mission that
will either see him killed or see him hailed as a hero.

She's Tired of Heroes

All they ever want to do is try to kill her. Ever since she
was born, Ophidia has been hunted like an animal and all
because of what she is: a beast that has the power to turn
people into stone.

Forced to hide in a cave her entire life with only the dead
heroes for company, Ophidia desperately wants her next
visitor to be a little less stabby.

And less inclined to look at her face.

And would it really kill them to just *talk* to her first?

But as the centuries pass, she's starting to lose hope that
such a man exists…